—— **BOOK ONE** ——
IN THE *Isles of Stone* **SERIES**

EMERALD'S FRACTURE

KATE KENNELLY

EMERALD LIGHT
PRESS

Published by Emerald Light Press
Copyright © 2018 by Kate Kennelly

Cover Art by Chrissy H. at damonza.com

Editing by KM Editorial, LLC

Map designed with Inkarnate

ISBN (paperback): 9780999097717
eISBN: 9780999097700

DEDICATION

In memory of my father, who read every single story I wrote when I was a little girl

*"Hold tight, Abuela, if you're up there
I'll make you proud of everything I know!
Thank you, for everything I know."*

- In the Heights (Lyrics: Lin-Manuel Miranda)

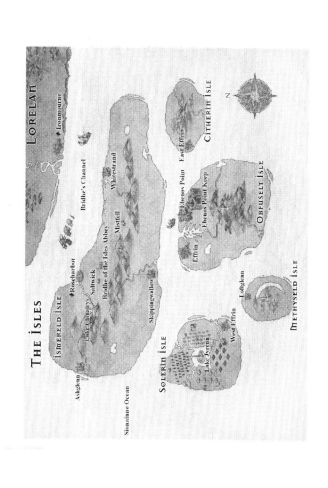

THE ISLES

LORELAN

Ironmourne

ISMERELD ISLE

Ashglenn

Roseharbor

Lake Chmairy

Saltwick

Bridhe of the Isles Abbey

Bridhe's Channel

Whitestrand

Mistfell

Skippingswallow

Stonanne Ocean

SOLERIN ISLE

Lake Arenna

West Effrin

Effrin

Ebenos Point

Ebenos Point Keep

East Effrin

Loftglenn

CITHERIN ISLE

OBFUSELT ISLE

METHYSELD ISLE

N

TABLE OF CONTENTS

Dedication iii

Table of Contents..v

Chapter 1 1

Chapter 2 9

Chapter 3 19

Chapter 4 27

Chapter 5 39

Chapter 6 45

Chapter 7 49

Chapter 8 59

Chapter 9 71

Chapter 10 81

Chapter 11 89

Chapter 12 97

Chapter 13 107

Chapter 14 117

Chapter 15 125

Chapter 16 133

Chapter 17 141

Chapter 18 151
Chapter 19 159
Chapter 20 169
Chapter 21 179
Chapter 22 187
Chapter 23 197
Chapter 24 205
Chapter 25 213
Chapter 26 223
Chapter 27 231
Sunstone's Secret 243
Acknowledgements 254
About the Author 255

CHAPTER 1

In the darkest hours of the night, Natalie Desmond rushed to the Abbey hospital, her dog, Jake, trotting behind her. "Good Goddess, why isn't the hospital closer to our rooms? I'll be lucky if the patient doesn't die before I get there." Jake glanced up at her, his tongue lolling out the side of his mouth. Entering the hospital at last, she spotted a familiar face, her good friend, Emmeline Arnold. "Em, Headmistress Gayla summoned me to treat a burn patient. Do you know which bed?"

Em turned from her own patient and nodded to the far hospital wall. "Bed twenty-four."

"Thanks," Natalie whispered. White knuckles gripping her satchel full of herbs, she walked through the room, careful not to disturb the other patients and Healers. In the four months since the war started, she'd kept careful watch on all the wounded who arrived at the hospital, waiting for the return of Healer Juliers Rayvenwood.

Could he be in twenty-four? She kept her eyes on the bed in question as she approached, searching for a glimpse of short, dark wavy hair and the familiar face with its high cheekbones. She swallowed, pushing her heart back out of her throat.

Reaching the bed, she let out a breath she didn't know she'd been holding. Long, sleek black hair and tan skin met her gaze. Juliers was still out there, in the war. Natalie covered her mouth with her hands and willed the tears away. *By the Five, please let me be able to Heal this man. And please keep Juliers safe and sound.*

Moving to the head of the bed, she rested a hand gently on the patient's forehead. "Hello, I'm Natalie, and I am a Healer. I'm going to take a look at your injuries now." After washing her hands, Natalie examined her patient for other visible injuries besides the severe burns along his left arm and torso, gingerly turning his body this way and that to make sure she didn't miss anything. *What's going on out there in the war that would result in burns such as these? Is Juliers in the same danger?*

Not spotting anything more than charred, blistered skin, she pulled a chair to the head of the bed, sat, and placed both her hands on the man's shoulders. It was time to see what maladies Naming would reveal. With a deep breath, she closed her eyes. Though she'd done this hundreds of times, she still marveled as energy rose from the Isle's ley lines and coursed into her body without effort.

For student Healers, accessing the rivers of magic—or ley lines—emanating from the tall emerald megalith in the middle of the Isle required a lengthy grounding meditation. Now a full Healer, Ismereld Isle's energy flowed into Natalie with ease. She directed it through her hands and into the burn patient before her. In her mind, a ghostly blue image of her patient formed as her energy sought and penetrated every corner of his body except the burns on his skin. Adjusting her hands and cocking her head a bit, she could tell the burns were severe but not as deep as she'd first feared.

"A solenloe poultice will have you right as rain, my

friend," Natalie informed the unconscious man, opening her eyes. She went to the hospital's herbal stock room that, due to the war Lorelan started with the Isles a few months ago, contained copious amounts of solenloe leaf, which was used to treat burn patients.

"I still don't understand why Lorelan started a war with us this year after centuries of peace," she grumbled to Jake, who had followed her to the stock room. She counted out the appropriate amount of leaves. "And Juliers volunteered to go to war? It just doesn't seem like the thing he would do." She'd said as much to her friends over the past few months, but even after some lively conversations about current politics between the Isles and Lorelan, it still didn't sit right in Natalie's mind.

Jake cocked his head, having no more answers than she.

Natalie placed the solenloe leaves on a nearby worktable and vented her frustrations by mashing the large, thick, dark green leaves into a viscous, gooey mess. She scraped this onto a clean cloth and carried it to her burn victim, then spread the leaf mash along his burns and covered them with clean cloths. She returned to her chair at the head of the bed and closed her eyes. Warm tingling filled her hands as the Healing energies of the two-thousand-year-old emerald megalith, wielded by her, melded with and Activated the solenloe on her patient's skin, intensifying the leaves' effect. The man's inherent energy grew and strengthened under the ministrations of the Healing energy and herbs—exactly what she wanted. The Activation finished, Natalie slumped back in her chair, wiped her forehead on her sleeve, and then pressed her hands to the small of her back.

Natalie moved her chair to bed twenty-four's side. This was the worst part of any treatment—waiting. She hoped her patient would regain consciousness within the next hour. She took the time to study the man she'd Healed. He was short but sturdy, with a few days' worth of beard growth on his chin. His sleek black hair and olive skin indicated he originated from the northern part of the main continent. He must be an Islander now, though, if he'd been brought to the Abbey. She peered under the bed and spotted a black cloak amongst his belongings. He was an Attuned of the Isle of Obfuselt, another one of the five Isles just south of Ismereld. "We'll have you up and back to your Isle soon, sir."

An hour later, Natalie rose from her chair to check the poultices. She peeked under one to find the burn underneath appeared much better. She placed her palm on her patient's forehead. He was feverish. "Hell in a kettle!" She bit her lip. Had infection set in? Holding her breath, she removed all the cloths, wincing as the man moaned. Everything seemed well on the mend; only the worst burns still showed signs of needing more time. She pressed gently on the edges of the burns; no pus, so no infection. Natalie swore under her breath and slumped in her chair.

Sighing, she ran her fingers through the hair that had fallen out of her braid and pressed it to her head. Letting her hands fall to her lap, she pushed herself out of the chair and paced back and forth beside the bed.

"I'm missing something. Come on, Nat, think." Natalie went to one of the many windows lining the hospital wall and ached to breathe in the crisp spring air on the other side of the glass. Instead, she rested her head against the window frame and stared out at the moon. "I must've missed something during the Naming," she told the moon and closed her eyes.

"You can't fail this man. You can't fail Headmistress Gayla. You have to figure it out." Naming an illness or injury always ate at Natalie's confidence. An illness must be accurately Named before herbs would truly help heal the patient. Herbs weren't a problem—plants spoke to her. Natalie fancied they whispered how to grow them best, how they could help and how she should prepare them. It was easy as breathing for Natalie to prepare an herb to treat an illness. Though the Abbey staff regarded her as one of the best Namers, in her opinion, Healer Juliers had always been the best Namer—her Naming teacher, in fact, five years ago when she first attended the Abbey as a student.

Natalie had learned more from Healer Juliers than she had from any other Abbey teacher. She'd watched as he'd laid his strong, confident hands on the sick and injured. Their bodies and their illnesses spoke to him the way herbs spoke to Natalie. And when he'd placed his hands on hers to show her new Naming skills … she sucked in a breath. Well, that was something best left alone. She'd been thirteen and he twenty. She a student and he a teacher. It had been a schoolgirl infatuation. That was all.

But now, she longed for his skills and confidence. She could picture his wide, capable hands with their long fingers as he placed them upon her patient's body. Juliers would find the problem, she was certain.

She shook her head. Juliers wasn't there. She glanced around the hospital, the thought of having someone else Name the patient flitting across her mind. No, this patient was hers. Besides, she shouldn't need anyone to double-check her. She would simply have to repeat the Naming process.

Sitting at the head of the bed once again, Natalie drew a shaky breath and began. Once more her energy flowed effortlessly into her patient's body, stopping, as she expected, at the burn sites. She clenched her fists to stop herself from banging them on the bedside when every sensation, every image in her mind was the same as before.

Biting her lip, she adjusted her hands and tried to ignore the trickles of sweat between her shoulder blades. She paid particular attention to the energy surrounding the burns; the shape and feel of it. She observed the boundaries between where the solenloe poultice had helped and where the burns were still healing. Head bent forward and a cramp forming in her back, Natalie waited to spot any differences from her first examination. Then, like stars materializing at twilight, three small, separate shadows appeared in his side in one of the worst parts of the burns. Either those were pockets of infected burn … or shrapnel.

Scrambling out of her chair, she grabbed her satchel and removed her surgery and suture kit. She placed everything next to the patient's side. Now for pain management. Thankfully, Em was still there and currently unoccupied.

Em noticed her attention. "Need help?"

Natalie nodded. "Can you keep him sedated while I remove shrapnel from his side?"

"Absolutely."

With brisk efficiency, the two women prepared for minor surgery.

"We're getting a little too good at this," Natalie commented as they washed their hands.

Em snorted. "I'm a midwife. I'm still wondering what I'm doing stitching up wounds in the hospital."

"All hands on deck when the going gets rough." Though she knew Em missed being a midwife exclusively, Natalie couldn't help but feel selfishly happy to be spending more time with her best friend. Since passing to full Healer status, their respective careers had made it hard to find time together. Sometimes Natalie longed to be a student again when most of her days had been spent in Em's company and there hadn't been a war showing her the worst of humanity every day.

Em scrubbed her hands with soap. "How many casualties do you think they bring in a day from the port triage in Roseharbor?"

Natalie dried her hands on a clean towel. "It must be close to twenty or thirty. Lorelan has never managed to invade the Isles by land, for which I'm grateful, don't get me wrong. But it's hard to see all the people lying in this room who pay the price for it."

Em shot her friend a look Natalie was all too familiar with. "How are you holding up, Nat?"

Natalie finished using the towel, her gaze intent on her hands. "I'm fine. Let's get to work."

Returning to the burn victim's bedside, Em covered the wounded man's face with a mask, into which flowed a controlled amount of fidelia weed smoke that would keep him unconscious.

"Ready," Em stated.

Natalie nodded, cleaned the area, selected a scalpel and began. Using her memories from Naming, she knew approximately where to look for the first piece of shrapnel. She made a small incision, cleaned fluids out of the way, and a victorious grin appeared on her face when her efforts revealed a small, dark piece of wood. Natalie removed the splinter and repeated the process for the other two wounds. She cleaned each hole and packed them with garlic paste to kill and prevent further infection, and then applied new solenloe poultices. She Activated the garlic mixtures and new poultices, her energy gliding in and around the wounds and her herbal applications. The harmony between the two resonated such that her heart felt full and the sides of her mouth curled up. Lifting her hands from her patient, she placed them on her heart and took a deep breath. She'd done her best by this man. Hopefully she—well, that would be enough.

Thanking Em, she wearily took a seat next to her patient's good side and held his hand. Jake came over and, with her permission, jumped on the bed and lay at the man's feet. Natalie was back to the worst part—waiting.

CHAPTER 2

Late the next morning, after sleeping in and availing herself of a bath, Natalie swirled her green Healer's cloak about her shoulders and skipped down the spiral staircase to the first floor of the Abbey. She strode toward the Headmistress's office, Jake trotting behind her. The Headmistress oversaw not only the school and its students, but also the activities of the Abbey Healers.

Natalie entered the Headmistress's office and opened the thick leather-bound volume in which each Healer logged their patients, treatments and any new, useful observations. She selected a quill, dipped it in the ink and began her notes. Her quill hovered above the parchment as she struggled to describe her experience with Naming her burn patient's injuries.

The return of the Headmistress startled Natalie out of her reverie. "How is your patient in bed twenty-four?"

"Much better. He should make a full recovery soon," Natalie replied. Frowning, she told the Headmistress about her difficulties Naming his injuries and how she'd missed the wooden shrapnel the first time around.

The Headmistress put her strong, wrinkled hand on Natalie's shoulder. "And that's how we learn, my dear. Excellent work."

Natalie shook her head. "I should have—"

"Come, have a seat." The Headmistress sat behind her desk, and Natalie took a seat in the overstuffed red chair in front of it, Jake curling up in a ball at her feet. "Would you like some tea?"

Natalie nodded her head and the Headmistress poured tea into Natalie's favorite teacup—a delicate china one with various plant specimens painted on it. Natalie's fingers wrapped around the familiar cup, and she savored the tea's delicious scent.

Headmistress Gayla sat and blew on her own tea to cool it. "Healers walk a difficult road. We often find ourselves isolated. As you know from your time in the hospital, even when surrounded by other Healers, one often ends up working alone. It's why we teach all students to Name and Heal patients without the assistance of other Healers. This, naturally, requires quite a bit of confidence.

"I, of all people, know why you doubt yourself. But remember, in that patient's case, there was nothing even an experienced Healer could've done. Good Healers think on their feet and look for the hidden amongst the ordinary. You have great ability, love. Trust it."

Natalie willed the tears pricking her eyes not to spill over. Goddess knows the Headmistress had seen her cry in her office often enough. If only trusting herself was as easy as just saying the words. Unfortunately, the dragon of self-doubt perched on her shoulders, its claws firmly dug in. Natalie stared at her tea and said nothing.

"I thought you'd look like that." Headmistress Gayla folded her arms and smiled like a cat about to pounce on a mouse. "I'm due at the hospital in a few minutes, but before I go, I have a request. Healer Giles is getting married and moving to Roseharbor in one week. Since the new semester is starting soon, that leaves me without an

Introduction to Naming professor. I would like you to take her place. You have a lot to offer as a Naming teacher and I think our newest students will gain much by learning from you."

Natalie blinked at her Headmistress, who sipped her tea calmly, a bemused expression on her aged face.

"Well, I do need to leave for the hospital now. I'm so glad we had tea, it's been too long." Gayla swept from the room, squeezing Natalie's shoulder as she passed, leaving Natalie staring after her.

Teach Naming? She'd just become a full Healer a year ago and never even considered being a professor. Well, to be honest, she'd never really considered what she wanted to do with her Healing career. She'd been so focused on Healing the next patient and making sure the Headmistress was happy with her work. *But teaching? And she wants me to take Healer Juliers's position? My Goddess.*

Natalie's head fell into her palms. Jake, sensing her distress, jumped into her lap.

"Oof!" She hugged him and closed her eyes against the sloppy dog kisses, not even minding his horrid dog breath. "Thanks, buddy." Never had she been so grateful for the late night she'd been Healing a patient in the nearby town of Saltwick and had found a sick puppy near death in the alley. Jake had made a full recovery under the care of the Abbey's animal sanctuary Healers, and Headmistress Gayla let Natalie keep the stray retriever mix. Amongst the Abbey staff, many of whom kept rescued stray animals themselves, Jake's friendly, outgoing personality and constantly wagging tail made him a particular favorite.

Natalie closed her eyes. Teaching Naming. How was she even going to do that? Well, letting the Headmistress down was not an option. She was just going to have to figure it out.

The Abbey bell tolled one hour after midnight. Natalie

wadded up yet another piece of parchment and threw it into the fireplace. "I still struggle to Name patients and now I'm Naming professor? Goddess's bloomers, how will this end well?"

Tomorrow was the first Naming class for which she would be Professor, and after one week of attempts to plan her class curriculum, she still had no bloody idea where to begin. When consulted for advice, Healer Giles had told Natalie that every night she thought about what the class needed to work on, and then had the students do that the during the next morning's class. Natalie hated working like that; she preferred to plan things out in advance. Yet in each attempt to plan the first week, she'd cast about and failed to find a place to begin.

Her spring semester class would consist of first-year students at Bridhe of the Isles Abbey who'd never accessed the ley lines on the Isle, let alone Named an illness. Her quill hovered over the parchment as she tried to come up with yet another teaching plan. How had her teachers guided her from a novice to someone who could Name a patient by herself?

When she'd first learned Naming, everyone had examined one sick student. Natalie rolled this idea around in her head and discarded it. As a student, being singled out in front of the class had embarrassed her; she had no wish to inflict the same upon her own students. "With my luck, no one would be sick anyway," she grumbled and plopped her head down on her elbow, breaking her quill in the process. "Argh!" She threw the quill across her desk.

Jake lifted his head, staring at her from his enviable position on her bed, curled up in a small ball on top of her pillow. Natalie wondered once again at the magical ability of large dogs to curl up in the smallest of balls. Satisfied she was not in danger, he rested his head on his paws and his eyes drifted closed.

Natalie obtained a new quill and chewed on the end thoughtfully. Once she got them going, once they got the feeling, it would be easy. But how did she get them in touch with their own Healing energy and that of Ismereld?

She put her hands on either side of her own head, whereupon her own Healing energy detected the headache growing there. She yanked her hands away and stared at them. Moving her hands so they were cupped, one right on top of the other, she sensed her own energy pulsing and tingling in the circle her two hands created. Perhaps she could start there? Just with a small demonstration of the power already in their hands.

Since it was better than anything she'd come up with so far, she collapsed into bed, curled around Jake and fell asleep.

Natalie stood outside the Naming classroom door with her back pressed up against the wall, eyes closed. This was a huge mistake. Surely Juliers would somehow stop haunting her dreams, appear beside her and take over so she could disappear to the sanctuary of the greenhouse tucked away down in the cloisters.

But no one appeared and she remained alone in the echoing hallway.

She blinked and huffed out a breath she didn't know she'd been holding. Jake peered at her, his warm brown eyes filled with unconditional love. "Hell and damn," she swore at him. Gulping, she pushed off the wall, tilted her chin up, drew her shoulders back and walked into the classroom. Her whole body tingled. Her legs felt like she was walking through deep sand. She hoped she didn't vomit in front of the entire class.

She reached her desk, turned and faced her students. A sea of eyes stared at her expectantly. She began speaking before she lost her nerve.

"Good morning class and welcome to Introductory Naming I'm Professor Natalie Desmond and I am replacing Healer Giles as your teacher," she blurted. *No run on sentences or they'll know you're nervous.*

She made eye contact with a girl whose skin was the color of strong tea. She took a breath, then spoke again. "As you know, all illnesses we encounter must be properly Named before they can be treated and our patients Healed. Proper Naming takes years of practice. This is just the beginning ..."

As she spoke, she selected different students in turn to look in the eye, speaking directly to them. This helped calm her nerves and communicate the importance of her lesson. When she concluded, she had the class practice on themselves. "First, cup your hands as if you were holding a small, imaginary ball of light. One hand is on the bottom of the ball and one hand on the top. Close your eyes and breathe. Tell me what you feel—don't raise your hand, just say it out loud."

"Tingling," said the girl Natalie had first made eye contact with.

"Like I'm holding my hands over a candle flame," said a boy with a shock of bright red hair and freckles.

"Like I've captured a river current," a tiny wisp of a girl piped up.

Natalie observed the students—her students—with wonder. Here they were, just starting. There was a long road ahead of them, but they'd just learned a bit more about the power within themselves. One day, they'd each be Naming patients on their own, with the full knowledge of what it meant to be Attuned to the magic of Ismereld and the green cloak to go along with it. And she would help them get started.

A boy with tan skin and long, curly hair stared at his hands, puzzled. "Professor, why can I do this and not my sister?"

"Excellent question. No one understands why some people Attune to this Isle and others do not. Some people never Attune to an Isle. Or, one day, your sister could visit one of the other four Isles, and, if the Isle's magic accepts her, she would be an Attuned of that Isle.

"In fact, not only do people travel from Isle to Isle to see if they become Attuned, but travelers come from far across the main continent to live here. It's one of the reasons our population is so diverse. Now, back to the subject at hand."

She moved around the room assisting and guiding, encouraging the class to place their hands on their own bodies or on Jake, who proved to be an excellent test subject with his lolling tongue and big dog smile. The looks of wonder on her students' faces made her heart swell with pride.

For the first time that morning, she wasn't yearning for the solitude of the greenhouse. Here in her classroom, the exchange of knowledge generated its own powerful energy. Warmth radiated through Natalie's body when she saw eager young people put knowledge to use, gratified that it was she who gave them that knowledge.

The class fell over one another to ask questions, which she did her best to answer in the context of the basic education level they had. When the hour passed, Natalie reluctantly dismissed the class.

The boy with the bright red hair stood in front of her after all the students left. He was so tiny, but even so Natalie could see the generous smattering of freckles across his face when she smiled down at him.

"When do I get my green cloak?" he asked.

Natalie knelt in front of him so she could look directly into his eyes. "The same time as all the Attuned on every Isle—after you get your education and pass your apprenticeship."

Smiling at the boy's disappointment, Natalie walked to her classroom desk and sat tall, eyes closed. How odd. Or amazing. Well, both. In the year since becoming a Healer, she'd started to wonder what she wanted to do with her life. She'd Healed the sick and injured. Such had been her calling since she was ten and her brother, Aaron, had fallen from a ladder and she hadn't known how to help.

Eight years later, she did know how to help. And a part of her had started to wonder what came next. And then the war had started and now there wasn't any time for wondering.

But here, in the silence of the room, her fingertips began to tingle. The tingling spread to her arms and suffused her whole body. It wasn't energy from the ley lines, it was energy from her students flowing in her and within her. It was the excitement of knowing she wanted to teach everything she knew to these children and help them be the best Healers possible. It was the desire to know that she'd been there to give these boys and girls the proper basics they'd need, when, some years from now, these same students would be scattered across Ismereld, Naming a patient in some remote fishing village, assigned as a Healer to a small town or in the hospital in the dead of night.

Her eyes snapped open. She fumbled through the desk drawers for some paper, an ink pot and a quill, and she wrote out a curriculum until her hand cramped and she had to stop writing.

Three weeks into her teaching career, Natalie made her way to the greenhouse after her Naming class. She had one blissful hour before dinner when she could be alone and at peace with her plants. Tucked in the corner of the cloisters, the greenhouse was a simple building. It was small, but the low cedar walls and glass ceiling surrounded her like an embrace when she entered. Rows of herbs grew in pots on the tables. Natalie checked the cast iron stove in the corner; it was emanating the right amount of heat for this time of year. Without the stove, they'd be unable to grow herbs out of season. Delicious green scents filled the room, and Natalie stopped to take a deep breath. Peace seeped into her bones. This was her home. She left the door open to let the spring breeze in and turned to the one table left empty—the worktable. Jake trotted to his usual corner, turned around in three meticulous circles, and lay down on the cool dirt floor with a sigh.

Natalie ran her fingertips along the thick boards of the polished wooden table at the center of the room debating what she should work on. Ah, dullanbark. Yes. She grabbed a mortar and pestle, selected some dullanbark from the drying room behind the main greenhouse and began crushing the bark. It was a tough, stubborn, stringy substance—good for reducing fevers—and in no time, her sweat clung to her skin with the effort. She doffed her cloak, hung it on the greenhouse doorknob so she wouldn't forget it, and then returned to the table.

Natalie closed her eyes and became aware of everything—the trickle of sweat right between her shoulder blades, the assorted scents of herbs—both growing and drying—surrounding her, the gritty texture of the dirt under her feet and the coolness on her toes as she spread them apart on the dirt. Contentment and joy suffused her whole being.

Natalie looked up when Jake lifted his head and stared at the greenhouse door, ears pricked. She'd been so lost in her work that she hadn't heard the footsteps echoing on the cloister walk. Jake stood and trotted to the door. Natalie placed her pestle down and followed her dog.

A tall man with short, dark wavy hair, dressed in a brilliant white shirt, impeccably tailored black riding pants and tall, shiny black riding boots approached the greenhouse. His green Healer's cloak rippled in the breeze behind him. Her heart pounded in her chest when he caught sight of her. A thin beard now covered his face, but his emerald green eyes left no doubt. Her jaw dropped.

Juliers.

CHAPTER 3

Unaware of his owner's discomfiture, Jake jumped around Juliers in circles, tail wagging.

"Jake," Juliers exclaimed and knelt to scratch whatever bit of dog wasn't wiggling with sheer delight. Natalie peered around the greenhouse doorframe, brushing the dirt off her mud brown pants and running a hand over her amber hair, which had mostly fallen out of its braid. Jules glanced up; blood rushed to her face as she gazed into those emerald eyes. Hell in a kettle, must her face betray her right now?

"Natalie? Is that you?" Juliers said.

"Yes," she croaked. Clearing her throat, she spoke again. "Welcome back, Healer Juliers." She grasped for ideas of what to say next like she was trying to catch minnows in a stream. The last time they'd had a real conversation, she'd been a student and he a teacher. Conversation about classroom topics had come easily. Now they were colleagues and a war separated them. *Should I ask about the war? Goddess, no, that's way too personal. The weather? Ugh, small talk would be so trite.*

As if he couldn't bear the silence, Jake jumped up and tugged on Juliers's cloak. Natalie smiled when Juliers laughed and tugged back. A tug-of-war ensued between the two, Juliers grinning and Jake growling playfully. Natalie's giggles stopped when he turned and looked into her eyes again. At that moment, Jake gave one big tug and Juliers's cloak slid off to the side, revealing only a sewn seam where his lower right arm should be.

The blood drained from Natalie's face. "You're injured," she stated. She hoped she conveyed the proper mix of acknowledgment and lack of pity. *For Goddess's sake, how did a Healer get close enough to combat to lose part of an arm?*

"Yes," he admitted, looking away.

Unable to stop her Healer's instincts, she approached him and took his right arm in her own hands for examination. From what she could tell, his hand was amputated just above his wrist.

"I was lucky," he continued. "My Healing abilities helped me prevent infection. However, the teachers here at the Abbey neglected to teach me how to restore a missing limb. Needs to be added to the curriculum, if you ask me."

She grinned up at him as he smiled wryly down at her. He stood so tall and entirely too close. She could just lift her fingers and brush his cheek … Natalie blushed and released his arm. "I'm glad the Five thought to spare the rest of you for us. But how do you Name with only one hand?"

Juliers looked away again. "It's why I've returned to the Abbey. I need to consult Healers I trust about my current … situation."

"Of course," Natalie said, cocking her head. He'd returned to the Abbey solely to consult other Healers about his arm? Not because he belonged there after he could no longer participate in the war? He raised his eyes to hers again, and Natalie saw, just for a moment, the panic his current situation caused him. "Please let me know if I might provide any assistance."

Juliers gave her a noncommittal nod. He spotted her green Healer's cloak and a broad grin spread across his face. "You've passed to the Healer rank, I see. Congratulations."

"Yes, I completed my apprenticeship a year ago. I'm part of the regular on-call and hospital rotation of Healers now. And of course, I can often be found here among my herbs."

Juliers laughed. "Naturally. I'm surprised you're not teaching Herbalism by now."

"I …" Natalie brushed an imaginary bit of dirt off her shirt, sighed and leveled her gaze at the man before her. "I'm teaching Naming."

"Naming? Why you?"

"I'm sorry?"

"Why are you teaching Naming? You're obviously more talented with Herbs than Naming. I can think of three Healers off the top of my head more qualified to teach Naming than you. What happened to Healer Giles?"

"Got married and moved to Roseharbor." Natalie lifted her chin. "The Headmistress herself selected me to replace her."

Juliers snorted. "Well, I'm back now. I'll go talk to the Headmistress. Miss Desmond." He bowed slightly and swept away, bootheels beating a staccato rhythm on the cobblestones.

Natalie pinched the bridge of her nose. That went well. Good Goddess, did he mean to take her teaching position away?

Shaking, Natalie returned to her worktable and pounded the dullanbark with a vengeance. She had no doubt that Juliers suffered a lot—physically and probably psychologically. Still, was it so much to ask that her old Naming teacher would be proud of her new position as a teacher within the school? Juliers had been so amiable as a teacher, explaining the most complex concepts simply, step by step. He'd stayed after class to help the students who'd needed it and cheerfully mentored the students, like Natalie, who'd excelled in the subject. Wouldn't such a man want to see his students succeed?

When twilight shrouded the greenhouse in shadow, she put her tools away. She closed the greenhouse, face flushed and arms shaking. As she traipsed to the bathroom to wash up, it dawned on Natalie that, while Juliers had not died in the war, the man she'd known was gone.

At mealtimes, the Abbey great hall filled with students, apprentices and Healers alike. Natalie entered with Jake, praying Healer Juliers was not there. Natalie snorted; the irony of that. Four months aching to see the man, now she'd do anything to avoid him.

And it's just Juliers now, she reminded herself. After all, they were equal in status, despite whatever he felt. She kept her eyes on the flagstone floor until she reached the large serving tables groaning with food. She ladled some venison stew into a bowl and selected a chunk of bread. Ordinarily, she might take a moment to admire the setting sun's rays shining through the Arcadian stained glass windows, but she didn't want to chance seeing Juliers. She spotted Em sitting at a small, out of the way table, her scirpa draping in lovely folds down her back.

Emmeline followed a particular Goddess tradition that required men and women to keep their heads covered with a long piece of cloth called a scirpa. The scirpa wrapped around the head at the top tied off in a complicated knot at the back of the neck. The two ends hung down about her shoulders. Fingers clutching the sides of her bowl, Natalie hastened over.

"Em. Please, tell me all about the new babies," Natalie begged, setting down her food and plopping into the chair opposite her friend.

Em smirked. "Ha, too late. I already know that a

certain Healer is back from the war. Have you seen him?" she stage-whispered, waggling her reddish eyebrows.

"Yes." Natalie kept her eyes on her plate.

"What? Healer Perfect is indeed not perfect? Do tell."

Natalie picked up her spoon and toyed with her stew. "It's not that he's not perfect, it's ... well, he was injured in the war." She dropped her voice. "He ... he lost the lower part of his right arm. I don't think he can Heal anymore— or at least not well. I think he came back expecting to teach since he can't Heal. But I have his job. He's gone to the Headmistress to see if he can take my place."

Em's alabaster complexion turned ghostly ashen. "By the Goddess. That's awful. On both counts. I feel terrible about his injury, but that's no excuse to take your position. Speaking of awful, two Healers were sent to Whitestrand today to deal with some sort of epidemic."

"What?" Natalie scoffed. "We haven't had an epidemic in over a hundred years. Do you know anything about the illness?"

Em's face was grim. "No, but given Whitestrand is on the coast and a port town, anything could've come in from anywhere."

The sound of the third chair at the table scraping across the flagstone floor interrupted their conversation.

"I heard it's spreading through Whitestrand like wildfire," said a deep voice. Natalie rolled her eyes up and glared at Juliers as he sat down across from her with his own meal. She just couldn't deal with him right now.

"We'd like to sit alone. Please sit somewhere else." Natalie said.

Juliers gave her an insolent look and changed the subject. "I spoke with Headmistress Gayla. I've got a room in the Healer's dormitory."

"Great," replied Natalie. "Did she personally invite you to sit down at our table as well?"

"No," Juliers grinned. "Did that myself."

"Well, you can just as easily undo it."

Juliers popped a bite of roll into his mouth. "What if I don't want to?"

Natalie gritted her teeth. She'd underestimated how much he'd changed. The man who'd left had been much more civil. "It's not down to you. Please leave our table now."

"And what about you, Healer Arnold? Would you like me to leave?"

Em clasped her hands in her lap. "Natalie asked you nicely to leave, twice. I suggest you do so."

Healer Juliers looked from Em to Nat. "Why do you want me to go?"

Natalie shot him a challenging look. "A gentleman and friend would wait until they're invited before sitting down at someone's table."

Juliers's jaw dropped open and he snapped it shut. "You wound me, good Naming Professor. I shall leave you two alone."

"Insufferable ass," Natalie muttered to his retreating back and put her bread in her mouth and tore out a bite.

Em leaned across the table. "Okay, so sitting down uninvited wasn't the politest thing, but it wasn't the end of the world. Would it have been so terrible to share a meal and maybe learn more about what's going on with him?"

Nat folded her arms, looking away. "Be careful, you're getting your scirpa in your food." Em hastily removed one end from her mashed potatoes.

"You be careful, Nat."

Nat glanced at Em's pale, freckled face full of concern, and nodded reluctantly.

After dinner, Natalie took Jake to the greenhouse. She paced the length of the building, the scent of growing plants not bringing the usual comfort to her burning temper. Although the near-full moon gave off enough light for her to avoid running into objects, it did not give off enough for her to do any serious work. Still, there was no place else she wanted to be, and she sat on the worn workbench while Jake curled up in his usual corner. The fight with Juliers kept replaying in her head. She tried to keep in mind he was a war veteran in hopes she could hold some compassion for him. She could deal with physical damage—she was a Healer after all—but not his attitude toward her. Implying she was unqualified to teach Naming. Trying to take her job and … and … being so unlike the man she used to know—the man who'd seemed drawn to her budding Healing skills like a moth to flame and then kindled them until her thirst for Healing knowledge had become insatiable. The sensation of hundreds of warm butterflies taking flight in her stomach and spiraling up around her chest made her close her eyes, heart pounding.

Natalie clamped down on the feeling right away. "Why doesn't he think I'm qualified to teach Naming? And what if he's right?" she murmured.

Jake growled and gave a soft woof. Natalie lifted her head. Footsteps sounded on the cloister walk. Jake sniffed the air and thumped his tail on the floor. A friend then.

Juliers poked his head in the doorway. Natalie folded her arms and stepped back. They'd fought both times they'd seen each other since he'd come back. *What does he want now?*

"May I come in?"

Natalie, expecting to be on the receiving end of his temper, dropped her hands to her sides. "Yes." She cringed inwardly at the timidity in her voice.

Juliers ducked under the doorway and sat next to her on the workbench in silence. His left hand rested on the table, idly drawing invisible patterns on it.

"I'm sorry," he whispered, then cleared his throat. "I'm sorry for what I said earlier. For how I acted at dinner. For pretty much all of today, actually."

Stunned, Natalie stared at him. The moonlight cast his face in gray and white shadow as he kept his gaze on the table. There in the shadows, she saw a glimpse of the man he'd once been, the man who'd recognized her talents and nurtured them. A man who now lay buried deep under the burdens he carried.

"I don't know how to do this," he whispered. "I don't fit in where I used to."

Natalie wanted to speak so many words of comfort that they all jammed up trying to come out. Which was just as well, because when she thought twice about it, what was there to say? Life wasn't going to be the same for him ever again. If she said it was going to be all right, he'd either laugh out loud or leave on the spot.

"I'm sorry for what I said at dinner as well." Sitting in the moonlit greenhouse, it was quite clear Natalie was no longer that bright-eyed student and he was no longer her teacher and mentor. Perhaps it was time they became something new.

Natalie took a deep breath and turned to face him. "I can't make your hand come back. And as you know, there's literally no magic fix for the situation you're in. But we can start over as friends. I can offer you my friendship, Juliers Rayvenwood. If you'll take it."

Juliers stared at her. She stared right back, entranced by the way the moonlight enchanted his emerald eyes. Her traitorous hands ached to reach out and stroke the stubble on his chin. She struggled to swallow past the tightness in her throat, but she kept her gaze on him, daring him to accept her offer.

"Jules," he said at last. "My friends call me Jules."

CHAPTER 4

The next morning, Natalie hunched over her classroom desk, jotting down notes about the day's class. Many things had gone wrong during the class period, and despite the beginnings of a headache, she wanted to update her lesson plans. She finished her notes and snorted. Notes be damned. The class's outcome had been a result of a teacher distracted by memories of moonlight shining on dark, wavy hair and enchanting green eyes.

She jumped when the classroom door banged open. Juliers—no, he said his friends called him Jules—stormed into the classroom and stalked up to her desk. He glared at her as if she'd committed some horrible crime, then strode over to glare out the window.

Her eyebrows rose. "To what do I owe this pleasure?"

"All the Healers I talk to say the same thing," he snapped.

"What do they suggest? Have they helped at all?" She leaned forward and rested her chin on her hands.

Shaking his head, he closed his eyes, and a muscle

bulged in his jaw.

Natalie remained at her desk, their moonlit camaraderie of the night before seeming years away. Perhaps it had been a dream, Natalie thought, pinching the bridge of her nose, her headache coming on full force.

"May I ask what they said then?" Sarcasm slipped into her voice, and she dropped her hands to the arms of her chair. The man was as forthcoming as a stone wall.

"They said," he parroted, turning on her, "I should see if I could use my Healing abilities if I partnered with another Healer. All of them suggested you."

The same green eyes that had bewitched her last night threatened to consume her in flame.

"Which Healers said this?" Natalie asked, anxious to know who thought so well of her. Jules simply glared at her. She sighed. "Is it such a terrible fate working with me? I thought we were friends."

"But I shouldn't have to … One Healer should be enough for a small village or town. Two Healers for smaller assignments would be wasteful. Besides, I don't want to have to rely on anyone. Especially you." He turned away from her, muttering. "I shouldn't have come back. I should leave."

Natalie sat speechless as he stalked out of the classroom. *How dare he? My students are learning. They enjoy being in my class. And whomever he talked to must have a reason for suggesting he work with me. I am not a terrible Healer or person, for Goddess's sake. Does he doubt my abilities?*

Her own temper, as it often did, went straight to her tear ducts. She swiped up her papers, called Jake and ran for her room before anyone saw her crying.

"Natalie?" A familiar voice called as Natalie sped along the cloisters walk to her room.

Natalie scrubbed the tears from her cheeks and looked over her shoulder. She spotted a stout man with carefully combed white hair, exquisite silk robes and a finely made green Healer's cloak.

"Healer Aldworth. It's good to see you."

"It's good to see you as well. I haven't seen enough of you since your apprenticeship. I do miss being your mentor. Though I seem to have stopped you on your way to someplace important. I apologize."

"Oh, uh, no. I was just—I'm fine."

"May I walk with you for a bit?"

"Certainly."

"I understand Healer Rayvenwood approached you about working together."

News travels fast. "Yes." She didn't want to say more lest the tears start falling again.

"Did he seem amenable?"

Natalie hesitated, not sure how to tell her former mentor and a member of the Council of Healers she'd been thoroughly rejected. "No, not really."

"That is unfortunate."

They walked along in silence. Healer Aldworth regarded her intently as they walked. Natalie studied the cobblestone walk at her feet with undue fascination.

"Might I suggest you try to convince him to work with you? I'd be very grateful if you did."

"Why? I mean, why me?"

Healer Aldworth smiled at her. "I believe if we are to have Healer Juliers restored to us, you are the best person for the job. And I know you won't let me down. After all, we both know your patient who went into a coma was just an anomaly."

That's what the Council of Healers decreed at the time. A patient with a severe head injury. It could have happened to any Healer. A lone blemish on the career of an apprentice with an otherwise stellar record. If only he knew how memories of that patient tortured her; playing over and over in her head with each patient she treated. Then he would know it would be the last thing to give her the confidence to approach Jules. But Healer Aldworth was her teacher; her mentor. She owed it to him to try. She couldn't disappoint him.

"Yes, sir," she whispered.

"Good morning, Healer Desmond. Do keep me posted on your work with Healer Rayvenwood."

Sitting on her bed with Jake licking her face, Natalie thought of all the things she should have said back to Jules. Many of them included words Natalie's mother would skin her alive for using. But it was useless; the moment was gone and the man was still as insufferable as ever—if not worse. Fantastic, she thought, flopping back onto the bed and glaring at the ceiling.

At the same time, she didn't want to let Healer Aldworth down. She'd already let him down so much when that patient had gone into a coma. And, much as it pained her to admit it, she'd rather Jules be safe here in the Abbey; she did not want him to leave again. Somehow, she had to convince him to stay and work with her. Her brain churned out ideas about how Naming could work with two people. Had anyone ever tried it before? She could neither recall learning about it as a student nor reading about it in any book. Jules was right: in general, the Abbey staffed Ismereld with as many Healers as possible, but that often meant Healers found themselves Healing alone in small towns and clusters of buildings barely large enough to be called a village. People helped each other in the hospital, but only with medical tasks. Magical tasks like Naming and Activation were done alone.

Natalie pushed the palms of her hands against her eyes. But why couldn't Jules Name by himself? She reached over to Jake, closed her eyes, placed a hand on him and attempted to get a clear picture of his body in her head. Seeing nothing but haze, she imagined her energy dipping farther into the Isle for more magic. The misty image of Jake swirled with small eddies drifting around the outside. Giving in, she placed two hands on him, breathing a sigh of relief when a crystal clear image of her dog's body appeared in her mind in its normal ghostly blue color.

Goddess above, if a cloudy mist was all Jules saw now after nearly a lifetime of Healing, no wonder he'd been in a horrible temper since his return. In his shoes, she'd be on the edge of giving up all hope.

Yet someone at the Abbey must feel there was some hope; otherwise, why would they want Jules to partner with her?

"It sure would be nice if that person would share their knowledge with the rest of the class," Natalie said to the empty room, rolling her eyes. "Like, do you expect us to both put our hands on someone at the same time? Would we see the blockages together? Would we detect the same illnesses?"

Natalie sat bolt upright. Wait a minute, she had been there when two Healers had put their hands on a patient at the same time. She and Jules had been those Healers. Well, she had been a student at the time, and Jules had been her Naming teacher showing her how to Name. It had been her first Naming class here at the Abbey when she was fourteen and a first-year student.

Juliers had started the lecture and Natalie, rather distracted by his handsomeness, hadn't been paying attention.

"So, let's start with you." Natalie's face flushed when he stopped in front of her. "What is your name?" he asked.

"Natalie Desmond," she whispered, suddenly finding her clasped fingers on the desk quite fascinating.

"All right Natalie, please join Emmeline."

Natalie traipsed to the front of the room and stood next to Emmeline Arnold, whom she'd never met before. Emmeline sat nervously at the front of the class. She had a cold that day, thus making her the perfect Naming practice subject.

"Good, now, place your hands on the sides of Miss Arnold's shoulders."

Biting her lip, Natalie put her trembling hands on Emmeline's shoulders, and the two girls giggled nervously.

Healer Juliers looked her in the eyes. "Obviously you'll ultimately do this by yourself, but I'm going to help you for now. It's going to be all right."

She nodded.

From behind her, Healer Juliers placed his hands over Natalie's. Natalie stared intently at the pattern of small flowers printed on the fabric of Em's dress. Her face felt like it was on fire, and her hands tingled.

"Close your eyes, Natalie," he said. Natalie was only too grateful to do so. "Now, center your awareness on your breath. Imagine that awareness dropping down through the floor and into the depths of Ismereld Isle itself. See if you can sense one of the ley lines I talked about at the start of class."

Hoping he couldn't tell she hadn't been paying attention and had no idea what a ley line was, Natalie took a deep breath in and out of her nose. She concentrated on the place just below her ribcage where her breath rose and fell, right next to the butterflies swooping about in her stomach. She imagined one of the butterflies flying down out of her feet, through the Abbey floor and into the earth, searching in the dark soil. Her awareness sharpened and clarified. She jumped as tingling in her fingers and hands increased tenfold and she became simultaneously aware of Healer Juliers's and Emmeline's energy as well as her own.

Healer Juliers seemed to sense her connection to the ley line. "When you are ready, reach your awareness out through your fingers into Emmeline."

With more confidence, she imagined her awareness traveling down through her arms and through Emmeline's body. As it did, she was less aware of Healer Juliers's energy—as if she'd left it behind. She opened her eyes a fraction and saw he'd removed his hands from Emmeline. Natalie bit her lip and tried not to frown. Why didn't he leave his hands on hers?

"When you are ready, Natalie, describe your experience."

Bringing her attention back to the connection between her fingers and Em's, Natalie whispered. "My hands tingle, especially the fingertips. Like I am holding starlight or moonlight in my hands and I am able to direct the light into Emmeline's whole body." She adjusted her hands and frowned. "But ... There are places the light won't go. As if the ... as if the way is blocked and my light can't get through. I can't form a picture of her entire body."

"Where is the way blocked?" Healer Juliers's voice brushed across her ear from far away.

"Her nose and throat," Natalie replied. She adjusted her hands. "And a bit of her lungs." She adjusted her hands one more time to ascertain if there were more blocks, but her energy flowed very clearly into Emmeline, except to the places she'd listed. She put her hands in her lap, then turned and sought her teacher's approval. Juliers pinned her with an intense, speculative gaze. Captivated, Natalie stared back. Healer Juliers blinked, the spell broke and he turned to the rest of the class.

"Fantastic," he said. "Next?"

How Juliers had haunted her dreams since that first class. How ironic, on her first day of class with him, he may have unwittingly given her the answer to help the man plaguing her now. What would have happened in that first Naming class if he'd left her hands on hers and they'd sent their awareness into Em together instead? And, would it still have worked if one party was missing the lower part of one arm? Her fingers itched for the pages of a book. She needed answers.

Natalie managed to get to the library around twilight that evening after her rounds in the Abbey hospital. Pushing open the large, wooden double doors, she entered her second favorite place on the Abbey grounds.

The Abbey library was a horseshoe-shaped, two-level structure on the eastern side of the transepts. It had plush red carpet and shelves of dark mahogany from floor to ceiling on each level, packed to the brim with tomes on all subjects from Healing to the history of the Isles. Worn mahogany tables and overstuffed red chairs allowed library visitors a comfortable place to sit and research topics of their choice.

She perused the stacks, gauging the best place to begin. She clutched her Healing diary to her chest as she scanned the titles on the shelves. She'd started keeping her Healing diary when she was a first-year, writing odd bits of class notes and excerpts from books she hadn't wanted to forget. Five years later, various bits of knowledge stuffed the well-worn book to bursting, and Natalie took it with her nearly everywhere she went. She'd read her notes from cover to cover looking for anything about Healers Naming together and she hadn't found a thing. Time to see if she could add more to her diary.

Deciding the Naming books were the logical place to start, she went to those shelves and scanned the titles on the spines. She selected a likely title, sat down on a chair nearby, found a promising chapter and began to read, one foot absentmindedly rubbing Jake's belly.

An hour later, the stack of discarded books next to her wobbled precariously, her patience with pompous authors and their ability to write long, dull tomes worn quite thin. Natalie rubbed her eyes and carefully lit the lantern on the table next to her. Hands braced on her back, she paced while searching the worn leather spines for another title. *An Illness by Any Other Name* by Healer Nestor Scroop stood out. She laughed, shrugged and pulled it off the shelf.

"Have you found anything?" a voice asked quietly behind her, making her jump.

The shadows cast on Jules's face by her lantern aged him several years.

"No," she replied. "Other than a rather pompous lot of dead old men droning on and on about things we both already know."

A grin ghosted across his face, and he sat down in the chair next to hers. "Is there nothing for it then?"

"Well, I had an idea," she ventured.

He cocked a dark eyebrow. "A brand new Healer outsmarting the pompous, dead old men?"

"If they'd been smarter, they would've written less dull books," she retorted, this time making Jules laugh out loud.

A sense of lightness filled Natalie at the deep sound. Could they actually get along?

"If I'm correct, when you try to Name with one hand, you only get about half of the mental input you used to, yes?"

Jules grimaced. "Yes. The images of patient's bodies in my head are severely blurred, no matter how hard I work to bring them into focus."

Natalie nodded and sat next to him and faced him. She held her left hand out, palm up. "I'd like to try an experiment. Put your hand above mine."

Jules frowned at her, his hand rubbing the stubble on his chin.

The silence stretched on, but Natalie kept her hand out as if trying to coax a bird to take seed from her palm. Jules stared at her hand, his expression unfathomable. At last, his hand dropped into his lap, then he lifted it and hovered over hers.

A pulse of energy snapped awake between their two hands. Natalie closed her eyes as the connection between them sparked and grew. The intensity spread up her arm and through her whole body. When laying hands on others, she'd often felt something in return, but never on this scale. Her whole being filled with intense light; she felt as if she could heal the sickest person, raise the dead, or even fly right off the ground if she held her arms out.

She opened her eyes; she and Jules had clasped hands as their shared Healing connection had brought them nearly nose-to-nose. Her heart ached at the pain and longing etched on his face, and suddenly, his pain— physical and emotional— became her own. Their connection was incredible—and taxing.

"Jake, come," she rasped. Her dog got up from his sleeping place and walked over. She put her free hand on Jake's head, closed her eyes again and imagined their joined energy going into Jake.

"Jules, can you feel where the light won't go?" she whispered. Her back itched where sweat trickled between her shoulder blades. "Jules. Focus on Jake. I have my hand on his head, can you see him? Where won't the light go?" She opened her eyes and saw Jules had his closed, concentrating. Beads of sweat glistened on his forehead and his head was cocked to the side.

"His front right shoulder?" Jules inquired.

"Yes," Natalie crowed and let go of both Jules's hand and Jake's head, slumping back in her chair. Panting, she pushed her damp hair out of her face. "He has arthritis in his front right shoulder. It bothers him more at the end of the day."

Jules leaned back in his own chair, wiping the sweat off his face with a handkerchief.

"It worked," she grinned. "I wasn't sure it would … but it did. You could Heal again. We could try to treat a person, someone with something simple like a cold or an ear infection. If … if you wanted."

Jules rested his chin on his palm. "We've done one test. And I'm not even sure what we did, Natalie."

"We combined our magical energies with the Isle's ley lines. I haven't been able to find any supporting evidence in these books, but I believe when we combine our magic together, it makes up for the loss of vision, if you will, that you experience with the loss of your hand. If you think about it, it's a new way of Naming entirely since it only requires one hand on the patient."

Jules considered this. "I think I see what you're getting at. But I think it needs some fine-tuning. Look at us. We're sweating like pigs and I'm sure I could eat the Royal Palace out of house and home. If we're going to do this, we have a lot to figure out."

Bloody realist. Sweat soaked her own clothes and she could probably eat five of her mother's apple pies without batting an eye. Yet, she also felt like she could take off, fly around the Abbey, and then land and run to the nearest town and back. She jumped out of her chair and paced back and forth.

"So we need to practice a lot and test thoroughly."

Jules nodded. "But first, we eat."

CHAPTER 5

After stopping by the kitchens, where they ate enough to feed four horses, Natalie and Jules returned to the library to experiment with their newfound connection. Trial and error led to several discoveries. Jules figured out he was transferring too much energy to Natalie. By slowing his energy flow into her, their partnership became less tiring for him and left Natalie feeling more stable, rather than like a firework about to explode. They learned holding hands, rather than hovering her hand above his, resulted in Jules having the best ability to "see" the patient's energy, though their patient, the long-suffering Jake, trotted away after the eleventh experiment.

"I think it's time to stop," Natalie yawned, observing her dog's retreating backside.

"I think you're right," Jules replied with a yawn of his own and stood up, stretching. "Best put away this cartload of books you pulled out first."

Natalie took a book and whacked his shoulder with it. "Careful, Healer, or you'll need some Healing."

Jules chuckled, but then his face became serious as he turned to take the book from her. They stood, her hands on one end of the book and his on the other. "Thank you. I've been a bit of an ass these past few days. I'm surprised you helped me at all."

Peering up at him, Natalie attempted to gauge his sincerity. Her heart softened at what she saw. His hair, normally so carefully groomed, was a mess and his jaw had dark stubble showing. Was it harder for him to shave with one hand? In how many simple ways was he still trying to adapt to being an amputee? Surely he still struggled with many mundane tasks.

Yet his eyes, shadowed with grief when he'd found her earlier, shone with life now. Of everything they'd accomplished during their experiment, seeing him look optimistic was, to her, the greatest achievement. The overwhelming urge to reach across the small distance separating them and touch him swirled in her stomach.

Taking a deep breath, Natalie let go of her end of the book and turned away to get the next one. "Thank you for apologizing. But don't thank me for solving anything yet. Let's see if it works on more than just my dog, first."

Rather than make her usual hospital rounds that afternoon, Natalie entered the cacophonous Abbey animal sanctuary with Jules. Snakes and other reptiles had a warm room with a cast iron fireplace, whereas birds and small mammals each had a room with separate indoor and caged outdoor sections for those animals well enough to partake of it.

The sanctuary was the domain of Healer Euphemia Bowers, a short, stout woman whose scowl made Natalie wonder if the Headmistress had been lying when she'd given her approval for her and Jules to practice their new technique on the animals there. They found Healer Bowers bent over an injured fawn in the treatment room.

"Hullo," Healer Bowers grunted. "Gayla said you'd be coming."

Unable to bear the awkward silence that followed, Natalie said, "Uh, yes. Do you have any animals on which we could practice Naming?"

"The rabbits and turtles might be best. Don't get in my way."

Natalie and Jules hastened out of the room and, after a few wrong turns, happened upon the small mammals' room. Large ventilated boxes with straw bedding each contained one injured rabbit. Natalie spotted one brown fellow lying morosely on his side.

Natalie took a breath to steady her nerves. "Ready?"

Jules nodded, his face inscrutable.

Closing her eyes, she clasped his hand and they established the correct balance of energy. Natalie opened her eyes to find Jules's gazing at her intently. Mesmerized by his emerald eyes, she instinctively pulled him toward her until his forehead rested gently on hers. His breath brushed across her lips and Natalie's knees nearly gave way as their energy went out of control. She closed her eyes to reestablish it. "Sorry," she muttered. "Ready?" she asked when she'd found equilibrium again.

"Yes," he croaked.

She reached her free hand into the rabbit's box. The creature looked at her but didn't move. Not a good sign. She placed her hand on its back and exhaled. Light flowed from them into their small patient. She closed her eyes again as her whole body suffused with warm energy and her entire being thrilled at being part of something new and magical. She brought her awareness to the rabbit, his body taking shape in her mind.

"Jules," she whispered. "Can you see the rabbit now that I'm touching it?"

"Yes," he squeezed her hand.

"What do you see?"

"His back is hurt. Not broken, but the energy flow is

interrupted along the muscles that support his spinal cord. I'd say severe back muscle strain—maybe an injury from a predator?"

"That's what I see." With care, she lifted her hand off the rabbit, thanking it mentally, then she gently let go of Jules's hand and opened her eyes and beamed at him.

"That was good, but we need to do more." Jules turned and strode out of the room, green cloak swirling behind him. Natalie rolled her eyes and followed.

Natalie struggled to keep her eyes open as she ate dinner with Em that night. She made sure there were no extra chairs at the table, as she was sick to death of a certain Healer she'd spent all afternoon with. Their only company was Jake, head resting on his front paws under the table, alert for any falling objects.

"I swear to the Goddess, Em," she said, stuffing mashed potatoes into her mouth, "we must've Named every bloody animal in the sanctuary. Healer Bowers nearly turned purple. The looks she gave us most likely melted the walls behind us. I should check to be sure all the sanctuary walls are still there."

Em grinned. "But did it work?"

"Of course it did. It worked from the first moment we tried it." Natalie blushed at the memory. "It's taken some practice—"

"Just what sort of practice?" Em arched an eyebrow.

Natalie threw her napkin at Em. "The kind where I nearly took a dagger and stabbed him repeatedly because he just wouldn't believe it. He insisted we try and try again, even though we got it right each time. We even found some things Healer Bowers had missed. That went over well." Natalie shoved a forkful of chicken into her mouth. "I wanted to try Naming and treating some of the patients here in the Abbey hospital. But he disagreed, saying those patients are often in critical condition. I rather think getting back into the swing of things here with other Healers around would be good. Build him some confidence, you know? So we parted ways badly. Again."

"Well, you certainly do have a way with men."

"Thanks."

Em jabbed her fork at Natalie. "Lucky me. I don't have to listen you mooning about him anymore. Now I just have to listen to you gripe about him."

Natalie picked at her food. "He is very much changed."

"War does that to so many. We Healers are often the first to see."

"He was so confident and sure of himself when we were students. It's hard to imagine that man changing. Being torn down and remade into the man who came back. What he must have experienced … I can't even begin to imagine. I try to keep that in mind when I'm with him, but it's like he blames me for it all. Or at least takes it out on me. I get angry right back; I can't seem to help it."

"Maybe being a Healer again will help him."

"I honestly don't know. But I need to go to bed. I'm exhausted." Natalie said goodnight to Em and stumbled back to her room.

That night, a knock on her door woke Natalie from a restless sleep. It was Headmistress Gayla with a report of a seriously ill man in the hospital. All the night shift Healers were busy with battle-wounded soldiers, so the hospital needed extra staff. Natalie got dressed, grabbed her herb satchel, called Jake and strode down the hall.

"Natalie," Gayla called after her. "Why don't you wake Healer Juliers and try your new method of Naming? I hear from Healer Bowers that it's rather successful."

Natalie froze and resisted the urge to pinch the bridge of her nose. "All right," she was proud when her voice sounded almost neutral. "Where is his room?"

"Downstairs," the Headmistress replied. "It's right

under yours."

Natalie gritted her teeth. Might as well do it. She was the one who thought a hospital case was the best to start with, after all. She traipsed down the spiral staircase and wandered the lower hall, reading the nameplates until she found Jules's room. Nothing for it. She took a deep breath and knocked. She stepped back from the door, fiddling with the handle of her herb satchel.

The door to the room swung open and Jules stood there, disheveled from sleep, wearing only trousers and his dark hair a mess. The candlelight from the hallway spilled across the well-shaped planes of his chest.

Oh, dear. Natalie clenched her fingers tighter around the handle of her satchel lest she reach out and brush her fingers along his bare skin.

"Natalie, are you all right?" Jules said when she didn't say anything.

Natalie blinked, cheeks flaming. She snapped her mouth closed—holy Goddess, had it been open? "Yes. Yes, sorry. There's a seriously ill man in the hospital. The Headmistress would like us to treat him."

Jules ducked his head and ran his fingers through his hair.

Will he do it? Does he believe in us enough? Does he think we have enough experience to treat this patient?

After what seemed an eternity, he shrugged. "I guess we might as well."

CHAPTER 6

The Headmistress led Natalie and Jules to the first patient they would treat together, a barely conscious man whose pallor matched the sheets upon which he lay.

Natalie took the patient's wrist and felt his pulse. "What do you know about him?"

"He started feeling lethargic and sick yesterday around mid-morning and he had trouble waking earlier this evening."

Jules felt the patient's forehead. "No fever. What is his name?"

"Malcolm Bartlett," the Headmistress replied and left them to their work.

"All right, Malcolm. Let's see if we can get you well again." They began by examining the rest of his body for any other symptoms.

"Natalie, look." Jules nodded his head—a rash spread ominously on Malcolm's torso. The rest of their search yielded nothing significant.

Natalie washed and dried her hands at a nearby

washstand. "Let's see what the Naming reveals."

After Jules washed his hand, they resumed their positions by the patient, Natalie placing her one hand on Malcolm and the other in Jules's hand. Natalie bit her lip; it was like Malcolm's body sipped their energy rather than devouring it as a healthy body should. Natalie's arms ached. The energy eventually permeated his whole body, but not his heart. She opened her eyes.

"His lungs," Jules said.

"His heart," Natalie said at the exact same time.

Natalie dropped his hand as if it had betrayed her. "Let's go over the symptoms," she began objectively. "Sudden symptom onset, no fever—"

"No fever *yet*," Jules said.

"He's pale, with severe lethargy and a rash on his torso. He didn't absorb our energy well either, and the only place it didn't go," she glared at Jules, "was his heart. It's tremosis. He's going to be dead by tonight or tomorrow if we don't treat him."

"Vell's fever has the same symptoms—"

"If he's got Vell's, the fever will take three days to come. He'll be dead by then." She almost slammed her fists on the bed but clenched them instead. Why wasn't he listening to her?

"I'm certain about what I saw. It was his lungs. Vell's attacks the lungs. It's only just started, that's why you thought it was the heart, since they are so close together."

Natalie crossed her arms over her chest and raised an eyebrow. "Should we do the Naming again to double-check?"

"No. It's Vell's."

"If we wait for the fever to confirm it's Vell's, the tremosis could give him the heart attack that kills him."

Jules clenched his teeth. "It's Vell's."

Gripping the edge of the bed, Natalie leaned over Malcolm's ailing body, hissing further arguments at Jules. Jules got in her face, debating right back. He would *not* make her doubt herself. Not this time. They stopped short when Malcolm's body contracted into a ball and he broke out in a sweat.

"It's the heart attack," Natalie snarled, reaching for her herb satchel and grabbing a vial of plennia elixir. "Hold him still," she ordered two Healers who'd rushed to their aid. "Tip his chin back and help me open his mouth," she snapped at Jules. She poured the vile-smelling elixir down Malcolm's throat, shoved his chin closed and held it there. In her head, she apologized to him for all of it. The taste of the medicine, for holding his mouth closed while he tried to sputter the vile-tasting stuff back out and for the delay in getting the medicine he needed because Jules wouldn't listen, damn the man.

Once she was sure he'd swallowed all the medicine, Natalie placed one hand on Malcolm's heart and another on his back, closed her eyes and let her energy flow through him. She reached out to the plennia elixir in his body and Activated it. Or tried. She kept her hands on his body until a horrible cramp formed in her neck, but she refused to remove her hands until her energy glowed brightly throughout Malcolm's body. Except it never did. She Activated what herbs she could detect, then turned to the Healer nearest her. "More plennia elixir," she demanded.

She forced another dose down Malcolm's throat and again tried to detect the elixir in his body. There was nothing but dimness in her mind.

Laying her ear on his chest, his heartbeat sounded irregular and muffled. A terrifying amount of time passed from one beat to the next.

"No. No." Natalie climbed atop Malcolm Bartlett, interlaced her two hands and began compressions on his heart, making his heart beat for him. Every five beats, she'd stop to see if she could detect any of the plennia elixir's energy. All she could detect was light fading into nothingness.

A gentle hand caressed her shoulder. "Natalie. He's dead."

"No, I can save him!" Natalie frantically continued the chest compressions, willing Malcolm Bartlett to come back to life.

Her arms aching, sweat dripping off her forehead and her back clenched in knots, Natalie placed her palms on Malcolm Bartlett's shoulders and rested her ear on his chest. She closed her eyes. Silence and darkness. Tears welling up in her eyes, she kept her head on his quiet chest.

"Natalie, I—" Jules began.

She glared up at him from Malcolm's chest. "Get. Out."

CHAPTER 7

Natalie spent the night at Malcolm's bedside, tending to his body. She washed him with cool water and wrapped his body in a linen shroud. She and several other Healers carried his remains to the morgue to await his family. As dawn touched the horizon, Natalie sat in a chair next to what had been his hospital bed, with her head resting on her folded arms. An emptiness filled her that transcended tears.

A gnarled hand touched her shoulder. "Natalie," Gayla whispered. "The Council of Healers has called you and Juliers to a review. They want to know what happened here yesterday."

Natalie sat up and pressed her palms to her eyes. She couldn't look at Gayla at all; she feared the disappointment she'd see in the face of the woman who was like a mother to her.

She rose and shuffled behind Gayla through the narrow passage leading to the main part of the Abbey. At the end of the passage, they entered an ornately decorated antechamber. Natalie's old, scuffed leather boots stepped on elegant carpets and she gaped at the elaborately carved wooden walls she'd only seen one other time. On their right stood the ornate wooden doors with large brass handles leading to the Council chamber.

Gayla paused with her hand on the chamber door. "Take a moment, my dear. Juliers and the rest of the Council are already inside." Her face inscrutable, Gayla turned and entered the chamber. The double doors closed with a bang behind her. Natalie flinched. Healer Aldworth and Headmistress Gayla sat on the Council of Healers. They must be so disappointed to see her under review again. And this time her patient died. Oh Goddess, she'd failed everyone. She'd be lucky if she made it out of this and kept her Healer status.

Blinking back tears, Natalie peered into a mirror in the antechamber. Her hair had come loose from its customary braid. She re-braided it, then licked her hands to help tame the wisps of hair that insisted on sticking out. She hoped she'd washed her hands recently. There were dark circles under her eyes from the stress she'd been under. Her high cheekbones, which normally made her look healthy and cheerful, made her look gaunt. She sighed. "Nothing for it," she said to her reflection, then turned to the imposing double doors and opened them.

The three members of the Council of Healers— Headmistress Gayla, Healer Aldworth and a Healer who Natalie did not know—sat at a long table at the back of the room. Juliers sat in a chair facing the table, his face carefully blank. The empty seat next to his was obviously meant for her. She lifted her chin and took the seat with as much dignity as she could.

"This review is now called to order," said Healer Aldworth, seated in the middle of the Council table. He tapped a gavel on the table three times. "First, I will introduce the Council. I am Healer Aldworth. You know Headmistress Gayla, of course," he gestured to the Headmistress on his right. "And Healer Hawkins is on my left." Healer Hawkins reminded Natalie of a wise owl with her brown hair sprinkled with gray, pulled back into a bun, and round spectacles perched on her nose.

"We are here to review the incident that occurred overnight in the Abbey hospital during which a patient, one"—he consulted the parchment on the table—"Malcolm Bartlett, died under your care. Healer Juliers Rayvenwood, as the senior Healer of the two, perhaps you might explain what happened." Healer Aldworth clasped his fingers on his desk. He awaited Jules's testimony with what Natalie felt was an almost gleeful manner. Natalie shot a glance at her former mentor. What the hell was going on?

Jules calmly presented the facts of Malcolm's case. Natalie tried not to turn and stare. His voice sounded foreign; wooden and completely devoid of feeling.

"So, you Named the illness. Now, Healer Rayvenwood, we understand you've been developing a way to Name with your current … condition … by working with Healer Desmond."

An uncomfortable silence filled the room. Natalie glanced at Jules; his clenched jaw betrayed his aloof manner. The thought of him breaking a tooth gave her a momentary feeling of satisfaction.

"Yes, sir," Natalie interjected, "I developed a way for the two of us to Name together. We practiced on all the animals in the animal sanctuary first. Last night, Headmistress Gayla asked us to treat Mr. Bartlett. When we Named him, it was the first time we detected different results. While we both detected slow absorption of our energy, the only place I felt my energy blocked was the heart. Healer Rayvenwood felt the energy blocked at the lungs."

"So that brought you to a choice of tremosis versus Vell's fever," said Healer Hawkins, speaking for the first time.

"Yes, ma'am. We—"

A frantic knock sounded at the doors.

"Come," Healer Aldworth's voice boomed.

A Royal messenger rushed into the room, caked with dust and sweat, and delivered a letter to the Headmistress. The Headmistress opened it and as she read, her face paled and her hand covered her mouth. Natalie gripped the arms of her chair. The Headmistress always seemed so calm and collected; seeing her otherwise sent a frisson of fear down Natalie's spine.

Trembling, the Headmistress pushed herself to her feet. "Healers Rayvenwood and Desmond, please await me in the antechamber. Council members, a word please."

"But, we haven't finished—" Healer Aldworth stood, his long, silk robes flowing about him.

"This takes precedence," Gayla interrupted with the same voice that commanded Healers, nurses and patients alike.

Deciding to listen to her Headmistress over Healer Aldworth, Natalie stood up and left the room, Jules right behind her.

In the antechamber, Natalie sat and studied the end of her braid. Jules paced back and forth. Natalie was convinced he'd wear a trench in the floor before the Headmistress came out.

The double doors opened at long last and Gayla rushed out, her face pale.

"Come here both of you and listen well. Your review has been canceled in light of a more urgent matter."

"What is it?"

"Be quiet." Gayla had not taken that tone with her since Natalie was fourteen.

"You two need to get your acts together now. I know figuring out the difference between Vell's fever and tremosis is hard, but the real reason Malcolm Bartlett died is because both of you had your heads stuck up your asses. Now, grow up and learn how to work together. Get back out there, practice more and get it right. We need you both at top form. Soon." Gayla glared at each of them, then turned on her heel, strode into the Council chamber and slammed the door behind her.

Natalie stared at the scuffed toes of her boots, feeling like she might throw up. The Headmistress was right, of course. They'd wasted precious minutes arguing. Though they wouldn't have been wasted if he'd just listened to her.

She grabbed her braid and twisted it viciously. Still, she was the one who'd thought they were ready for a hospital patient. She couldn't have been more wrong. And yet the Headmistress wanted them to continue working together? How could they ... how could she even think that would work after a man had died?

Unable to face Jules—or anyone—Natalie raced to her room, found Jake, grabbed her summer-weight cloak and left the building. Tears flowed freely as she walked away from the Abbey and toward the woods nearby. It was a cloudy day, with a warm, misty rain moving in off the sea. The forest provided some shelter from the mist and wind, but also made the day even darker. She pulled her cloak's hood over her head and aimlessly followed a trail through the wood, occasionally giving a sullen kick to a nearby stone.

When she came to a large fallen oak tree, she sat on it, sobbing in earnest. She grabbed a nearby rock and threw it as hard as she could into the forest, screaming as she threw it. It hit a nearby tree trunk with a satisfying thunk.

"Just once," she shouted at the forest. "The one time I was confident in my Naming! And look what came of it. A patient died, a review with the Council of Healers and ..." she couldn't voice the rest aloud. She folded her arms over her heart. She could just imagine Gayla and Aldworth talking in the Council chamber even now about their disappointment in her. How would she ever earn their respect back? She hadn't seen Healer Aldworth much since her apprenticeship—he always seemed to be traveling— but she and Gayla often took tea together in the

Headmistress's office. Sometimes they would discuss Healing, with Gayla doling out advice here and there, but other times they would chat about ordinary things. Natalie cherished their friendship. She prayed she had not damaged it beyond repair.

And now she was under orders to patch things up with Jules. Honestly, she didn't want to see him ever again.

She stomped repeatedly on a nearby branch, breaking it into small bits. "In-suff-er-a-ble. ASS!"

Jake barked. Natalie picked up one of the remaining sticks from the branch and threw it as hard as she could. Jake raced after it and brought it back to her. She threw the stick until the mist and her own emotions had her wiping her raw nose on her cloak.

She headed back to the Abbey, Jake prancing next to her with his stick. Natalie blew out a sigh. What should she do about Jules? He'd been in the wrong, yes. However, he wouldn't have been Healing in the hospital if she hadn't suggested they were ready. And the Headmistress was right; they obviously needed more experience working together. Approaching the main entrance, she eyed the worn "Bridhe of the Isles Abbey" carved in stone above the door. What would the ancient mage who imbued Ismereld with magic have to say about her predicament?

Dammit, she supposed she should apologize.

Natalie returned to her room, changed into dry clothes and dried off Jake as best she could. Where would she find Jules? Since his return, he had always sought her out. Making sure Jake's paws were extra clean—or perhaps delaying the inevitable—Natalie headed for the library.

She pushed open the library's double wooden doors, stepping into the yellow light cast by the table and wall lamps. She couldn't find Jules on the first floor, so she climbed the spiral staircase at the back of the library to the second. She spotted tucked in a corner a pair of spotless black riding boots crossed one over the other and a dark head bent over a book. Natalie paused, tugging on her braid. There was a lump in her throat and her tongue felt too big for her mouth. She'd apologized to him once; she could do it again.

Picking one foot up off the floor and then the other, she approached Jules, hands clasped behind her back, wringing her fingers together.

He looked up from his book and spotted her, his expression guarded.

"Hello," she gulped. "I wanted to say I'm sorry, I shouldn't have told you to leave yesterday, he was your patient, too, and I had no right to throw you out, after all, I was the one who thought we were ready for a hospital patient and I was wrong about that wasn't I?" There she went with the run-on sentences again. Natalie bit her lip.

Jules arched an eyebrow at her. "That's quite an apology."

"I tend to speak too much when I'm nervous. I've done that ever since I was a child. S-sorry."

Jules set his book on a nearby table and rested his head in his hand, elbows on his knees. "No. I should apologize to you. Malcolm Bartlett would be alive if I had listened to you." He pulled his left hand away from his face and stared at what remained of his right arm as if it had betrayed him. "You should go on without me," he whispered.

Natalie considered this for a moment. "That would be easier," she mused aloud. "But not what's best for our patients."

Jules scowled at her. "I killed a man, Natalie."

Wanting to defuse another fight, Natalie shook her head. "We. We killed a man. Did you get one image from the Naming and I another? Sure. But the real issue was us fighting instead of staying calm and taking the next logical steps to clarify our diagnosis. That's what got Malcolm killed. Gayla was right—he lay there dying because you and I couldn't get our heads out of our own asses for two seconds." Natalie swore one side of his mouth curled up in a smile before Jules rubbed his jaw with his hand.

"We've discovered an amazing way to Heal patients. But if we're going to do this, you and I? Not only do we have to get the Naming right but we have to get ordinary things right, too. Like communication."

Jules's haggard face regarded her with skepticism. "Are we going to do this? *Should* we? Wouldn't you be better off as a normal Healer and not chained to me?"

Natalie looked down at her shoes. He'd just offered her a way out. She didn't have to work with him anymore if she didn't want to. She could go back to her life as it was, before he came back.

"Natalie?"

She gave her braid a savage twist. "I—let me think." *I don't know. I don't have all the answers. You came into my life like a shooting star and your light sat in my heart for years. Then you left and I just went through the motions of my life, constantly wondering if you'd turn up dead. Now you're in my life so much it hurts. I don't like being hurt by you, and I have every reason in the Isles to leave you alone in this library and get on with my life.*

She paced back and forth. They'd also discovered something new; a system of Naming that made Healing accessible to amputees like Jules, or to people who, for whatever reason, could not work alone. It would be a shame not to discover its true potential and even teach it to others if they became skilled enough.

As for going back to her old life? It was the easy way out. But it also meant Jules would have to try working with someone else—or stop Healing entirely. Her chest squeezed tight at the very thought of the former and she rejected it immediately. As for the latter, well, frankly she couldn't stomach seeing that deadness return to his eyes ever again.

Natalie took a deep breath and faced the man in the shadows. "I think we're better—" Natalie swallowed, blood rushing to her cheeks at what she'd almost said. "I mean we work better together than we do apart. *Should* we do this? I think the answer is up to us and how hard we try to make our system of Healing work."

Jules considered her words. "I didn't like the Council's reaction to whatever news that Royal messenger delivered. I have a feeling it's about what's going on in Whitestrand." For the first time during the conversation, he looked her in the eyes.

She squeezed her fingers extra hard behind her back, but she was able to meet his gaze in return. "It's bad news, no doubt. We have work to do before they call on us." After several seconds of awkward silence, Natalie said, "Well, my esteemed Healer Rayvenwood, I will make every attempt to pull my head out of my own ass. For the good of our patients."

Jules chuckled. "My dear Healer Desmond, I, too, will attempt to remove my head from my same orifice. For the greater good of our patients."

CHAPTER 8

The next day, Natalie and Jules returned to the animal sanctuary, much to Healer Bowers' dismay. Once again, they Named every single animal; their confidence got a large boost when they helped cure a foal Healer Bowers had been struggling to Heal.

To avoid further miscommunication, they started a log of their patients in which they noted in detail the images they observed during the Naming process. In addition, they visited patients during recovery to ensure their Healing went well and observe how their technique might be improved.

Once they regained their confidence with animals, they began treating people again. Any calls from Saltwick Natalie got as a Healer, she found Jules and they rode into town together. For the time being, they stayed away from the hospital. Between teaching, her hospital rounds and working with Jules, Natalie's face hit the pillow hard at the end of each day and she prayed she'd not be needed overnight.

Occasionally, they encountered a patient where

Naming revealed different things to each of them as it had the night of Malcolm Bartlett's death. They each wrote down their observations in the log. Natalie noted with relief that Jules contributed to the log with ease; whatever had happened in the war, it had not taken the hand he wrote with.

Having learned their lesson the hard way, they calmly discussed the similarities and differences in their Naming perceptions. It was Jules who spotted the pattern that predicted which patients would give them different results. People who took in Healing energy at a slower than normal rate presented one picture to Natalie and a differing one to Jules. Although this didn't happen often, it was a situation for which they needed to be prepared.

"Is there any way we could boost the uptake of the Healing energy to reduce our chance of error?" Natalie asked Jules late one night in the library. She chewed on the end of a quill while paging through her own Healing diary to see if she'd ever taken notes on such a thing.

Jules looked up from the stack of open books in front of him and rubbed his eyes. "To my knowledge, it's not possible for one person to do it. Do you think it's possible for two?"

Natalie blinked. Her scholarly opinion mattered to him. She spoke carefully, handling the precious gift of his respect with care. "I haven't found anything that says it is. Thinking back to our early experiments, it's rather easy to transfer energy between the two of us. So you, therefore, could likely transfer more energy into me than you currently do. But can we force a body to take that energy in when it's reluctant to do so?"

"And would that even be a good idea?" Jules mused.

"Probably not. Since people whose bodies take up energy slowly are usually very weak, I'd have to say flooding them with extra energy could be dangerous."

"I agree."

"So we're back in the same place—how do we handle

the Malcolm Bartletts of the world?"

Jules abruptly stood and began pacing, rubbing the stump of his arm.

Natalie bit her lip. "Is your arm all right?"

"Well, apart from being still missing, it's just dandy."

Natalie decided to let him walk off his mad. After several minutes, he stopped pacing and stopped in front of his chair with his hand covering his face.

"We handle the Malcolm Bartletts of the world by having you Name them by yourself. I am a liability."

"No, I still think there's— "

Jules slammed his hand on the table. "Natalie, I'm still trying to figure out how to use a straight razor one-handed without slicing my face to shreds."

"I'm sure you are. And if you had a student in your Naming class, Juliers Rayvenwood, who was missing part of an arm, would you consider that student less than the other students or would you move the Isle itself until that student could Name as well as every other student in the class?"

Natalie gathered her things and left for her room, leaving Jules to his thoughts.

After two weeks of intense work, they reported back to the Headmistress. Gayla looked uncharacteristically weary. Though Natalie knew her Headmistress was well along in years, this was the first time she seemed old. Her eyes, normally sparkling with a bit of mischief, seemed dull and listless. New lines seemed permanently etched around her eyes and upon her brows.

"Good work. Please report to the hospital right away. Be sure you can work on patients there as well as you've been doing here." She tapped their log with one bony finger.

"Yes, ma'am. Is there any patient you'd like us to work on first?" Jules asked.

"No. Please. Any of them. Just make sure you're at your best. You're dismissed."

Frightened by the despair in Gayla's voice, Natalie followed Jules out the door of the Headmistress's office.

"What is going on?" Natalie wondered, sitting with Jules and Em at lunch in the great hall.

"If the rumors I've heard are true, it's horrible," Em said in between bites. "The Midwives' Guild has forbidden us from going to Whitestrand. They say the city is quarantined."

"That would explain the Royal messenger," Jules took a sip of ale. "Roseharbor is just up the coast from Whitestrand, and I doubt Their Royal Majesties want the contagion getting any closer."

Natalie glared at him. "Or maybe King Gerhard and Queen Phillipa just care that their subjects are dying."

He raised one dark eyebrow. "Their subjects die in the war with Lorelan all the time and they don't stop the war."

Natalie had no response, so she turned back to Em.

"Has there been any word from the Council of the Isles? Surely, the Headmistress, as the representative of Council of Healers, must've told the other four councils what's happening. Head Councilwoman Ramesh must take some sort of action."

Em shook her head. "Well that's the catch, isn't it? The Council of the Isles and the monarchy are always butting heads about what's right for the Isles. What you hear or read depends on whether or not it's coming from a monarchist or someone who's pro-council. Even though we're just an hour or so from Roseharbor, most people will be pro-council since the Council of the Isles, on the whole, tends to look out for the best interest of the Isles' citizens. Or most people have that perception, at any rate. And you know the Headmistress can't talk about Council of the Isles business with us."

Natalie scowled. "Have your patients told you anything about the nature of the illness?"

"No. But, if it's bad enough for an entire port city to be quarantined …"

"… it's bad," Natalie finished unnecessarily.

"What?" Natalie jumped awake. She glanced out the window. It was the middle of the night, but she couldn't recall Gayla's voice summoning her to Heal a patient.

"Natalie," a deeper voice called as someone knocked on her door.

"Jules?" she went to the door and opened it. "What's wrong?"

"They want us to go to Whitestrand. The Healers the Council sent are … are dead. They want us to go to replace them. The Council is downstairs with more information now."

Natalie covered her mouth. "Dear Goddess."

"I know. Get dressed. We've got to get moving."

Natalie's Healer's instincts took over. "Right. Hang on." She grabbed the nearest clothes, threw them on, braided her hair, tossed her cloak around her shoulders, called Jake and joined Jules in the hall.

"What do you know?" Natalie asked.

"Nothing so far. The Headmistress told us to be in the Council chamber in fifteen minutes."

"I've never been to Whitestrand. How far is it from here?"

"Roughly four days' ride," Jules replied

"A lot can happen to a city in four days."

Natalie's grim observation kept them quiet until they knocked on the door of the council chamber. Once summoned inside, they were once again greeted by the same three councilors who had conducted their review.

"Welcome back," Healer Aldworth smirked. "Headmistress Gayla reports you've made excellent progress since your review."

"We have," Jules replied in a tone that made it clear he was in no mood for dancing around the subject at hand. "We understand you have an assignment for us in Whitestrand. We'd like the details so we can get underway."

"The first two Healers we sent were unable to make much progress Naming or treating the disease. We do have the symptoms, though." Healer Hawkins consulted her notes, her mouth forming a thin line. "Whatever this is kills quickly. Patients present with a headache, soon followed by other muscle pains, vomiting, chest pains, shortness of breath and profuse sweating. Most patients die within twenty hours of symptom onset—or less."

Jules rubbed his jaw with his hand. "What did the Naming reveal?"

"No notes were sent regarding the Naming," Gayla replied.

Jules swore.

"How much of the city is sick? Are the other Isles in danger? Do you know how it spreads?" Natalie asked.

"The city is currently under quarantine and the port is shut down. We've notified the other Isles what symptoms to be on the lookout for, but so far we haven't heard any word," Healer Aldworth replied. "You and Healer Rayvenwood will be given special permission to enter and stay there. The Abbey has a Royal army liaison who will see to it you receive supplies and instructions for your journey. And Healers?" Healer Aldworth looked pointedly at both of them. "Do not let us down this time."

Clearly dismissed, they left the chamber. Natalie made sure the heavy double doors were closed. "He didn't answer the most important question. How does this disease spread?" she muttered.

Jules bent his head close to hers. "I think that's for the best. I don't trust him and I wouldn't have believed the answer he gave us, anyway."

"Why don't you trust him? And why would the Council keep details from us? Especially if two Healers are dead and now our lives are on the line."

"Frankly, I trust our judgment rather than theirs. Or Aldworth's, at least. Let's get on the road and see for ourselves what's going on."

Natalie followed Jules out of the antechamber, only belatedly realizing that Jules hadn't answered her questions either.

Natalie fussed with her summer-weight cloak for the umpteenth time as the sun rose over Ismereld. No matter how she adjusted it, it pulled on her throat as she and Jules rode along the road to Whitestrand. Jules rode his tall, sleek bay horse, whose name was Elric, with regal confidence. She rode Benji, who, despite being her favorite pony in the Abbey stables, would never be regal. Eventually, she and her errant piece of clothing seemed to find some sort of truce.

Natalie snorted. They must look an odd pair. The tall, dashing man on the beautiful horse beside the shorter woman, cloak askew, riding the fat chestnut pony. Off to save a city. Or so they hoped.

She eyed the longer cylindrical bundle tied behind Jules's saddle. "Why do you have more baggage than I do?"

"I brought my tent. From my time in the army."

Natalie thought back to when she received her provisions, and she distinctly recalled receiving the token that would allow them to stay at the inn in Whitestrand. The Abbey kept tokens for Healers needing shelter in remote towns. Healers gave the tokens to innkeepers who, in turn, sent the tokens to the Abbey. The Abbey then paid the innkeepers for all expenses incurred. "I thought we were staying at inns."

"We are—until we get to Whitestrand."

"You don't think it's safe to stay in the town."

Jules shrugged. "Two Healers are dead. I don't know what to think, other than I want to be alive to keep thinking. I say we stay out of Whitestrand as much as possible. We go in and take care of patients, but we sleep, eat and drink outside of town."

Natalie nodded.

Summer was upon Ismereld in full now. They rode along paths surrounded by tall, lush grasses, seed heads bobbing on the tops of their stalks. Trees in full leaf offered the occasional bit of shade. It got so hot, Natalie gave in and removed her cloak, securing it to the back of her saddle. They stopped often to water the horses and take long pulls of water from their waterskins themselves. However, not even the heat could dampen Natalie's joy of being outside surrounded by the smell of grasses, trees and shrubs, with the blue sky stretching above her. She made a mental note to try and spend more time outside when she returned to the Abbey.

After the third stop to water the horses, the silence between her and Jules got under Natalie's skin. A four-day journey stretched in front of them. She hoped their fragile friendship could take it. Should she start a conversation? What was there to talk about? What did they have in common besides Healing anyway? Stories from her time as a student seemed awkward, and she sure as hell wasn't going to ask him about the war. Books? Should she ask about books? Would that be—

"What do you remember about epidemics from history?" Jules asked, making her jump.

Relieved to have something to talk about, Natalie seized on the conversation topic, and between them, they recalled quite a few epidemics they'd studied while at the Abbey.

Natalie mentioned the Healing diary she kept and that she had several sections devoted to epidemics. "My grandparents used to tell us stories of the last epidemic to strike the Isles; it killed several of their friends and loved ones. I'll never forget the haunted look on their faces when they told us what it was like. I made a special point to keep notes on epidemics, I think, because of them."

"What do you remember from your notes?"

A few epidemics in particular stood out, such as one where a Healer traced the cause of a citywide stomach illness to one polluted water well. Once sealed off, people couldn't consume the polluted water and stopped falling ill. Basic hygiene and the advent of plumbing advances from the Isle of Obfuselt put an end to most of the recurrent epidemics the Isles experienced in the past, but they were good reminders of what patterns to look for in Whitestrand.

Unfortunately, that topic of conversation ran out and silence descended once again. Natalie fidgeted with Benji's reins.

"Where are you from?" Jules asked. She managed not to jump this time.

"Uh, Mistfell. We'll be passing somewhat near there on the way to Whitestrand."

"Indeed. You said you had a brother. Any more brothers? Or sisters?"

"No, just my brother, my parents and me. I grew up on an apple farm there. It was a wonderful place to grow up." She smiled as images of home, the scent of her mother's hearty dinners, the sound of her father's booming laugh and memories of playing with her brother in the apple groves filled her head.

"How did you find out you were a Healer?"

Natalie's lips curved in a wistful smile. "Well, I had always had an herb garden—"

Jules laughed out loud.

"Yes, no surprise to anyone." She laughed. "Anyway, I knew some remedies, but when I was ten, our family had a puppy. He came into my garden limping one day. I picked him up and it was like my hands caught fire, they tingled so much. In my mind this image appeared and I could see the small crack in a bone in his front right leg. Poor thing, I almost dropped him because it scared the hell out of me."

"I can imagine."

"I was pretty spooked and didn't really want to become a Healer. But then my little brother fell from a ladder and hit his head. I felt so helpless. I never wanted to feel that way again; I wanted to know how to help. So I started at the Abbey three years later."

They rode in silence for some time before Natalie got up the courage to return the question. "How about you; where are you from?"

Jules's mouth hardened into a thin line. "A few days' ride from Mistfell. I'm from Roseharbor. I grew up in the shadow of Roseharbor Castle, the eldest son of clothing merchants. My parents are tailors to much of the upper class of Roseharbor. They were quite disappointed when I told them I was a Healer."

Natalie grimaced. She wanted a word or two with Jules's parents. "Do you have any brothers or sisters?"

"One sister. She married a wealthy man who is as vain and frivolous as she is."

"Ah. I gather you two had a pleasant childhood frolicking in fields and making mud pies," Natalie jested.

Jules laughed again. It was a deep, baritone laugh that sent an unexpected thrill of desire through Natalie's middle. She peeked out of the corners of her eyes; he was quite at home riding his tall, sleek horse. The sun shone down on his dark wavy hair, his cloak billowing behind him, and he looked like a knight straight from a bard's tale. Hoping the summer heat hid her blushing face, she kept her eyes on the road ahead.

"Oh, Mother would have needed a ship full of smelling salts if one of us even got near mud. No, it was tutors, manners and governesses all the time for my sister and me."

"Well, obviously you need to make up for lost time. Once we solve this thing in Whitestrand, I insist we go frolic in a field and make a mud pie. I'm sorry to break it to you, but your pristine clothes will get filthy."

Jules turned his emerald gaze on her and gave her a lopsided grin. "Is that a promise?"

Was it? Did she want to be with him as a friend … or more? Her stomach flip-flopped at the thought. Pretending to love someone for years was one thing. But everything between them had changed. The man she'd dreamed about was now her partner. They'd Healed, fought, made up and—perhaps—even become friends together. *Is all this a prelude of things to come? I have no bloody idea.*

Natalie turned to Jules and nodded, managing to swallow past the lump in her throat. "I promise."

CHAPTER 9

R umors of the horrors awaiting them did nothing but increase along the way to Whitestrand.

"I hear the carts removing the dead from houses aren't big enough to carry all the dead," said one barkeep.

"I hear the whole city smells like death," responded one of his patrons.

"Aye, well it already smelt o' fish. How would you tell the diff'rence?" said another customer, well into his cups.

The stories grew and changed at each inn, and both Natalie and Jules found themselves reminding each other rumors would not help them solve anything in advance. Despite this reassurance, Natalie often spent her nights, stomach in knots, poring over her Healing diary, searching for clues based on the scanty information she had and trying to find all the notes she'd ever taken about epidemics. None of her research seemed to fit and sleep often eluded her until the early hours of the morning.

Four days after leaving the Abbey, Natalie and Jules arrived at the cape above Whitestrand. Natalie followed

Jules as he scouted for a campsite. He eventually found a rock outcropping surrounded by tall grass that would give them shelter from the sea winds.

"Let's get our campsite set up and something to eat. That way we'll be prepared for what we find in town," Jules looked down at his hand. "I'm going to need your help pitching the tent."

Natalie shrugged. "Just tell me what to do."

It took several attempts and a lot of swearing, but between the two of them, they got the tent set up.

"I used to be able to do this by myself in four minutes," Jules grumbled, reaching for his bedroll. Not for the first time, Natalie wished she could see his demons and remove them the way she removed shrapnel from her battle-wounded patients.

As they tossed their bedrolls inside the tent, Natalie's stomach danced when she imagined sleeping with Jules, his warm body so close to hers. *Does he snore? Do I snore? Should I stay as far away from him as I can or if I'm cold, should I … could we get … closer?* She concentrated on keeping a straight face and prayed it didn't blush.

They ate a simple lunch of dried meat and fruit washed down with water from their waterskins. They ate without speaking, each lost in their own thoughts. Natalie missed Jake's comforting presence, but for his own safety, she'd left him with Em.

She could barely eat her food; swallowing was like trying to eat a pulpfish whole. She gave it up as a bad job, shoved the food into her pack and dusted her hands on her pants. She grabbed her herb satchel and checked its contents for the umpteenth time. Her Healing diary was there, and she'd remembered to add a kerchief to tie around her face in case the mystery disease was transmitted by air. She secured the satchel to her pony, Benji. She triple-checked his tack, ensuring every single buckle and strap lay precisely in place. At least Benji was ready; she wished she could say the same.

They rode down the steep road to Whitestrand, the first sea winds blowing against her face. Natalie wrinkled her nose. The air did smell of fish—and something more insidious. Whitestrand was a port town, its buildings built of out of the plentiful gray stone that made up the cliffs and capes towering for miles over this part of Ismereld's coastline. Its buildings sat huddled together along streets paved with the same stone. The stone construction had stood the town well over centuries of vicious sea storms.

It was not a long road down the cape, and they soon encountered the campsite of the Royal Guard maintaining the quarantine on the town.

One guard, a burly, whiskered fellow, stepped into the road. "Halt," he bellowed.

Jules's horse, Elric, tossed his head imperiously when Jules halted him. Jules scrutinized the guard. "Healers Rayvenwood and Desmond from Bridhe of the Isles Abbey. You've been expecting us."

The guard raised his eyebrows, nodded and removed himself from their path. "I'm glad I'm not you, meself," he shook his head. "I wouldn't set a foot in that town if you paid me fifty gold coins."

Just past the quarantine campsite, they entered the town proper. An ominous silence filled the streets. The horrible smell became so overwhelming that both Natalie and Jules tied kerchiefs over their faces. Every once in a while, flakes resembling snow fell from the gray sky, even though it was summer.

Natalie peered at Jules. "Do you know where the center of town is?"

He nodded. "Near the Temple of the Five Mages. We're heading that way now."

They spoke in whispers. It was as if a powerful

vengeful spirit had wiped the town's people right off the earth.

Natalie despaired of finding anyone on the grim march through the twists and turns of Whitestrand's gray streets, until one turn revealed the Temple. They spotted a young boy, no more than twelve, walking with buckets of water toward the Temple doors. He spotted them at the same time.

"Healers!" he almost dropped his water. "Greatmother! Greatmother! More Healers have come," he shouted, running into the Temple.

Natalie raised her eyebrows at Jules. They tethered the horses outside the Temple, gathered their supplies, double-checked their kerchiefs, and entered the large, gray building. Natalie clenched her teeth together to stop her jaw from dropping. Sick people lay upon rows and rows of pallets in Whitestrand's enormous temple. Several elderly folk tended to the sick, doling out water, changing bedding and wiping brows. High fevers reddened the faces of most of the ill. Several patients sweated profusely, their pallets soaking wet. She spotted the boy from the street speaking with one of the elder women who she assumed was his greatmother.

The boy tugged his greatmother toward them. "See, Greatmother, I told you."

Natalie extended her hand. "Healer Natalie Desmond, and this is Healer Juliers Rayvenwood."

"Simona Halis. We are so grateful you are here." She shook Jules's hand as well. "However, I'm afraid there aren't many of us left for you to Heal."

"You've not become ill yourself?" Jules pulled out their journal, a quill and inkpot.

"No, only some of the elderly and young have. And when they do, for the most part, they survive." She dabbed her eyes with her apron. "We've—we've had to set up an orphanage in the town hall for the time being. You see, this sweating sickness affects only grown folk in the prime of life. Have you heard of such a thing?"

"It doesn't sound familiar as yet, but we'll know more once we examine the patients. Is there anything else you can tell us? How it's transmitted? When it started?" Natalie asked.

Simona bunched her apron in her fists. "I don't know how it's transmitted—nothing makes sense. If it were sneezing or touch, I'd have it by now, wouldn't I? And it started about four weeks ago when the weather turned warm. So many have died. We've … we've been holding mass funerals down on the beaches near the docks, burning the bodies."

Natalie suppressed a shudder recalling the mysterious snow-like flakes falling on her during the ride into town. It had not been snow; it had been ash. She put her arm around Simona's shoulders. "All right, we're going to examine patients. Why don't you get some rest and something to eat? We will let you know what we find."

Simona nodded, tears flowing freely now. "Be careful. The first two Healers died soon after they got here."

Natalie managed a weak smile beneath her kerchief. "We will."

Natalie and Jules sat on either side of the first patient they selected.

"Simona says her name is Ella. She's nineteen and she was just brought in a few hours ago. Her headache started at breakfast, the fever and vomiting half an hour later." Natalie observed Ella between them struggling to draw breath and sweating profusely.

Jules's quill scratched across the page. "Any sign of a rash? Or bruising?"

Natalie placed her hand gently on Ella's arm. "Ella? My name is Healer Natalie. I'm going to check under your clothes for a rash, all right?" Natalie lifted Ella's shirt and checked her torso and chest for a rash. Rocking her from side to side, she checked her back. Ella groaned. "No rash. No bruising." Natalie wiped Ella's brow with a cool cloth. Ella muttered incoherent words and her eyes couldn't quite focus on any one thing. "Add delirium to the list of symptoms. Though whether it's from the fever or the illness itself, I don't know."

Jules nodded. "Any swollen glands?"

Natalie gently pressed under Ella's chin and along her neck. "No."

Jules set the log down. "We've got to do the Naming."

They grasped hands across Ella's prostrate form. Natalie took several breaths to calm herself; Jules's energy flowing in her and within her, anchoring her to the ley lines of Ismereld, comforted her like an old friend. Her heart rate slowed and her anxiety dissipated. When she was ready, she caught Jules's glance. He gave her a nod, his emerald eyes encouraging over the kerchief covering his nose and mouth, and she placed her free hand on Ella, sending their energy inward along the bones, ligaments, tendons, nerves, blood vessels and tissues of the patient's body.

Natalie closed her eyes and focused as she never had before.

"Her lungs," Jules muttered.

Natalie's eyes flew open. "Yes. Almost like pneumonia. But it can't be pneumonia because—"

"—Simona said the elderly survive the disease for the most part." Jules finished her sentence.

"And pneumonia takes a lot longer to kill. So what acts similar to pneumonia but kills in a day or less and ignores children and elder folk?"

"Damned if I know," Jules whispered. "And how are we going to find out? We didn't bring the Abbey library with us. Do you remember anything similar to this from your diary?"

"No. I'd give anything to stop and read it right now, but if I do, we'll lose a lot more patients." Natalie surveyed the full Temple-turned-sick ward. "Let's start with tanyaroot tea. Perhaps what helps people overcome pneumonia will help them survive this."

For the rest of the day, Natalie and Jules labored in the Temple. Jules made a list of all the patients in the building, while Natalie enlisted Simona's help preparing the tanyaroot tea. To be certain, they performed Naming on each patient they treated, but the results were the same each time. Natalie recorded in their log when patients got a dose of tea and left a space to record any observations.

"Tanyaroot tea helps pneumonia patients within a few hours," she told Simona whilst helping one patient drink his dose.

Simona frowned. "Well, we'll soon know for sure, won't we? Folk until now have either died or gotten better in just a few hours' time. And I can't tell you why they got better, either."

"Could you give us the names of some of the people who've gotten better? So we can talk to them?" Natalie asked. Simona nodded and gave the names to Jules.

They toiled well into the night. Much to Natalie's dismay, the tanyaroot tea helped patients breathe easier but they died nonetheless. Simona Halis and the group of people working with her went home for some much needed rest, and a new group of people arrived, led by a wonderful old gentleman named Jarvis Humphrey.

Jarvis rested a hand on both Natalie and Jules when he found them, heads bowed, over a newly deceased patient. "Healers, you've done what you can for today. Go, get some rest. You cannot take care of us if you are not taking care of yourselves first."

Jules nodded. "Our campsite is just past the quarantine, up the road and to the right. Send a rider to the guards and have the guards fetch us if you need us."

They gathered their belongings and Jarvis gave them a

lantern to take along the road. Natalie's legs shook as she mounted Benji. She was certain the trip to the campsite took five days, though in reality, it only took about twenty minutes. When they passed by the quarantine camp, only one guard was awake; he raised the bottle he was drinking from to cheerily toast them as they passed, tripping over his own feet as he did. Anger boiled in Natalie's chest at his carelessness. The rest of Ismereld depended on maintaining this quarantine, and the guards, it would seem, could care less. Natalie thought she just might have some energy left to dismount and shove the bottle someplace from where he'd require a surgeon's services to remove it. But that would leave the road unguarded. Such as it was.

Once at the campsite, they tethered and untacked the horses. Natalie sniffed her cloak. Her nose scrunched; she literally smelled like death.

They took turns bathing in a nearby pond. Natalie stepped in, clothes and all, wanting to get everything clean. It disconcerted her, stepping into a dark pond in the middle of the night. She managed not to shriek when something slithered around her ankle. She shivered, despite the warmth of the water, and finished her ablutions quickly.

After donning a change of clothes, she entered the tent first and sat on her bedroll, knees to her chest and arms hugging her legs. As she listened to Jules splash around in the pond, uncertainty crept up and sank its claws into her. The specter of Healer Aldworth saying not to let him down rose before her. The frustration of Naming the disease grated on her nerves. She—well, they—Named every patient in the Temple properly. Right? But how could they Name a disease they'd never seen? So many people had died today. Aldworth would be so disappointed.

A few moments later, Jules came in with the lantern. Carefully avoiding stepping on her—no small feat considering how far he had to bend over—he got into his own bedroll. He noticed her distress right away. "Are you all right?"

Did her tears have to start now? "No, I mean, yes. Yes, we did all right today. I mean, I think. We did, right?" Her death grip on her legs increased as she turned to him. "Did we miss anything? Think back to the Naming, what you saw. Did we miss anything? It's nothing we've ever seen, right? Should we go back and double-check?"

Jules crawled over, sat in front of her and rested his hand on her shoulder. "Natalie. It's an epidemic unlike anything I've ever seen. We did our very best. What's going on?"

Natalie bit her lip. "I … I always get this way after I Heal someone." She stared at the green tent wall. "My third time out as a full-fledged Healer was for a boy who fell and hit his head. His name was Aaron, the same name as my brother. I Named his injuries, I gave him all the right herbs. And … and he went into a coma and is now paralyzed." Tears flowed down her face and she wiped her nose on her sleeve. "The Council of Healers reviewed my actions and found I'd done nothing wrong. But I must have missed something. If I'd been as good a Namer as you are, I would have seen it. He'd be just fine—"

"Hey," Jules slowly cupped her face with his hand and stroked her damp cheek with his thumb. "You are more than capable. You were one of my best students and you are one of the best Healers now. What happened was terrible, but it wasn't your fault." Natalie turned her head away, trying to swallow the tears. Hesitantly, Jules put one arm around her, then the other, and then rested his dark head on top of her brown one.

Her tears dried on the soft fabric of Jules's shirt as she closed her eyes. His heart beat against her ear. It seemed to resonate in her head and settle within her soul. She drew her lips into a smile and inhaled deeply, attempting to memorize Jules's smell—the sweet tang of his shirt, the faint smell of horse. She let the breath out slowly, savoring every moment.

"Head wounds will always be tricky, for the best of Healers," he whispered. He ran his forearms from her shoulders down to her elbows, pushed her away gently and looked into her eyes. "And I wouldn't want to work with anyone else at the Abbey, got it?"

Natalie half laughed and half sobbed. "Got it." She wiped her nose on her sleeve again. "Thank you."

He stroked her cheek again with the utmost gentleness. The compassion in his eyes made her breath hitch. "No, you must allow me to thank you. I came back broken. I wanted to quit and leave. Despite my pushing you away, you persisted and—well, I'm not whole, but I'm starting to find the pieces again. Because of you. Now, lie down and get some sleep."

She obeyed, climbing into her bedroll, a thrill running up her spine as Jules tenderly pulled a blanket over her and said good night.

Before succumbing to exhaustion, it occurred to her that she was falling in love with the man. Again.

CHAPTER 10

The next morning, Natalie drifted awake, eyes still closed, and relished how comfortable she was. Odd, considering she'd slept on the ground in a bedroll in a tent. She knew a room full of dying people awaited her, but for the moment, she mentally shoved that to the side. Just a bit of breeze shifted through the tent, bringing with it the salt scent of the sea. The early morning sunlight filtered by the canvas of the tent rested on her eyelids. Lying on her right side, snuggled under her bedroll with her head nestled against Jules's shoulder, she was cozy and warm. *Wait*—

Her eyes flew open. Jules slept on his side, facing her. Natalie delicately maneuvered her body back little by little so they no longer touched. The early morning sun on his face made him seem younger, although the occasional scar and dark circles under his eyes were proof of his time in the army and the stress he'd been under. This close to his dark hair, she could see tiny copper highlights glint in the sun. He kept his hair cut short, but given its waviness, she thought it might be curly if he ever grew it out. Her fingers ached to thread through his hair and—

"Am I very fascinating?" His deep voice startled her.

Natalie found his emerald eyes looking at hers, crinkled at the edges, and a smile on his face.

Blood rushed to her cheeks. "I … well, I …"

He laughed. "Goddess, woman, you should see your face."

She punched him in the arm and flopped onto her back on her bedroll, only to have Jules's face appear above hers.

"What?" she demanded.

"Well, it seems only fair," he whispered, "since you had time to study my face, I should have time to study yours."

"Oh," she said, her heart beating out of rhythm.

His startling eyes studied her. He reached up and brushed a bit of her hair off to the side. Natalie swallowed, their energies connecting with that merest brush of skin. She wanted to close her eyes and arch against him like a cat, but she feared the moment would scatter like so many butterflies if she so much as moved.

"Am I very fascinating?" she whispered.

His eyes widened, hearing his own question repeated back to him. He closed his eyes, then ever so gently rested his forehead on hers. "Fascinating isn't the word I would use," He sighed.

Natalie squeezed her eyes shut. *What does he mean? We're friends now—I think. Is he saying he wants more? Do I want more?* His breath caressed her face and she relished the feeling of his forehead against hers. *Oh, Goddess, yes. Yes, I want more. Now.*

One of the horses whinnied, shattering the moment. "Someone's here." Jules jumped up, grabbed something Natalie couldn't see, darted to the tent doorway and peered out. "It's one of the quarantine guards," he said. He turned to her, a dagger clenched in his fist. Did he sleep with a dagger nearby? "Stay here. I'll be right back."

When he closed the tent flap behind him, she crept over to listen in. Apparently one of the illness survivors was an ale brewer asking if he could resume trade with the other cities on Ismereld.

Natalie pinched the bridge of her nose. "Does he not know the meaning of the word 'quarantine'?" she muttered. She began rolling up the bedrolls in her frustration.

Jules denied the request and asked the name of the brewer so they might talk to him; he could prove useful in their efforts to heal others. Once the guard was on his way, the tent flap opened again. "Time to start the day, I suppose," Jules said.

"Way ahead of you." Natalie nodded to his rolled bedroll and pretended nothing had happened between them that morning at all.

On the way back into the city, Natalie lectured the quarantine guards that no one but she and Jules should enter or leave the city. Only they, as Healers, could lift the quarantine. The guards glowered through the entire lecture. Natalie glanced at them over her shoulder as she and Jules rode away. Surly she could handle; incompetent she could not.

The situation at the Temple was no better. The fever had taken fifteen more patients overnight. Each loss was like a dagger to Natalie's heart. Looking around the large room, she wondered just how much more her heart could take.

Jules updated the patient log with the people who'd died. Natalie nearly burned herself brewing a large pot of tanyaroot tea, transfixed by the sight of him rubbing the stubble on his chin as he worked. Heat pooled in her stomach as visions filled her head of her face leaning in close to his, and the feel of his breath on her cheek. Stretching up on her tiptoes to finally explore the planes and textures of his face. Heat blossomed across her cheeks, and it was not from the steaming pot of tea she'd just finished preparing.

Jules laid down his quill. "I think it's time to talk to the survivors to see if we can spot what's different about them."

Natalie shook her head and ordered herself to get it together. "I agree. Let's start with that brewer who tried to break quarantine. I'd first like to help some of the people here, though. And I still need to find time to read my diary. Now that we know so much, I've got to see if I wrote down something about a disease similar to this one."

After administering herbs and elixirs to bring down fevers and loosen chest congestion, they were off to the home of one Briggs Morley, Brewer, who had recovered from the fever.

Mr. Morley was well off. He had a large house in the finer part of town, and Natalie got the distinct impression if it hadn't been for the epidemic, a servant, not Mr. Morley himself, would have answered the door. As it was, the door swung open and a large, beefy man with thick arms filled the doorframe.

"Healers?" Morley said without preamble, "Have you come to tell me I can leave the city? As you see, I am quite well, and I don't want to lose any more money. There's no one here to buy my ale."

Natalie put her hands on her hips. "Have you been oversampling your own product, sir? Most of Whitestrand is dead, and you're worried about profits."

Morley stepped into Natalie's face and looked down upon her. "You'd best control your woman, Healer," he said to Jules.

Natalie opened her mouth to tell him off, but Jules beat her to it. "Actually, Mr. Morley, my fellow Healer—who happens to be a woman—made an excellent point. We have some important questions and, with your permission, we'd like to examine you. We must determine why some people survived this epidemic."

Natalie glared at Morley. "Think of it this way, Mr.

Morley: any life you help save is the life of a potential customer. And make no mistake, *sir*—if you leave Whitestrand and take this epidemic with you to another town, those deaths will be on you."

Morley clenched his meaty fists. "Fine. Come in."

Jules and Natalie examined Morley from head to toe. The Naming revealed a slight weakness in his lungs leftover from his bout with the illness but that was it.

Natalie wrote in the log while Jules asked questions. The last time he'd traveled to the main continent was three months ago. He did most of his trading within the Isles. No, he hadn't eaten or drunk anything out of the ordinary. He had not had any other strange illnesses before this one. If he didn't eat at his own house, he tended to patronize three of the more well-to-do pubs in Whitestrand. He didn't know anyone who was ill before he became ill himself, and he had not taken any remedies for the illness when it came on; he simply got better.

They thanked Mr. Morley for his time and barely missed being hit by his front door on the way out.

Natalie glared back at his house. "What an insufferable man." She kicked a rock in the empty street.

Jules feigned offense. "I thought that was your nickname for me."

Natalie's eyes grew wide and she gaped at him.

Jules roared with laughter. "Goddess, woman, you should see your face," he said for the second time that day.

Natalie closed her eyes and regained her dignity. "It's not my fault if you were being an insufferable ass. That, sir, is entirely upon you. I was merely being observant."

"True. I was quite insufferable when I got back. And an ass. I do apologize, my lady."

"Don't 'my lady' me." Natalie whacked him with their log. "You're being insufferable right now."

He laughed. "At least things are better now."

Natalie gestured to the Temple, where they'd just arrived. "A Temple full of dying people and things are better?"

"Better than what I saw in the war, I mean." Jules rubbed the stump of his arm.

"How so?"

Jules's face darkened. "It's difficult to explain. There's a lot more going on in the war than people know about. It—they tried to—"

The door opened behind them and Simona Halis poked her head out. "Oh good, you're back. We need the extra hands."

What? Natalie longed to ask. What had they tried to do that had left Jules so broken?

Inside the Temple, things hadn't changed. Natalie treated patients until her legs turned to jelly and her back ached something fierce. All her herbs seemed to do was ease the people's suffering as they died. It was a blessing but did nothing to cure people or stop the spread of the disease.

She spoke words of kindness and comfort to her patients as she doled out tea and Activated the herbs within them. But behind her kind words and gentle touches, she was losing hope. She wanted to ask the Council of Healers if they'd sent her just to watch these people die. Or did they send her here to punish her for Malcolm Bartlett's death? What did they expect her to learn from a disease as impossible to treat as this? That sometimes Healers end up in no-win situations?

Stumbling to the stove to fix more tea, it was all she could do not to cover her ears to drown out the sound of moaning and vomiting. The smell of the Temple itself made her claustrophobic, and the urge to walk out the door welled up in her chest and nearly choked her. Anything to get away from the sweating, pain, helplessness and death. She grasped the wooden teapot handle and dug her fingernails into it. She must stay. She must.

They received few new patients, though Natalie

suspected that was due more to the epidemic having decimated Whitestrand's population than anything else.

Natalie and Jules worked late into the night, eating from their own packs and drinking from their own waterskins. Natalie was administering tanyaroot tea to one patient when the Temple doors burst open and one of the quarantine guards nearly fell in. Natalie rushed to him and Jules quickly got to his other side; the man had been beaten quite badly.

As they tended his wounds, the guard grabbed Natalie's hand. "'Twas Morley the brewer, it was. Came upon us in the dark with his wagon full o' goods demanding to pass. When we said no, two lads came out o' the wagon an' them an' Morley himself set upon us. He's long gone."

Jules swore. Several of the Temple nurses shot him a look. "Did he say where he was headed?"

"Said he was goin' to Mistfell."

Natalie dropped the bandages she was holding. Her knees buckled. She fell, hard, into a sitting position on the ground. The room spun. A strange buzzing filled her ears.

Mistfell.

"Simona, can you send people to get the other injured guard and bring him here?"

Was that Jules's voice? She stared at her empty hands. Sounds floated in and out, competing with the buzzing.

Through the static, a voice in the distance called out, "Natalie. Nat."

Two emerald eyes came into view, breaking contact with her useless hands. Hands that had failed her so far. Hands that had failed this town. Hands that would fail her family too.

Her shoulders shook. "Natalie." Jules was shaking her. He was talking to her now. His lips moved but what was he saying?

Mother. Da. Aaron.

Suddenly, the buzzing stopped. "Jules." Her voice wasn't at all raspy like she thought it would be. It was strong. Solid. Sure.

Her shoulders stilled in his grip.

"If Morley took the epidemic with him ... my family. We've got to go to Mistfell."

CHAPTER 11

"Nat, come on, let's go outside and get some fresh air." Jules helped her to her feet, put an arm around her shoulders, and helped her outside the Temple.

"Fresh air. Fresh air?" She rounded on Jules and gestured to the nearby buildings. "This isn't fresh air. This is air that smells like dead and burnt bodies. This whole town is dead and we couldn't stop it. And now Mistfell will fall."

"You don't know that. And what of the people here? The Council ordered us to this city. We have no orders to leave. We'll face the inquiry of a lifetime if we abandon Whitestrand. We could even be stripped of our Healer status. Everything we've worked for our entire lives will be lost."

"The Abbey wants us to stop the epidemic, right? To have any chance of doing that, we'll go to Mistfell," Natalie countered.

Jules threw his arms in the air. "We don't know for sure Morley took it with him. We don't know how this fever is transmitted. Maybe we carry the disease. Nat, if we follow Morley, what if we take the disease to Mistfell ourselves?"

"Dammit," Natalie turned on her heel and started pacing. "There hasn't been any time for me to do my research."

"You're sure the answer is in that little book you have?"

"I don't know for sure, but it's the best resource we have."

Jules stroked his chin and started pacing. "Well, I'm not sure we have time to do research now, but I do think we have time to do a little process of elimination. What are the different methods of disease transmission?"

Natalie counted off on her fingers. "People touching each other, bodily fluids, contaminated surfaces or objects, food or water, and insect bites."

Jules nodded. "Have we been able to eliminate any of those yet?"

Natalie bit her thumbnail. "I've got a few bug bites and I'm not sick."

"Same. So that's one method off the list. We're down to five. Can we safely eliminate more before leaving for Mistfell?"

Natalie's head snapped up. "You ... you think we should go?"

Jules looked up at the night sky. "I stand by what I said earlier. We were ordered here. Leaving could be a terrible decision—professionally, that is. On the other hand, what will we do here? Raise orphans and care for the elderly? There's what, forty patients left in that Temple? What can we do for them? You are right; we have to assume the disease is on its way to Mistfell. We have to put Mistfell in quarantine or the whole Isle stands to fall. And with a war going on, that would allow Lorelan easy access to all the other Isles. I think I will sleep better at night knowing we're trying to save our home Isle. We'll just have to deal with the council when they come for us. And they will."

Natalie nodded. "In that case, I have an idea how we can eliminate the other methods of disease transmission. But you're not going to like it."

"Try me."

"Before we leave, we make sure the patients inside are comfortable. And I'll take off my kerchief and won't wash my hands. It's two days between here and Mistfell. If I get sick, we know it's person to person contact, bodily fluids, or contaminated surfaces."

Jules's eyes narrowed. "Why just you? We should both do it."

Natalie raised her chin. "It's my family. It's my home. There's no need for you to sacrifice yourself for them. Besides if I … if something happens, you'll need to ride ahead to warn them about Morley. And set up the quarantine."

Jules reached for her, his hand cupping her face. "You don't have to do this," he whispered.

His palm on her cheek shot frissons of warmth down the core of her body. Natalie gave in to one her greatest desires and stroked her fingers along the stubble on his cheek. "I do," she said. "I can't have the death of my family and hometown on my conscience."

Jules rested his forehead on hers. "I can't let you do this. I can't let you die."

Natalie huffed a small laugh. "Maybe I won't die. You know me, I'm stubborn and hard to get rid of."

One side of Jules's mouth curled up, and then he sighed. "I don't like it. But it is a logical plan—and the only one we have."

Jules took her hand, and they walked into the Temple.

"Jules? Before we leave, I want to visit the pyres on the beach and honor the people who were lost. The ones we couldn't save."

Inside the Temple, Natalie removed her kerchief, then set about ensuring each patient was as comfortable as possible. Not only did she give them the herbs to reduce their coughing and fevers, but she also placed her hands on their foreheads, not to Heal, but to apologize and say goodbye. Although no one had ever confirmed that dying or delirious patients could hear people talking, Natalie had always believed they could. She murmured in their ears all she wished she'd been able to do for them and all she planned to do in their memories. She would stop the disease at Mistfell. Somehow, she would find a way.

They packed their belongings in the Temple, said a fond goodbye to Simona Halis and wished her well.

Simona shook each of their hands warmly. "Thank you for all you've done for us. I hope you can stop Mistfell from suffering our fate."

Jules returned her handshake. "Thank you. We are so grateful for all your help. If we may, Mistress Halis, we'd like to pay our respects. Can you direct us to the pyres on the beach?"

Dawn broke over Whitestrand as Natalie and Jules walked in silence toward the beach. The gray stone buildings of Whitestrand acted as a somber escort to the mass grave of its fallen citizens. As they approached, the stench of rotting and burning flesh overwhelmed their senses. Soon, they didn't need Mistress Halis's directions; they simply followed the column of smoke arcing toward the sky. As they came around the last turn, the sea winds blew in their faces, swirling the street with the ashes of the dead.

Bile rose in Natalie's throat and she broke out in a cold sweat. She whirled, ran back around the corner and emptied the contents of her stomach in the gutter. Jules held her hair back out of her face. When she was done, he held one of their waterskins out for her and she swished her mouth out.

"Thank you."

He nodded and took the waterskin, tucking it under his cloak. Wordlessly, he continued toward their destination, gripping the stump of his right arm with his left hand as if it were the only thing holding him together.

They joined the people on the beach, many who cried or comforted loved ones. A Temple priestess prayed over the large pyre. Natalie kept her head bowed, not just out of respect, but also because the flames licked and roared through skulls and around leg bones. Were her colleagues amongst this macabre pile?

Tears flowed down her face. She wanted to collapse to the ground and rage at the sky. Where did she even begin with such a disease? A little over a year ago, she took a vow to save lives; to heal. The pile of bodies in front of her, stacked and burning like so much wood, taunted her. How was she to keep her vow when a disease killed so fast?

Jules gently took her arm. "Come, Nat. Let's go to Mistfell. There are no answers here."

Back at their campsite, Natalie and Jules made quick work of packing and loading their horses with their gear. Natalie avoided smelling her clothes for fear she might vomit again. The fresh air of the campsite did much to clear her head. She mounted Benji, fidgeting in the saddle while Jules finished getting ready. Benji, sensing her mood, tossed his head and pawed the ground.

Jules secured the last of the gear to Elric's saddle and then mounted up, looking down at her. "We'll need to hunt along the way. Our food is almost out. Did you learn how to hunt growing up?"

Natalie shook her head. "No. We always traded for the food we needed. Don't tell me you learned to hunt in Roseharbor?"

Jules laughed. "Oh, no. Mother would've died before

letting us run that wild. A friend in the war taught me. However," he added with a significant look at her, "I'm going to pass the knowledge along since I'm less handsome than I was in the war." He waved his stump at her, grinning wickedly.

Natalie snorted. "Only one less handsome."

Jules raised one eyebrow. "So you still think I'm half handsome?"

Natalie rolled her eyes. "All right, enough puns. Why don't you just tell me what I'll need to do, Half Handsome?"

Given the territory they rode through, the best game was rabbits and squirrels. A deer would be too heavy to carry.

Natalie examined the plant life. "Luckily, it's summer and there are plenty of edible plants to gather, as well. All right, how do I catch a rabbit?"

They made camp that night within walking distance of a stream.

"This is a good place. We'll be far enough away that we won't scare the game off as they come to take a drink, and there are good places nearby to set traps," Jules explained. "We're going to need several sticks about the length of your foot. I'm going to teach you how to build a spring snare trap."

Once they had sufficient supplies, Jules showed Natalie how to build the basic trap structure. They secured several of these structures in the ground near the stream, next to young trees that bent over easily when grasped. The trees would spring up when released, and thus the unsuspecting animals would be captured in the traps.

The traps baited and camouflaged, Natalie squatted next to the stream and washed her hands. "You've survived using traps like this before?"

Jules nodded, rinsing his hand next to her. "Yes. It's

not as quick as, say, a bow and arrow, but it works. We'll check our traps in the morning. We'd better catch something; tonight, we'll be finishing off all the food we brought with us."

"We won't go entirely without. I gathered some food for us while looking for bait," Natalie replied.

"Good thinking. Gather as much as you can, in fact. Let's think ahead going into Mistfell."

Natalie nodded. "I'd love a bath and to wash all my clothes as well."

Jules eyed her skeptically. "This freezing stream is all you have for a bathtub."

"I don't even care. I'm tired of smelling foul."

"You do smell foul."

She splashed him. "Pot, meet kettle, Half Handy."

"Hey," he ducked. "Keep going and you'll get a bath and your clothes washed all at once." Jules splashed her back and she shrieked as a wave of freezing cold water doused her.

He splashed her again. "Shush, woman! We won't catch any food with you screaming like a banshee."

She splashed him back. "You started it."

Jules shook the water out of his hair and helped her up. "Come on, Healer Banshee. Let's move downstream a bit if we're going to do some serious bathing."

Natalie tripped. Did he just say "we"? Bathing with Jules together? Is that what he meant? Blood rushed to her face and she prayed Jules wouldn't look her way as she wordlessly went to get her bathing supplies.

Thankfully, Natalie had thrown a bar of her own homemade herbal soap in her satchel before leaving the Abbey. She grabbed that and every single bit of clothing she owned and headed downstream. Jules, proving her imagination overactive, stayed at the campsite and built a fire.

"You'll need it when you get back," Jules waggled his eyebrows at her.

Nat turned and stuck her tongue out at him and then walked a safe distance downstream. She didn't want to be out of earshot of Jules, but she wanted her privacy nonetheless. She selected a rock to work with and soaped and rinsed all her clothes, imagining all the horrors of the past week washing away downstream with the soapy bubbles. Clothes finished and hung out to dry, she herself stepped into the stream with the soap, letting out a long string of curses as she did so.

Teeth chattering, she pulled her damp Healer's cloak around her as best she could, grabbed the rest of her clothes and headed back to camp.

Jules sat next to the fire and stared at her as she approached. She stared back, clutching her cloak tightly around her. She looked away first, warmth pooling in her belly. *Thank Goddess my face is too frozen to blush. What are we to each other?* Their relationship edged closer to a precipice every day. When she thought of what lay over that precipice, her breath caught in her throat. She wasn't sure if it was too good to be true or if she should turn and run. What she wouldn't give to talk to Em.

Natalie hung her clothes to dry on bushes near their tent. Clad in only her cloak, she huddled close to the fire and tried to keep her teeth from chattering.

After a few moments, she could no longer stand the weight of Jules's stare. "What?"

"You have an impressive vocabulary for someone who comes from a nice family in Mistfell and grew up at the Abbey," he smirked.

Natalie raised her chin, seriously doubting that's all that was on his mind with her sitting there in only her cloak. "Well, the water is bloody cold. Best bathe fast so your bollocks don't freeze off."

CHAPTER 12

Natalie startled awake the next morning as the hairs on the back of her neck stood on end. Someone or something watched her. She opened her eyes and scanned her surroundings, only to find Jules staring at her with a bemused expression on his face.

"Well, this is awkward," he drawled.

She was about to ask what was, and then she bit her lip. All her clothes—and likely his—were outside out on the bushes. Natalie thought back; she had gone to sleep before he did and climbed into her bedroll naked, but she did have her cloak nearby. She pulled her bedroll up to her chin.

"Yes, it is," she agreed. *Two can play at this game.*

"Who is going to get out of bed first?" he taunted.

"I don't mind," she retorted. "I've got my cloak in here."

"You act like you've woken up with a man before."

"So what if I have? I'll bet you've woken up with women before. You were the one in the army."

Jules's face darkened and he got up and left the tent,

not caring one bit about nudity. Natalie sat transfixed by the lean muscles in his shoulders and back tapering down to his rounded, firm buttocks.

Natalie rubbed her eyes with the heels of her hands. Hell in a kettle, she always spoke first and thought later around this man. It was one of the reasons they hadn't gotten along since he'd returned from the war; her tongue always got the better of her. *Whatever we were growing into— I've ruined it entirely. I'll never get a chance to run my fingers along the skin of his back and feel those muscles or his skin against mine.*

Shaking her head, she stood, wrapped her cloak around her and exited the tent. Once dressed, she found Jules, fully dressed, down at the stream splashing his face off. She opened her mouth to apologize, but he cut her off. "We need to check the traps." He began walking. She had no choice but to follow.

When the first and second traps came up empty, Natalie began to worry. The third trap, however, had a rabbit dangling from it.

"It's still alive," she covered her mouth with her hands.

"Yes. Best kill it quickly," Jules handed her his dagger, hilt first.

She took a step back as if he'd handed her a venomous snake. "I can't kill it."

Jules scowled at her. "Natalie, it's suffering. Kill it before it suffers any more. You have two choices: break its neck with your two hands or slit its throat."

Natalie stared up at the thrashing animal. Its panicked eyes begged for her help much as the rabbits in Healer Bowers's animal sanctuary had. She could not kill this rabbit; she simply couldn't.

Jules rubbed the bridge of his nose with his fingers. "You mean to tell me you grew up on a farm and never killed an animal? You know where the meat in your stew comes from, right?"

"Of course I know," she snapped. "I just never did the killing."

"Well you'd best do the killing now or you and I will starve to death. That's one thing I learned the hard way when I was in the war, Healer. When I had to kill so I could live another day."

Natalie stared at him. She turned back to the rabbit, which writhed in pain, and swallowed with some difficulty. Mother or Da had always killed the farm animals when she was growing up; she'd always cried and hidden in her room. But it had meant Aaron and she could eat. Now she and her partner needed food. She had to do this.

She closed her eyes in a brief prayer for strength, then held out her hand for his dagger. "I'm sorry. Thank you," she told the rabbit. With hands that only shook a little, she slit the rabbit's throat.

In all, they caught three rabbits. Clenching her teeth, Natalie killed them all, then did her best to follow Jules's instructions on how to skin them. Tears stained her cheeks. She did not wipe them away and Jules did not mention them.

When the silence between them grew too much to bear, she left Jules turning the rabbits on a spit over the campfire and went to gather some fresh, edible plant life. She found a patch of wine berries and picked amongst them, tears still streaming down her cheeks.

She'd taken lives with intention for the first time in her life. What did that make her? A killer? A survivor? A hunter? As a Healer who'd made a vow to do no harm, she hoped she'd not betrayed her oath today. It was a fine line between killing an animal yourself for food and letting others do the killing and eating that food later. But Jules was right; they would show signs of malnutrition if they didn't replenish their meat supplies today. Much to her dismay, her stomach growled at the thought of roast rabbit.

Judging by what he'd said, Jules had had to kill more

than animals in the war. No wonder something inside him had broken. She'd always assumed he'd only been a Healer for the soldiers; she'd never imagined him in a position where he'd had to kill another human being. Had he?

Natalie gathered more edible plants than strictly necessary, delaying the inevitable return to camp. But her satchel was full and she decided she might as well face him and get it over with.

The sight that greeted her upon her return to camp stopped her in her tracks. Jules sat at the campfire laughing—with two strange people. She wanted to turn and disappear into the forest again, but Jules spotted her.

"Nat, come meet my friends, Anli and Onlo." He waved her over, grinning.

He was calling her Nat again, was he? Natalie plastered a smile on her face and approached the campfire. The woman sitting next to Jules had sleek, dark hair, brown eyes and an olive complexion, indicating she hailed from the northern part of the main continent. The man on Jules's other side had dark skin and long ropes of hair, meaning he was from much farther east on the continent. They wore black cloaks. Did Attuned from Obfuselt randomly materialize out of the woods? She held out her hand to the woman first. "Hello, nice to meet you."

"Hey." Anli nodded curtly and did not take her hand.

The man took her hand instead. "Nice to meet you."

Natalie liked Onlo instantly. His voice was deep and his eyes were merry.

Jules began removing the rabbits from the fire. "I met Anli and Onlo in the war."

"Met," Anli scoffed. "I saved your life."

"True," Jules shook a cooked rabbit at her. "But I seem to recall saving your ass a time or two myself."

Anli laughed, a beautiful lilting sound that, for some reason, grated on Natalie. "True enough."

Jules passed the rabbits around and Natalie gave everyone a portion of berries and vegetables. They ate while Onlo, Anli and Jules traded war stories. Natalie sat off to the side, chewing moodily on her food.

"I didn't realize Obfuselt took such an active part in the war," Natalie interjected at one point.

The three veterans grinned. "Obfuselt is why Lorelan has never invaded our country by land," Anli said, her chest swelling with pride.

Natalie shook her head in confusion. "I thought King Gerhard and Queen Phillipa's navy kept Lorelan from invading. And, growing up, my da would tell us stories of great sea monsters sinking Lorelan ships." Though truth be told, she'd always found those stories a bit far-fetched.

Onlo nodded. "That's what we want people to think."

"The Attuned shipwrights of Obfuselt build ships that are light, fast and hard to see in the dark. Attuned sailors, who have an easier time spotting ships at night, sail those ships with great skill," Jules supplied.

Anli threw a rabbit bone in the fire. "Over the centuries, we've made an art out of sabotaging Lorelan's ships at night and getting away unnoticed. It's Obfuselt's best-kept secret—even Their Royal Majesties don't know."

Natalie's eyes widened. Well, that changed a lot of the history she'd learned. But why were they talking about long-kept secrets in front of a complete stranger? "Why tell me?"

Jules and Onlo glanced at each other. "This war is different," Jules began. "The war Lorelan waged on the Isles two hundred years ago was, shall we say, a much more straightforward war. Lorelan tried to invade us for our resources, and after seven years, they gave up thanks in large part to Obfuselt."

Anli's grin had a hint of madness in it.

"But this war ..." Jules began.

"There are some folk in power from our country—on at least one Isle, maybe more— working with Lorelan." Onlo continued when Jules could not.

Natalie's jaw dropped. "What?"

"One of them is Healer Aldworth," Jules said. Anli spat on the ground.

"Not possible," Natalie scoffed. "He was my mentor during my apprenticeship. He's a great Healer."

Jules held up his missing right hand. "He's responsible for this."

Natalie's stomach clenched and its contents rose. *No. No, I don't believe it.*

Anli hissed. "Jules was on a mission for us when Aldworth kidnapped him. At the time, we didn't know Aldworth and his associates wanted to abduct descendants of the mages who created the megaliths on the Isles. We also didn't know Jules was one of them."

Natalie's jaw fell open again. "You're a descendant of Bridhe herself?"

Jules raised his eyebrows and smirked. "Apparently I have green eyes for a reason. Anyway, Aldworth is trying to create a new megalith in Lorelan so Healers can Heal on the continent."

Natalie rubbed her face with her hands. "He's trying to duplicate our megalith? Did he succeed? Is there a megalith on Lorelan now?"

Jules sighed. "Well, it didn't quite go as he'd planned. I didn't cooperate as he liked, so he drugged me and held a knife to my throat. Then, during the ritual, when they made me do my part, something happened and the megalith burned my hand off and knocked us all out."

Natalie felt like she'd been punched in the stomach. She'd worked with Aldworth for a year and learned so much from him. He was a good man. She … she thought he was. How could he have done that to Jules? Why hadn't Jules told her this sooner?

Natalie put her hand on the back of her neck. "Why didn't you tell anyone about Aldworth? Headmistress Gayla, Healer Hawkins, someone needs to know."

"He's one of the most respected Healers at the Abbey and the head of the Council of Healers." Jules sighed.

"And I have no proof."

"You have our word," said Onlo.

"Would my word, yours and Anli's be enough to convince the entire Abbey of the depth of his treachery?" Jules shrugged. "At any rate, that's why I sent word to you before we left the Abbey. If an epidemic sweeps the Isles, we'll be weak, especially with our own working to take us down from the inside."

Natalie's jaw dropped open. "You three planned to meet up here?" Yet another secret he'd failed to share with his partner. Natalie snapped her mouth shut and glared at Jules.

Jules shrugged. "We need Obfuselt to know what's going on. I asked Onlo and Anli to meet us in Whitestrand, but here we are instead."

Natalie frowned. "Whitestrand is a point of weakness—perfect for a land invasion. It's a port city, and its remaining inhabitants are children and the elderly."

Onlo glanced at Anli. "We should get word to our Naval Guild to send the coast guard there."

Jules popped the last of his rabbit into his mouth. "We're on our way to Mistfell today. We have reason to believe the epidemic may have spread there. Tell anyone you encounter to avoid it, just in case."

Natalie rested her forehead on her hand. "Should we even tell the Abbey we've left Whitestrand for Mistfell?"

"We'll have to if we get there and we need a quarantine," Jules pointed out.

"I guess we'll have to hope they'll understand why we left Whitestrand without permission," Natalie sighed.

"Don't count on it."

Natalie finished putting her items into her pack and secured it to Benji. She observed Jules, Anli, and Onlo deep in conversation closer to the stream, their dark heads bent together, faces sober. She rolled her eyes. After all they'd revealed, now they didn't trust her? She double-checked Benji's tack, then mounted up and directed Benji toward the three of them. She was determined to join the conversation whether they liked it or not.

As soon as she approached, the three of them shook hands with each other and dispersed. Natalie huffed. Goddess forbid she disrupt their little secret society.

Onlo approached her on his dark stallion, smiling broadly. "It was good to meet you, Natalie. Take good care of my brother for us."

Natalie raised her eyebrows. "I will if he lets me."

Onlo chuckled at Jules's snort, then rode off down the road. Anli was already riding down the path, having only said farewell to Jules.

Natalie turned Benji to face Jules, who was loading up Elric with his gear. "Where are they off to?"

"To spread the word about what's happening here to their fellow Islanders so they can prepare extra defense measures for Ismereld," Jules said.

Natalie nodded and they rode off toward Mistfell in silence. She loathed the awkwardness between them but had no idea how to fix it. It would be easier if his moods stopped swinging like the clock pendulum in Headmistress Gayla's office. She knew it was normal for someone who had experienced trauma; she just wished she could help him in some way.

"Now you know," Jules said, "some of my war experiences and what lies between Aldworth and me. Now that we've disobeyed Council orders, he will be angry, which makes him a greater threat to me. And if I am in danger, then you are in danger by virtue of being my partner." He stared down at the stump of his arm. "I'm not certain I can protect you if he comes for us."

"Why did you go back to the Abbey if he is such a danger to you? And if he wants you so badly, why did he let you go to Whitestrand?" Natalie still couldn't believe it. Why hadn't Jules told her about Aldworth before now?

"After his megalith … did whatever it did to me, it disintegrated. I was covered in dust when I came to. I figured, with no megalith, he didn't need me anymore, so I returned. Besides, he'd be foolish to move against me so overtly at the Abbey. Which is why I think he sent me to Whitestrand. Revenge, I think. He hoped I would die there, you see."

Lifting her chin to contradict such an astonishing accusation, Natalie took one look at the guilt and pain etched on his face, and the words stuck in her throat. She stared at the road ahead, letting the silence cloak them for miles.

CHAPTER 13

The next morning, Natalie and Jules rode over a hill on the outskirts of Mistfell. A familiar grove of trees and a wooden red house came into view. Unable to contain herself, she signaled Benji to speed up.

"Nat, wait," Jules called after her.

Natalie brought Benji up in a tight circle.

"What?" she demanded.

"We need to do one last check for symptoms. You exposed yourself to all those patients in Whitestrand. We—we need to be absolutely sure before we go riding into town."

Natalie looked at her home and back at Jules. Dammit, he was right.

She guided Benji back to Jules. "I haven't had a headache or stomach issues. No fever or sweating beyond what's normal for summer. I think we can rule out contact with people or surfaces, or bodily fluids. Why don't you Name me just to be sure?"

Jules nodded and they dismounted and tied the horses to a nearby tree. Standing in the sun-dappled shade, Jules approached Natalie and offered her his hand. Keeping her eyes on the thick blades of grass beneath her boots, Natalie took his hand. She placed her free hand on her head and breathed deeply, letting Jules do all the work.

"You're just fine," Jules whispered.

Natalie removed her hand from her head and opened her eyes. He still grasped her hand.

"I'm sorry, for how I behaved at the campsite."

"I'm sorry, too. I shouldn't have said what I did about your time in the army."

He squeezed her hand.

She squeezed his hand in return. "You can tell me things, you know. It's hard being your partner if I'm left in the dark."

Jules bowed his head. "Trusting people is hard. After what happened with Aldworth ... He was my Cultural Studies professor and so well regarded. I trusted him. And he ..."

Natalie bit her lip. "I'm still not sure I believe it myself."

"I know. It's hard when people we respect turn out to be rotten at the core. But I will try to trust you more if you try to trust me and believe what happened to me at his hands. Now"—Jules led her over to the horses—"come on. I'd like to meet your family."

Natalie cantered down the lane, right to the front porch of her childhood home.

"Mother?" She leaped off Benji, ran to the door and knocked repeatedly. "Da? It's me, Nat," she pushed the door just as her mother pulled it open from the inside, and she flew into her mother's arms and squeezed her as hard as she could.

"Nat, how are you doing, love? We didn't expect you; what are you doing here?" Mother said into her shoulder.

"It's a really long story. See we were sent to

Whitestrand and … and …" The sobs Natalie had held back for days came out just then. She cried on her mother's apron much as she'd done when she was twelve and the baker's son had broken her heart.

"Nat, is that you?" Da came in the back door of the house, wiping the dirt off his boots. He was just as large and burly as she remembered him, though perhaps there were a few more lines on his face and some grey hairs sprinkled in his beard.

Natalie flew at him and squeezed him hard; she'd missed the tickle of his whiskers when hugging him. "I've missed you so much, Da."

Loud footfalls sounded on the stairs. "Nat?" Her brother, Aaron, jumped down the rest of the flight and joined their embrace, nearly knocking her and her father over. Her mother hugged them all, and for the first time in a long time, all was right with the world. She closed her eyes and wished time would stop for a bit.

When she opened her eyes, a tall, dark figure hovered at the door. "Oh, I'm sorry. Jules, please come in. Mother, Da, Aaron, please meet Healer Juliers." She led her family by the hand to the door and let Jules in. "Jules, this is my mother, Anna, my father, Gerard, and my brother, Aaron."

Jules greeted each of her family in turn. "It's nice to meet you."

She watched Jules take in the kitchen with its large cast iron stove—perfect for making Natalie's favorite apple tarts— its worn curtains, multicolored braided rug, and roughhewn wooden table and chairs. She wondered what someone who'd grown up as part of Roseharbor's upper crust thought of an apple farming family's humble house.

When her mother offered them lunch, Natalie declined. "We're unfortunately here on official business. We're looking for a brewer named Morley. We just came from Whitestrand where there is an epidemic. The town is under quarantine and he left there without permission."

Each one of Natalie's family backed away from her.

Natalie held up her hands. "We know the illness isn't spread from person to person, but we haven't eliminated food or water as a source yet. Have any of you seen Morley? He would have come to town a few days ago with a wagon and ale. Has a horrible attitude toward women."

Natalie's father shook his head. "I didn't see him, Nat, but you know the best place to go for information around here."

Natalie rolled her eyes. "The Leaking Dragon."

"The Leaking Dragon? Really? How is that a name for a tavern?" Jules hissed at her as they walked down the main street of Mistfell proper.

"Look, I didn't name it; the demented barkeep did. And besides, we need the information."

Jules grunted and followed Natalie and her father into the tavern. Natalie's father ordered an ale from the barkeep. The barkeep, Oswald, was a short man; his cropped, red hair stuck out in all directions, and he wore one half of a pair of orange-tinted goggles to cover up what Natalie knew was his missing eye. Natalie had no idea how he lost it and she'd always been hesitant to ask; Oswald had a habit of sharing a little too much information. She hoped that habit would help them now.

He squinted at Natalie. "I know you."

Natalie smiled. "Yes, I'm Natalie, Gerard's daughter."

"Mmph. The Healer. What can I get you and your man?"

"Oh, no, he's not—I mean, nothing, thank you," she replied, blushing. "This is Healer Juliers and we're looking for information on a brewer who might have come this way recently. A Mr. Morley?"

Oswald rolled his eye. "Large man resembling a horse's ass?"

Jules grinned. "That's the one."

"Was here yesterday. He's tried to sell me some of his

donkey piss another time. Told him I'd have none of it this time either. He stayed here for the night and moved on this morning."

"Did he say where he was going?"

"Roseharbor, I think."

Natalie and Jules blanched.

"Has anyone in town been sick?" Jules asked.

Oswald grinned conspiratorially. "Well, ol' Ron the Butcher took himself on a trip to Whitestrand a month or two back and spent the night with a lady and now he's got a pox. His wife ain't none too pleased."

"Thank you, Oswald," Natalie said. Jules nodded to the door and Natalie bobbed her head to show she understood. "Da, we'll be right back."

She and Jules stepped into the street and found an alcove in which they could speak without being overheard.

Jules threw his hands up in the air. "Because what we needed is more guesswork."

Natalie nodded. "The illness could be here, on its way to Roseharbor, or nowhere. Dammit."

Jules shook his head and shrugged. "There's nothing for it—we're going to have to tell the Abbey now. The more eyes and ears we have, the better. We can send word by rider and head back there ourselves in the morning."

"I agree. Let's go to the town hall and see if any riders are available."

At the town hall, a fourteen-year-old girl named Becca with a sleek, dapple gray horse said she could make the trip to the Abbey in two days. The Healers borrowed paper and a quill from the town hall and wrote a letter to the Abbey detailing their experience at Whitestrand, all they knew about the sweating fever, the escape of Morley and his suspected location.

Once sealed, Natalie handed the letter directly to Becca, who took it and tucked it safely in her saddlebag. "Deliver the letter directly to Headmistress Gayla herself." Becca nodded, her long, dark brown braids bobbing as she did.

Natalie reached into her pockets and handed Becca several coins and an Abbey token. "Here," she said "for your upkeep along the way and payment once you get there. You have our gratitude. May the Five light your path and keep you safe."

"Thank you," Becca said and cantered off.

That night, Natalie got to do something she'd hated as a child and horribly missed once she was at the Abbey: she helped her family cook dinner. She and Jules agreed it would be safe as long as the food supply came from the forest and not the town. The aroma of the cooking venison, for which she'd selected seasonings from her old herb garden, wafted through the house. Da and Aaron prepared root vegetables, while Natalie and her mother tended the venison.

It was a hot summer evening inside, despite all the windows in the house being flung as wide open as possible. Still, Natalie's heart swelled taking in the smells and sounds of her family preparing food. Da talked about how this year's apple trees were doing well. Aaron told Jules about school and his desire to travel to Obfuselt to see if the island's stone would Attune him.

"So young and already he talks about going so far away," Mother murmured to Natalie as they checked the meat. "But, I can't deny he loves building things. He's constantly fixing broken equipment around the farm."

Natalie wiped sweat from her forehead. "Luckily, I became Attuned right here. I love this island and I can't imagine ever leaving."

Her mother handed her a glass of water, and they stepped out onto the porch to escape the kitchen's heat. "But it's hard, yes? Your life as a Healer?"

Natalie rested her crossed arms on the porch railing and took in the sight of the farm before her. "It can be, yes. This past week has been the most difficult of all. I've seen and done things I never imagined … I mean, when I left here to attend the Abbey, I imagined helping people. And I have. But this week …" Natalie shook her head.

"If anyone can solve this problem, it's you. I believe in you, Nat," her mother said.

Tears spilled over onto Natalie's cheeks as she thought of a Temple full of dying people and a pyre on the beach with the ashes of the dead swirling around her. "I don't think I can."

"I know. That's why it's good, in our darkest hours, to have someone strong to rely on." Mother nodded back to the house. "You seem to have found a good person to have at your side."

Natalie nodded. Despite their ups and downs and their struggle to trust each other, she would not have made it this far without Jules. *Actually, since we've set out from the Abbey, he's had my back without fail. Maybe … maybe I can trust him more after all. He promised to start trusting me more. My Goddess, if Healer Aldworth really did that to him …* Natalie put her hands on her cheeks. It was too terrible to comprehend.

"Are you and he—?"

Natalie shook her head quickly. "No. I thought maybe there was a chance, but—it's complicated."

Her mother smiled and took her arm. "It always is. Come, let's see if dinner is ready."

Dinner was an amicable affair, with everyone crammed in elbow to elbow at the table, trying to eat and converse at the same time. Once again, Natalie wanted to freeze time so she could savor the taste of the food, the sound of her family and the fullness of her heart.

Even Jules joined in the conversation. He told Aaron a funny story from his boyhood in Roseharbor. Natalie found herself just as entranced by the story as Aaron. She caught herself grinning like a fool and quickly wiped her mouth with her napkin. Jules arched an eyebrow at her, one side of his mouth curling up in a smirk of his own.

Da told them it was just as well they hadn't arrived during harvest season, and all four Desmonds told stories of apple harvest seasons past, working from dawn to dusk, selecting the proper apples, getting stung by a variety of insects and never getting enough sleep for weeks.

"It isn't all bad, though," Natalie pointed out. "Fresh apple pies and tarts are possibly the best things in the world."

Jules smiled. "See, now I insist upon coming here during harvest season."

"Ha," Natalie's father said. "We'll just put you to work."

"No problem. I take pies as payment." Jules waggled his eyebrows.

Natalie stood and began to clear the table. Aaron came along to help with the dishes. Natalie listened for the sound of her mother fainting at the sight of them doing the dishes and not fighting.

"Mr. Desmond, are you all right?" Jules asked. Natalie froze, suds dripping from the plate she was washing.

"It's nothing. Just a headache I've had for a bit has suddenly gotten much worse."

Natalie dropped the plate and ran to her father. No. No, no, no, no, no. She reached her father's side soon after Jules did and put her hand to his forehead. It was burning up. But was that a fever or the warm evening? Dammit, she wasn't sure.

Natalie took her father's arm. "Come, Da, you need to lie down. Jules and I need to treat you."

"Nonsense, it's just a headache. Give me one of your teas, Nat, I'll be fine."

Jules took her father's other arm. "Mr. Desmond, I agree with your daughter. I think you need to lay down. We need to do something called Naming on you. Has Nat described it to you?"

Her Da nodded and as he did so, he began to slump out of his chair. Natalie and Jules grabbed him and helped him stumble over to the couch, which was near some open windows. Natalie pulled some chairs over next to the couch. Her mother and Aaron watched her, hugging each other with terrified expressions. "Mother, please boil some water. Aaron, if you can, find something to help cool Da down."

As they rushed off, Natalie and Jules sat next to the couch. They exchanged a helpless look before joining hands and placing them on Natalie's father. When they finished Naming, a deep, terrifying chasm opened in Natalie's chest. "Five help us," was all she could say.

CHAPTER 14

Holding a torch in one hand, Natalie rooted through her old herb garden, digging up all the tanyaroot she possibly could. She couldn't believe Da had this Five-damned disease. She wanted to lay down and cry until no more tears came. She wanted to grab a stick and smash everything in sight. But Da's life was in danger. She had to save him. She had to.

When she had all the tanyaroot she could find, she ran into the house and set it on the counter. She'd prepare it later; there was no time now. The rest of what she had left in her satchel already sat steeping in a mug on the counter.

Peering into her satchel, she took stock of her dullanbark supply; she had only a little left. She'd need more for Da's fever.

Aaron appeared at her side, out of breath. "I've got some ice from the cellar."

The ice cellar. She forgot Da cut ice out of the nearby river every winter. He stored it in an underground cellar packed in sawdust for use throughout the year.

She hugged him. "Aaron, you're a genius. Are there still

dullan trees near here?"

He nodded.

"Good. Take a basket, a sharp knife and a torch—be careful. I need you to shave off bits of the top layer of bark to make tea for Da's fever."

He ran off and she turned to observe her father. The fever had progressed. Soon, he'd be vomiting. She grabbed a bowl from the kitchen and handed it to Jules, who'd remained next to her father's side.

Jules gently touched her arm. "We're going to need sheets or blankets for when he starts sweating."

"I'll get them," her mother said from behind her.

Between the four of them, they soon had everything they needed. Natalie got her father to drink the tanyaroot and dullanbark tea, and together, she and Jules Activated it.

Then there was nothing to do but wait. Natalie sat next to her father and held his hand, his eyes closed against the pain of his headache. Jules alternately paced and unnecessarily reorganized their supplies.

"Nat," her father whispered.

She held his hand tighter and leaned forward. "Yes, Da?"

"Is this…what they had…in Whitestrand?"

"Yes, Da," she replied. Jules put a reassuring hand on her shoulder. She reached back with her free hand to grasp his. They both let go when her father heaved to the side; she and Jules got the bowl under him just in time as he lost the contents of his stomach.

For the next several hours, Natalie did things for her father she'd done thousands of times for other people. She cleaned up his vomit. She helped change his sheets and clothes when the illness made him lose control of his bowels. She whispered comforting things to him and told him to keep fighting. She helped keep him packed with ice to keep the fever down.

In the early hours of the morning, the sweating started.

Natalie and Jules changed his sheets once again and handed them to Aaron and Natalie's mother who took them off to be washed. They were running out of sheets, Natalie worried.

"Nat," Jules called softly from her father's side. She went and sat next to him.

He brushed her jaw with his fingers. "How are you holding up?" he asked.

Tears pricked her eyes, but she held her chin up. "I'm doing all right. I'm determined to see him through this."

Jules smiled at her.

She turned back to her father. In his delirium, he'd stopped recognizing her or any of the family. His incoherent mumblings filled the house, though they did seem to get better the lower they could keep the fever. Natalie put a new round of ice on. She applied the ice judiciously since, as much as he was sweating, the ice also tended to make him shiver.

Hell in a kettle, between the sweating, vomiting and diarrhea, he was losing so much fluid, Natalie thought. It's like the tea isn't enough.

"Jules," she began, "what if the tea *isn't* enough?"

He finished shifting one of the ice packs. "What do you mean?"

"He's losing so much of his bodily fluids, right? What if the medicinal teas aren't replacing what he's lost?"

Jules sat back. "Almost like he's a heat exhaustion patient. Or a patient who has had vomiting or diarrhea so long, they're dehydrated."

Natalie nodded, warming to her idea. "Exactly. What if we added honey and salt to what he drinks next?"

Jules stared at her and nodded. "I think you're right. Dammit, we didn't even consider dehydration in Whitestrand." He pounded his fist on his knee.

Natalie ran to the kitchen and flew through the cupboards until she found a pot of honey. Salt, she had in her satchel. She mixed honey and salt with some tea, and together, she and Jules helped her father drink it.

Jules handed the cup to her when they were done. "We'll have to make sure he gets a lot. He's lost a great deal of fluids so far, and with the constant sweating he'll continue to lose more."

Natalie nodded. "I'll go fix a big batch and we'll make him sip some constantly." In the kitchen, she found a pot and began to mix her ingredients. She smiled when her mother and Aaron came in from doing the laundry, but her smile faded when she saw her mother's face. "Mother, are you all right?"

Mother's face was gaunt and red. "I'm exhausted, sweetheart." She stumbled to her husband's side and held his hand.

Jules caught Natalie's eye over Anna's head, concern on his face. "Mrs. Desmond, we can make a place for you to lie down. You can't care for your husband if you do not care for yourself."

Mother rubbed her temples. "Perhaps I will lie down. Just for a bit."

Natalie walked over and knelt next to her mother. "Mother. Do you have a headache?"

Tears spilled down her mother's cheeks when she nodded.

"It's all right, we'll take care of you," Natalie cupped her mother's face with her two hands and brushed her tears away with her thumb. "Aaron, do we still have a trundle cot upstairs?" She turned and saw her brother looking petrified, one tear rolling down his own cheek. She strode over and hugged him. What a change, she thought grimly. Yesterday afternoon, sunlight shone in this room upon all four of them hugging together. Now, she and Aaron clung to each other as Da fought for his life and Mother began her fight.

"Will they die, Nat?" Aaron asked.

Natalie closed her eyes and buried her face in her brother's hair. "Not if Jules and I have anything to say about it."

"Will I get sick, too?"

Natalie sighed. "Well, that's the odd thing. In Whitestrand, none of the children got sick at all. So, I think you're safe. Come on, let's get the cot for Mother."

Dawn broke on the Desmond household. Coughs racked Da's body as his lungs filled with fluid despite the tanyaroot tea. Mother made it through the worst of the digestive symptoms, her body beginning to sweat. Natalie and Jules ran themselves ragged taking care of two patients and doing all the laundry with Aaron's help. They rejoiced that Mother received the honey and salt mixture from the beginning to help keep her hydrated and could not help but be optimistic about the difference it might make in her outcome.

Natalie observed Jules tending her father. His face was haggard from lack of sleep. Thick stubble grew along his chin. He'd discarded his cloak and rolled up his shirt sleeves in an effort to remain cool. Yet he cared for her father and mother with the utmost gentleness and patience under the most trying of circumstances.

Jules caught her staring. "What is it?"

For once, she did not hesitate to hold his gaze. "Thank you. From the bottom of my heart. I am so grateful to you."

He tilted his head to the side and considered what she said. "This," he gestured around the room, "is what I was born to do. When I became Attuned and then a Healer, it was the happiest time of my life. But I'm not tending to your parents because I am a Healer and I took an oath. Yesterday afternoon and evening, when I spent time with your family, it was one of the happiest times of my life. I have never felt so at home or welcome."

Natalie smiled at him. She was glad her family had been able to give him such a gift, if only for a short while. Five willing, it was a gift they could all give him again. She turned to give her mother some more tea.

"I hate to bring this up, but we must send word to the Abbey; Mistfell needs an Imperial quarantine," Jules said.

Natalie sighed. "Yes, I've been thinking the same thing. And, what do we tell the townsfolk without causing a panic? Furthermore, I still don't understand how Morley transmitted the disease. Oswald said he didn't buy any of his beer.

Jules rested his head in his hand. "I haven't the foggiest idea. Obviously, Morley brought it with him somehow."

"Oswald said he stayed for the night at his tavern. Maybe when Mother and Da are stable, we should take a look at where he stayed. See if there's anything that might help us figure it out."

Jules nodded, then reached to help Da as a new round of coughing came on.

"Nat," Da gasped as the spell passed. "Aaron." Jules and Natalie stared at him. Usually the delirium didn't let up.

Natalie fetched Aaron, who had fallen asleep on a stool in the corner, and placed her hand on his shoulder to wake him. "Da is asking for us."

She and Aaron went to Da's side. Jules stood behind them with his hand on Natalie's shoulder. Natalie and Aaron both grabbed their father's hand. To Natalie's amazement, he was able to open his eyes and focus on them.

"Got a ... short time here." Da rasped. "I love you. Take care ... of Mother. And the farm. So ... proud ... of you both." His eyes lost focus, his mouth gaped open and he stared at the ceiling.

Tears poured down Aaron's face. "Is he really dying, Nat?"

Natalie observed her father's body as a Healer would. His breathing changed from congested wheezes to unpredictable, rattling, sporadic breaths. The part of his body facing the ceiling was pale and cold. Lifting his shirt gently, she could see the skin resting on the couch was mottled and purple; his heart was no longer pumping blood properly. She took a shaky breath and said, "Yes. Da is dying."

"What can you do?" he cried.

Tears fell down Natalie's own face. "We can hold his hand and tell him how much we love him. We can tell him stories from when we were growing up. We can tell him we'll take care of Mother and the farm and it's okay to go to the Goddess when it's time."

"But that won't save his life. You said you could save him!" Aaron accused.

Natalie bowed her head, dimly aware of Jules's hand squeezing her shoulder. "I can't save him. We … I tried," she said, her voice tinged with defeat. "Being with him and talking to him will ease his transition into the next world. That's our job now."

CHAPTER 15

Jules cared for her mother while Natalie talked to her father. Aaron, after some time standing off to the side, arms folded and eyes boring holes in the floor, joined his sister.

Aaron put his hand on his father's shoulder. "I love you so much, Da," he said.

Natalie rubbed her father's thumb with her own. "I love you, too, Da. I'll make sure to take care of Mother and Aaron."

Aaron sniffed. "And I'll run the farm."

Natalie smiled. "And I'll Heal him when he falls off the ladder and breaks his arm like he did when he was seven."

"Hey," Aaron said.

"Do you remember that, Da?"

"Of course he remembers. He's the one who carried me to the Healer."

"Aaron, do you remember the harvest when we accidentally knocked down a hornet's nest?"

"I've never run so fast in my life. You made compresses for us for days. Those buggers really hurt."

Aaron stared at his father, who lay staring at the ceiling. "Can he hear us, Nat?"

"I believe he can," she said.

"Shouldn't Mother be with us?"

Natalie turned to Jules. "Is it safe to wake Mother?"

Jules ran his hand through his hair and then shook his head. "No. She's too weak, It's all I can do to get her to drink. I'm so sorry."

Natalie nodded, blinking back tears. "Da? Mother loves you, too. She's sick and can't be with you now, but she has loved you for so long. She says to go be with the Goddess when you are ready. We will take care of her, don't you worry." Natalie wiped her tears away with one hand.

Natalie and Aaron held their father's hand, either telling stories or holding hands in silence. Over the course of the morning, Gerard's breathing slowed until he took a breath and it seemed like another would not come.

Aaron stood up. "Nat? Is it—what's happening?

Natalie hugged her brother. "His body is shutting down and dying. Soon he won't be suffering anymore."

Aaron turned away, and she cradled his head against her. Natalie, having witnessed the process many times, watched her father's last sporadic, fitful attempts to gasp for air; his body relaxed when it stopped trying and let go. She closed her eyes. "He's gone, sweetheart. He's with the Goddess now."

Aaron looked at his dead father. Natalie put her arm around his shoulders and held him tight; she wasn't sure if he'd ever seen a dead human body. Aaron reached out with a shaking hand and gently closed his father's eyes. The eyelids popped right back open and Aaron jumped. "It's okay, it's okay, they don't stay closed, it's normal," Natalie hugged him as he sobbed, and she buried her face in his hair, a few of her own tears falling. She'd failed. She'd failed to save her own father.

Another pair of arms embraced the two of them. She reached out to squeeze Jules tight, rested her forehead on his shoulder and leaned on him as if her life depended on it. She wanted to cry—let all the pain out—but the sobs stuck in her chest and refused to move.

After a few minutes, Jules turned around and covered Da with a sheet. "I wrote a letter to the Abbey telling them of the situation here and asking for an Imperial quarantine and more Healers. I'll ride into town and get a rider to take it to the Abbey. I'll also get the undertaker and tell the town Healer what to watch out for."

Natalie nodded. "Thank you." Exhausted, she sat next to her mother. *Please, Mother*, she prayed. *Please live. I don't know what I'll do if you die, too.*

When Jules returned from town, he suggested Natalie set up their tent near the house and get some rest. The undertaker had come and gone, taking Da's body with him. Aaron fell asleep in his bed upstairs. Jules kept watch over her sleeping mother, who coughed from time to time, but Jules and Natalie had heard worse from patients with this disease. With everything in as much order as it could be, Natalie staggered out to the tent and was asleep before her head hit her bedroll.

She woke when the sun's rays were setting behind the apple grove. Taking in the beauty of her father's life's work, it was hard to believe it would live on long past him. Before the tears could fall, she reminded herself she, Aaron and Jules needed to eat. She grabbed the equipment to make snares and set up several in the nearby woods. Returning to the house, she found Jules dozing in his seat next to her mother's bedside.

She squatted in front of him and brushed a hand across his leg. "Jules."

He jumped awake and ran a hand through his hair, which stood out at all angles. "Wha? I'm sorry I dozed off. Is she all right?"

They both examined her mother. Natalie shook her

127

head in wonder. "She's sleeping still." She put her ear on her mother's chest. "I can hear congestion, but I've heard worse. Why don't you go get sleep now? I've set snares in the woods. Hopefully, we'll eat well soon."

Jules nodded wearily. "She hasn't woken up since your father … She still doesn't know."

Natalie bit her lip and nodded.

Jules staggered out the door to the tent, and Natalie took an inventory of the tea and supplies, keeping an ear out for her mother. She alternated plying her mother with medicinal teas and reading her Healing diary, desperately searching for information that might help them treat or understand the sweating fever. There must be something in her notes; some clue as to why the young and old did not die from a similar disease or how the disease was transmitted.

Near dawn, a small whisper came from the trundle cot. "Nat."

Natalie ran to her mother's side and grasped her hand. "Mother. How are you feeling?"

"Chest. Hurts."

"Do you want some tea?"

Her mother made a face. "So. Sick. Of. Tea."

Natalie laughed. She touched her mother's head. It felt much cooler than earlier.

"Starting. To. Feel. Better. I think." Anna swallowed. "How is Da?"

Natalie bowed her head and swallowed as the tears spilled down her cheeks. "I'm so sorry, Mother. I tr-tr-tried so hard."

Mother looked like a deer that had been shot by an arrow and did not yet know the wound was mortal.

Unable to face her, Natalie rested her head on her mother's chest, the sobs that had refused to come earlier now rushing out in full force. "I'm so sorry, I d-d-did my best."

The feeling of her mother trembling beneath her made

Natalie cry all the harder.

Aaron came downstairs. "Is Mother all right?" His voice sounded terrified.

Natalie lifted her head and nodded, wiping her eyes with her sleeve. "I've only just told her about Da. She's awake, you see."

Aaron joined his mother and sister, and they clasped one another in a small circle sharing their sorrow with one another. Natalie had to put a stop to it, though, when the crying irritated Mother's coughing. She helped her mother drink some more tea to settle her cough.

Jules came in for the morning and helped reposition her mother. "Nat, it's dawn. Best walk the trapline and see if we've got some breakfast." He handed her his dagger.

She nodded, took his dagger, grabbed her cloak and went out onto the porch. She turned in surprise when the door opened and closed behind her.

Jules took her elbow and turned her gently toward him. He took her face in his hand and tilted her chin up so she gazed right into his eyes. The shimmering light of dawn shifted Jules's emerald eyes in a bewitching manner, distracting Natalie from her bleak thoughts. "Nat. It's not your fault. We tried our best."

It was. Oh, Goddess, it was. If she'd only thought of the honey and salt sooner, if she'd just … but if she said this out loud, he would contradict her. So she slowly leaned forward and rested her cheek on his chest. She'd take the comfort for now. One of his arms carefully came around her back and then another. She slid her arms around him until she was clinging on to him for dear life. Her body couldn't cry anymore; all she could do was breathe deeply. Jules smelled like the soap they'd used to wash clothes their clothes in the stream, horses, and fresh morning grass. She longed to stay here, safe in the comfort of his arms. She craved more than a partner and friend. She wanted a deep love like Mother and Da. She wanted— oh, hell in a kettle, if Jules knew what she wanted with him, he'd fly away like a frightened bird and never come back. Her chest tightened and she stepped out of the embrace, hastily tidying her hair as she did so. "Thanks," she said, looking away. "I have to walk the trapline."

Aaron, Natalie and Jules feasted on fresh cooked squirrel and berries as they watched her mother slowly recover. Mother was awake more and more and even able to sip a bit of broth by the evening's end. By the next morning, she could sit propped up and converse with a bit more ease.

"I'd like to bury Gerard near the apple orchard," she said after breakfast. "It was his life's work; he should be buried near it."

Natalie nodded.

"I'll dig the grave," Aaron said.

Natalie put her arm around his shoulders. "I'll help."

After another round of coughing, her mother continued, "I need to contact the Isle of Solerin to ask for someone who can help run an apple farm."

"Solerin Attuned can work on other Isles?" Aaron asked. "They don't need their megalith?"

Jules shook his head. "Solerin Attuned only need their sunstone megalith to help the plant life grow on Solerin itself. They often lend services to farmers in need on the other Isles; they hate to see a good farm go to waste. Besides, as your father proved so well, non-magical plant skills can accomplish quite a lot."

"I'll send a message to Solerin as soon as possible, Mother," Natalie offered.

Aaron cocked his head to the side. "It's going to be weird having a stranger living here at the farm."

Natalie nodded. "Yes. However, better that than losing the farm entirely. Isle folk look out for their own."

Aaron nodded and stood. "C'mon, Nat. We should start digging."

"Sure. Where do you want to—"

A frantic knock sounded at the door. Upon opening it, she found a gangly girl, red-faced and out of breath, whose sweaty pony was tied to the front porch.

"Healer Desmond. Healer Edgewood would like you to come immediately. Many town folk have headaches and are throwing up." Natalie almost questioned the rider about the Healer's name and then she remembered Mistfell's Healer from when she was growing up, Healer Wallace, passed away a few years ago. The memory carved a fresh wound in her heart; her childhood seemed to be disappearing in front of her.

"Yes, sweetheart, tell him we'll be there right away. See to your pony and you can head back to town," Natalie replied and turned to gather her things.

Jules put his hand on her arm. "Nat, wait. Stay and see your father buried. That is where you belong. I'll go help Healer Edgewood."

She put a hand on his shoulder. "Are you sure?"

"Yes, absolutely. We're going to start them all off as we did your mother—with medication and hydration."

Natalie strode across the room. "Come, take my satchel. All we need here is a bit of tanyaroot for Mother's cough. You take the rest of the root and the dullanbark. I'll put the salt and honey in there, too. You'll also need food. Aaron, pack some of the leftover squirrel for Jules. Some of the berries, too, if they're still good."

The house was a flurry of activity as they got Jules ready to travel into Mistfell town. Soon, she and Aaron had Elric's saddlebags packed and Jules mounted up.

Natalie put her hands on her hips. "Stay alive, Juliers Rayvenwood," she ordered.

He gazed at her with a look she couldn't decipher but made her stomach flutter nonetheless. "Come to me when you are ready," he said.

Natalie crossed her arms over her stomach and put his words away in her mind to savor for later.

"I will."

CHAPTER 16

Natalie and Aaron grabbed shovels, selected a site near the apple tree grove and began digging. Their mother kept watch from the back porch, carefully propped up in chairs and resting with her feet elevated.

It was sweaty, wretched work; stinging blisters formed on Natalie's hands, and the muscles in her back protested loudly. Yet it was also soothing and meditative, moving the dirt from one place to another; she found the smell of the dirt preferable to the smell of sweat, sickness and death that had been stuck in her nose these past few weeks.

She and Aaron took a break only for lunch. Natalie bandaged their blistered hands with a poultice of her own making. By early afternoon, they could both stand in the hole facing each other.

Natalie was lost in thought when a shovel full of dirt from Aaron's shovel landed right in her face. She dropped her shovel, coughing and sputtering, trying to spit out the dirt and wipe it away at the same time. She definitely swallowed some, too.

Aaron not-so-helpfully pounded on her back. "Nat? Are you okay? I'm sorry, I didn't mean to get you. The shovel slipped."

She flapped a hand at him, batting him away, and reached for the waterskin of water she'd set next to the hole. She sat on a nearby boulder, rinsed her mouth and spat out dirt. She stared at the ground, eyes watering, and concentrated very hard on breathing in and out.

Using a fingernail to pick the rest of the dirt from her eyes, she caught Aaron's glance. The expression on his face made her burst out laughing. Then, like a dam breaking, she couldn't stop laughing. Holding her sides and tears running down her face, she pointed at her brother. "Y-y-you should s-s-see your f-f-face!"

He giggled, and then he was laughing as hard as she was. "My f-face, what about y-yours? It looks like you lost a b-battle with a p-pig!"

They both lost it, gales of laughter washing over them until they were lying on the ground, faces streaked with tears, with stitches in their sides and lungs aching for air.

When the laughter subsided, Aaron turned to face her. "I feel sorta bad. Laughing so hard while we're digging Da's grave."

Natalie sighed. "Well, if it makes you feel any better, I learned at the Abbey that laughter is as normal a part of grieving as crying. It confused me when I learned it in class, but it makes sense now. I think Da would like us to laugh when we remember him."

"I also feel a lot better now," Aaron confessed.

After a bit more rest, Aaron stood, offered a hand to Natalie, helping her to her feet, and they resumed digging their father's grave.

Early the next afternoon, Natalie sat on Benji, all ready to ride into town and join Jules. Except. Except she was tired of treating the same illness over and over and losing. She longed for a cold or a broken bone or a cut that needed to be stitched. Anything but this blasted sweating fever that killed everyone in its path. Sighing, she squeezed Benji's sides. There was nothing for it. It was time to go. Luckily, her tears stopped before she reached the town proper.

Mistfell's town hall, Natalie discovered, was now a treatment facility for victims of the sweating fever. The compassion in Jules's eyes when she walked in almost made her sob again. So she bit her lip when smiling back at him, put on her kerchief and got to work. The endless cycle of keeping patients alive kept her occupied, though it was a fresh stab to her heart each time she discovered someone she knew from her childhood lying sick on a pallet.

By evening, every single muscle in her body cried out in agony every time she knelt down next to a patient. Each new fever victim picked at the feeble scab her soul had put over the wound left by her trials in Whitestrand and her father's death. If she knew the person she treated, the wound opened wider.

She hauled herself in a stupor from pallet to pallet, pouring tea into mouths and whispering words of comfort. *It's too late. They're all going to die anyway.* She collapsed next to her belongings. She knew she should take something for her own aches. She pulled her herb satchel over with her fingertips and stared into it. For sore muscles, she should take … what was it called again?

"Nat," Jules's voice came from somewhere nearby. "Do you have a headache?"

"No. No, I just hurt all over."

Jules's forehead wrinkled in worry. "I'm going to do Naming on you. I need you to hold my hand, okay?" She nodded and held his hand, putting her other hand on her head. Jules's energy flowed comfortably through her, but her own moved like mud.

His fingers brushed her cheek. "Just muscle strain and exhaustion. I'll go get some dullanbark tea for you. It will help with the aches."

She opened her eyes and saw Jules smiling with relief.

"All right."

He brought her tea, which she obediently sipped with shaking hands. "I just talked with Healer Edgewood. He has enough helpers. He says we can go home for the night."

She nodded gratefully. Jules gathered their personal belongings while she finished her tea. Her arms felt like bags of sand as she lifted her hands to Activate the tea; she frowned at her still-trembling hands.

"Here, let me help." Jules took her hand once more to Activate the tea and her aches lessened considerably. At least she'd be able to ride Benji home without falling face first onto the road.

"Thank you," she whispered.

Jules helped her stand and put an arm around her to help her out of the town hall.

"I shouldn't be leaving," she muttered to Jules. "Others have been here longer than I."

Jules squeezed her shoulders. "You've been through a lot. You need rest. If you don't care for yourself, you cannot care for others."

Natalie smiled. "Oh, Goddess, do I remember Headmistress Gayla saying that over and over in—"

They stopped in their tracks outside the town hall doors. A large mob pressed against the steps of the front hall, torches raised and faces angry.

"There they are," someone shouted, and like a spark to a fire the whole mob began shouting at once. Natalie couldn't understand anything at first; then she heard: "They brought the sickness with them! They're leaving us now! It's their fault."

"HEY!" Jules shouted. He stepped to the edge of the town hall steps and stood tall, glaring at the mob, his cloak billowing slightly in the breeze. The shouting died down to mutters. Natalie stepped up beside her partner, standing shoulder to shoulder with him. She doubted she appeared as impressive, but hopefully solidarity counted for something with this lot.

"Healer Desmond and I did not bring the illness with us. This illness has yet to infect us," he scowled at all of them.

"But it was Gerard Desmond who died first," shouted one woman.

"We believe a brewer from Whitestrand brought the illness here. Did any of you see a brewer named Morley in town this week past? He stayed at The Leaking Dragon for a night."

Natalie scanned the crowd. They all looked at each other nervously. No one seemed inclined to answer.

"Fine. Here's what you need to know," Jules said. "It isn't passed from person to person. We suspect it's transmitted somehow via food, water, or animals, but we really haven't stopped treating patients since we arrived in Whitestrand about a week ago and we are, frankly, exhausted. We need rest, and I assure you, we've told Healer Edgewood all we know and he has our full trust."

Natalie put her hands on her hips and glowered at all of them. "The first symptoms are a headache followed by vomiting. If that happens to you or your kin, come to the town hall right away. The earlier we can treat people, the better."

"Now go home." Jules descended the stairs, making a space through the crowd as he went.

Aaron greeted them when they arrived home. Both Natalie and Jules thanked him for taking care of the horses. Natalie inquired after her mother, who raised an eyebrow and said "My dear, I do believe I look better than you. Go get sleep. Now."

Instinct made Natalie obey that tone of voice immediately. She froze at the bottom of the stairs. Since arriving in Mistfell, she'd been by someone's bedside all night. Now, with no emergency at hand, Mother and

Aaron would sleep in their beds. She peered up the worn, wooden stairs. Her old bedroom and a blessedly comfortable bed lay upstairs. But outside was the tent and the man she'd slept next to for more than a week; a man whose comfort she sorely needed.

Indecision ruled her mind for several minutes. She sighed and put one foot on the stairs to go to bed. Without realizing what had happened, she found herself outside in front of the tent. She made sure to approach the tent audibly so as not to meet Jules with his dagger. Biting her lip, she opened the flap.

Jules sat on his bedroll, hugging his knees to his chest and resting his head on them. Concern clouded his expression. "You should be in bed."

Natalie shrugged, stepped into the tent and closed the flap behind her. "Earlier, you took care of me and made sure I was all right. I wanted to be sure and return the favor." The real reason she'd come to him seemed stuck in between her heart and throat.

Jules put his face on his knees and snorted. "I'm fine."

Natalie raised an eyebrow and waited.

"I'm not fine," he gave in. "I'm exhausted, angry, and tired of this Five-damned sweating fever. The mob at the town hall pushed me over the edge." He flopped onto his bedroll and stared at the tent ceiling.

"A fine bunch of humanity," Natalie nodded. "I'd give anything to treat an ear infection right now."

"An infected cut," Jules sighed wistfully.

"Food poisoning," Natalie said dreamily and lay next to him, intensely aware of the close distance between them.

"There's no favor to return," Jules whispered.

"What?"

Jules turned his head to face her. "When you came into the tent. You said I took care of you and you wanted to return the favor. But really, Nat"—he reached out to run his fingers along her jawline—"you helped me first. You were right, I was an insufferable ass when I got back to the

Abbey. I'd thought I'd lost everything. You helped me find my way out. Look at all I'm able to do now. I never would've believed it if you'd told me then."

The intensity on his face penetrated the tent's darkness. It sent a shockwave of yearning down her body; she longed to press herself against him and arch her back. She reached for his face when he gathered her against his side so her head rested in the crook of his shoulder and chest. A short time later, Jules's snores filled the tent, but Natalie lay awake long into the night, her body burning with need.

CHAPTER 17

*S*unshine, birdsong and a gentle breeze is a wonderful way to wake up, Natalie smiled to herself. Keeping her eyes closed, she let the comforting sensations wash away the last of her exhaustion. A suspicion someone watched her nudged at her subconscious. She opened her eyes and gasped when she found a pair of startling emerald eyes inches from her face.

"Why were you smiling?" Jules whispered.

She lifted a hand and ran her fingers along the rough stubble on his chin. "Because I'm happy." Her smile broadened as she explored more of his face with her fingers. His eyes closed and he tilted his head to the side as her hand cupped his face. Need washed over her like waves on a beach and she ached to kiss him.

Taking a breath for courage, she moved to pull his face to hers when he took her hand in his, smiled regretfully at her and said, "We'd best get going for the day. When you're ready, let's walk the traplines." Jules stood and left the tent.

Natalie fell back on her bedroll and let out a sigh. Hell

141

in a kettle, she'd bet this entire farm he'd wanted to kiss her just then. So why hadn't he? Why had he pushed her away?

"Is it me or are things not as bad here as they were in Whitestrand?" Natalie said to Jules over a patient that morning.

Although they had several new patients, only two current patients had died overnight.

Jules nodded while helping a patient drink tanyaroot tea. "I agree."

"Why do you suppose that is?" Natalie asked as they moved to the next patient. "Is it because Mistfell has a smaller population? Or because we're treating the illness earlier? Or we're treating the dehydration as well?"

Jules raised his eyebrows. "It could be all three, although I'd guess population is rather farther down on the list. I don't think this illness discriminates based on the size of the town."

"Hmm," Natalie thought as she helped the next patient drink dullanbark tea. "But the population here isn't stacked one on top of the other like it is in Whitestrand. The buildings and housing are more spread out. Could that have something to do with it?"

Jules considered for a moment. "Possibly."

The doors of the town hall opened. Expecting a new patient, Jules and Natalie moved toward the front to help bring the person in. They paused at the sight of two men in green cloaks. Two Healers, a short, balding man and a taller man with skin the color of coffee, stood in the doorway.

"Healers Desmond and Rayvenwood?" the taller of the two inquired.

"Yes?" Natalie said.

The Healer strode forward. "I'm Healer Kone and I have a message for you from the Council of Healers." He handed her an envelope.

Natalie glanced nervously at Jules as she tore open the envelope.

Healers Desmond and Rayvenwood: You are hereby summoned to the Bridhe of the Isles Abbey to face a review by the Council of Healers. The charges against you are: abandoning your assigned post and neglecting your duties contributing to significant loss of life.

Until the review, you are prohibited from treating patients on all Five Isles. Healers Kone and Schonberg will take over patient treatment in Mistfell.

Yours, etc. Healer Roderick Aldworth, Council of Healers

Jules let out a string of curses.

"Why did you leave Whitestrand?" Healer Schonberg asked.

Natalie pinched the bridge of her nose. "Whitestrand was already dead. This disease"—she gestured to the room—"had already killed the people it was going to kill. Someone escaped quarantine and came here. We couldn't save Whitestrand, but we could save Mistfell. Or at least try."

Jules ran his hand through his hair and dropped it to his side. "We sent them a letter to the Abbey explaining our decision, but it would seem it didn't go over well with the Council. I'm *shocked*."

"You'd best get going, then. The sooner you can sort it out with the Council, the better." Kone said. Jules snorted at that, but nonetheless, they imparted all they'd learned about the disease to Kone and Schonberg, including what they'd learned about transmission of the disease. Natalie reluctantly turned over her stores of tanyaroot and dullanbark and told the Healers where they could find more.

"Good luck," Natalie said to the new Healers, and they turned and left their patients.

Jules kicked a rock in the street. "I know I said I was sick of treating this disease but this is bloody ridiculous."

A burning, raw anger boiled up in Natalie. Healer Aldworth's words from before they'd left the Abbey rang in her mind. "Do not let us down this time." But then he had sent them to a city that was too late to save. She and Jules had done the only logical thing when someone had broken quarantine, which had been to move on to the town they could save. And by the looks of it, at least as of this morning, Mistfell was faring better than Whitestrand. Maybe they hadn't obeyed the letter of their orders but they'd done what Healers should do—try to save innocent people from disease.

And apparently, that was a terrible sin according to the great Healer Aldworth.

Who had seriously hurt her friend Jules. *Ugh, I can't believe he was my mentor that whole year and I never realized what a horse's ass he is.*

Natalie let out a string of curses. "The review I can understand, but not being able to Heal at all? What is Aldworth playing at?" Natalie said.

"Oh, Aldworth is always playing at something." The look in his eyes was almost feral.

Natalie shuddered. Of course Aldworth wanted them back at the Abbey. He'd kidnapped Jules before, and now Jules had disobeyed orders. But what then? What would happen when they returned?

"Well," she bumped Jules with her shoulder. "Aldworth's message didn't say when we had to return. I say we take our bloody time about it."

He grinned at her and then stopped short.

"What is it?" Natalie asked.

"The Leaking Dragon," Jules said.

"What about it?"

"We're standing right in front of it. Let's see if we can

get a look around where Morley stayed." Jules grinned at her. "We haven't had time to investigate food, water, and animal methods of transmission. We've got plenty of time on our hands now."

Natalie grinned. "Good point. Plus, Mother and Da used to eat here a few times a week. If The Leaking Dragon is the original point of infection for Mistfell, they could've gotten the disease here.

Oswald sat morosely behind his empty bar and brightened when they walked in. "Can I get you something to drink or eat? Business has been slow since the illness came."

"I'm sorry, Oswald," Natalie said. "We just need your help. The brewer from Whitestrand, Morley, what room did he stay in while he was here? We'd like to take a look around. And can you show us where he kept his cart and horses?"

"His cart and horses?" Jules eyed her with curiosity.

Natalie shrugged. "It's where he would've kept his own food and water. We should take a look."

Jules raised his eyebrows and nodded.

They searched the room first and didn't find much except for a large quantity of dust that made Natalie sneeze.

Oswald took them to the barn next. "His horses stayed in those stalls there. And his cart was on the outside of the barn on the other side of the wall from his horses."

Oswald left them to their own devices. They wandered through the dark, musty barn. Natalie looked up at a faint skittering sound; likely mice or rats in the hayloft, she thought. Hopefully, Oswald had barn cats.

All the hay and dust had Natalie sneezing again, so they walked outside to the alley where Morley had parked his cart. The alley's surface was gravel, pockmarked with holes filled with a rancid, brownish-yellow liquid best left unidentified. Bits of hay leaked out of large holes from the barn's hayloft. They walked to the end of the alley, searching for clues. Natalie almost fell into one of the brownish puddles when a cat scampered out of the barn right in front of her.

"Ugh." Holding her nose and regaining her balance, Natalie asked: "Do you think there's anything transmittable in stale horse urine?"

Jules wrinkled his nose. "Not that I've ever heard of. Unfortunately, I don't see any answers here."

Heads together at the kitchen table, Natalie and Jules pored over Natalie's worn Healing diary. Having given up temporarily on finding the source of the epidemic in Mistfell, they decided to try some research. Natalie expertly navigated to the pages with the entries on epidemics.

She tapped her finger on one page. "Here's the one I told you about on the way to Whitestrand, the one with the well." She thumbed through to another section. "Here's another one, the one my grandparents always told stories about. But it doesn't really have a lot in common with our epidemic." When Jules finished reading, she flipped the pages again. "Here's another one. I haven't read this one in a while. Let's see."

Natalie skimmed the left side of the book, then the right. Her eyes caught sight of a doodle she'd drawn in the margins; a heart with ND + JR written inside. Hell in a kettle, Goddess's bloomers, and damn it all to hell. She casually covered the initials with her hand, shifted in her seat, and returned her eyes to the content of the page as if her life depended on it.

"Are you done reading?"

"Not yet," Jules muttered.

Natalie's foot twitched back and forth.

"Can you move your hand, please? I can't read what's underneath."

Natalie shifted her hand a smidge to the right.

Jules raised his eyebrows. "Thank you."

Natalie nibbled her pinky nail.

"Natalie?"

"Done reading?"

Jules smirked. "What's under your hand?"

Natalie looked at him with her best innocent expression. "Nothing. Why?"

"Nat. I was a teacher for quite some time. I know when someone is hiding something."

"Look do you want to read about epidemics or not?"

"Fine, turn the page."

Natalie turned the page, tension draining out of her stomach when Jules's hand shot out and grabbed hers and flattened the page once more. Fire suffused her cheeks as he saw her drawing and comprehended its meaning.

Saying nothing, Jules turned the page, his face carefully expressionless. An awkward silence descended; Natalie tried not to crawl out of her skin. She lowered her eyes and kept reading, but the words jumbled together.

She'd been betrayed by her own hand from long ago; Jules now knew her feelings for certain. This would change things between them forever. And right now, she had the feeling it wouldn't be for the better.

"So that's it?" her mother asked, helping Natalie hang her laundry on the line. "No more Healing until you see the Council?"

"Yes," Natalie said.

"Well, I'm sure this Healer Aldworth will decide in your favor. What else could you have done? I would have died had you not arrived when you did."

"Mmm," was all Natalie said.

She and Jules put off leaving by cleaning all their possessions. The farmyard fluttered with bits of laundry, and even now Jules was off in a nearby stream bathing. Natalie ducked behind a hanging shirt to hide her blush as she thought about the cool water sliding over his warm skin. She dully reminded herself there was no point in thinking such thoughts. He'd barely spoken two words to her since they'd sat to read her diary together.

Aaron came back just then with a brace of rabbits. He'd become quite adept at making spring snare traps after she and Jules had shown him the technique. Natalie wanted to make sure her family wouldn't starve after they left. It would be several more days until they got a response from Solerin Isle, and Mother and Aaron needed to be able to obtain food independently until they had more help for the farm. Luckily, her Mother had always been a proficient vegetable gardener. The vegetable garden only needed some extra tending after a few days of neglect. Natalie also showed her family safe plants to gather and eat in the wild. Natalie swelled with pride as the shelves of the family larder filled to bursting.

Dinner that night was a somber affair. Natalie and Jules had put it off long enough; they must leave the next morning. The food was sawdust in her mouth and sat like rocks in her stomach. She hated leaving her family. The hole in her heart left by her father's death stuck out like a large thread that had been pulled out of a tapestry. She wanted to stay with her mother and Aaron and help her hometown through the epidemic. But the Abbey had called, and she must obey—especially if she wanted to Heal again.

Natalie sighed. She missed being a plain, simple Healer. She fiercely missed Jake and her sanctuary of the greenhouse where everything felt normal—where people weren't dying by the hundreds. And even though she'd only been one for a few weeks, she wanted to be a teacher again. She wanted to see her students' eyes lighting up with the knowledge she imparted; it was something she hadn't known she'd needed in her life.

At the end of dinner, she kissed her family goodnight, and against her own good judgment, followed Jules out to the tent. She lay next to him. She inhaled, smelling the clean scent of his clothes and the faint scent of forest and horses. Her heart pounded and she was all too aware of how close he lay. She inhaled to start explaining what he'd seen in her diary. If he could just understand, if she could just ask him how he felt ...

But Jules's dark head turned away from her and he went to sleep without a word.

Natalie blinked at the tent ceiling. They kept dancing toward each other and then spinning away. *Why does he hug me, flirt with me and confide in me, only to push me out when we get too close?* The awful weight of rejection sat heavily on her, and it was quite a while before sleep found Natalie, her pillow damp with tears.

CHAPTER 18

Natalie told herself she wouldn't cry when she said goodbye to her family, but her tears fell on her mother's shoulder nonetheless as they hugged the next morning.

"I'll miss you. Take care of yourself and keep getting better." She wanted to apologize about Da but the words gummed up in her throat.

She hugged Aaron. "Take care of Mother for me, okay?"

"Take me with you, please, Nat. I can build things and hunt."

"I know you can. You're amazing. But Mother needs you and I would feel so much better knowing you're here taking care of the farm and her."

Frowning, Aaron turned to Jules. Jules cocked his head thoughtfully. "One day, perhaps, it will be time for you to leave the farm and further your talents. But I believe your mother needs your talents the most right now."

Aaron looked slightly mollified as he shook Jules's hand.

They mounted the horses and departed, meandering along the road to the Abbey. It was a relief to not be in a rush, attending to patients nonstop. For the first time in years, Natalie got a chance to truly admire the verdant summer landscape of Ismereld. What was summer like on the other four Isles? She'd never left Ismereld, but she always imagined Solerin, with its Attuned skilled at tending plants and crops, covered in fields of flowers, vegetables and grains.

It was harder to guess with an Isle like Citherin. What was life even like on an Isle full of jewelers, potters, sculptors, artists and writers? Maybe, one day, she'd have the chance to visit. Methyseld must be a crazy place to live, with its dancers, singers, musicians and actors. Methyseld's Attuned often traveled in troupes to the other Isles, putting on amazing shows. Natalie cherished the memories of the few shows she'd seen growing up.

"Jules, have you ever been to any of the other Isles?" she asked, breaking the silence for the first time in hours. Relief washed over her when he answered.

"Obfuselt, mostly. Though that's the hardest Isle to visit. They guard their talents with a vengeance, as well they should. Amongst their Attuned are excellent builders and craftspeople, yes, but there are also exceptional shipwrights, weaponsmiths, hunters, and spies. They are easily taken advantage of by those in power. Other than that, I've been to Solerin once." He was silent for a moment, then added, "When I was working with Anli and Onlo, we mainly traveled between Lorelan and Obfuselt."

Natalie gathered her courage and extended the conversation. *Come out of your shell, my turtle.* "You said you met Onlo and Anli during the war. How did you meet? That is … if you don't mind telling the story."

"No, it's all right. I was on Lorelan, traveling with Aldworth. This was before I knew what he was trying to accomplish there. He kept handing me ancient manuscripts and asking me to read them out loud. Most of it was in a language I didn't know, so he had to teach me how to say the words. Reciting them always gave me terrible headaches. He never would give me an answer when I asked what we were doing. After a while, I realized the situation was dangerous, and I decided to run away." Jules laughed.

Natalie smiled. "What?"

"A Roseharbor-raised man, educated at the Abbey, and I ran off into the forests of Lorelan. How well do you think that went for me?" Jules smiled ruefully over at her.

"Oh, dear."

"Yes, well, so it would have been if it hadn't been for Anli. She wasn't kidding; she saved my life. She and Onlo took me in with a group of soldiers from Obfuselt. It was they who taught me to hunt and survive. Before I lost my hand, I was rather good with a bow and arrow. I really miss archery sometimes."

Natalie smiled over at him. "I'm glad they found you."

Jules nodded. "Me, too. I only wish I'd paid attention more and not let my overconfidence in my skills get the better of me. If I had done so, Aldworth might not have recaptured me and I might still have my hand. Anli still blames herself, but it was really my fault."

Natalie took a deep breath. She still had trouble wrapping her mind around her mentor's treachery, but she felt the need to speak up. "The only one to blame for your capture is Aldworth himself. It's not your fault, or Anli's."

"But—"

"Jules, if I got robbed on the street in Mistfell, would that be my fault or the thief's fault?"

Jules's mouth formed a thin line. "It's not the same."

"Isn't it?"

Jules ground his teeth. "No."

"Why not?"

Jules grimaced. "Because I volunteered to go with him. Aldworth approached me one day and told me he was assembling an elite squad of Healers to travel to Lorelan and Heal Isle troops there. Although we'd be without the power of Ismereld's megalith, our troops needed the skills of the Abbey's top Healers. Since I was one of the best, he needed me. And the gang of men he sent to capture me told me they'd captured Aldworth, too. It was all lies. Oh, he knew exactly how to reel me in." Jules shook his head, his shoulders hunched.

Natalie's heart broke to see the burden of guilt weighing so heavily on Jules. "Jules, I would've believed him, too. I didn't even believe you the first time you told me he was plotting against Ismereld. He was my mentor from my apprenticeship, and there was absolutely no indication he was a traitor. My dear partner, I hate to break this to you, but you are human, not all-knowing. And what happened to you is not your fault."

Natalie wasn't sure, but she swore one corner of Jules's mouth turned up. They spent the rest of the day ambling along the road, stopping to rest or eat whenever they desired. Natalie gathered herbs when she spotted them. Her satchel, which had been rather empty lately, brimmed with herbs again. They stopped when the sun hung low in the sky next to a lovely pond. Their bellies full from dinner and the cooking fire settling low, they lay on blankets outside the tent and stared at the stars.

Natalie sighed as the cool night air brushed her skin. "I wish I could still help Mistfell. And I know what awaits us at the Abbey won't be pleasant. And I miss my Da something awful. But at the same time, I feel like everything is right with the world. Just in this moment."

When Jules didn't respond, she turned to face him. He stared back at her with an unfathomable expression on his face.

A streak of light darted in the corner of Natalie's eye. "Was that—it is! Look, there's another! A shooting star." Natalie jumped up, scanning the sky for more. Soon, the sky was peppered with streaks of light and she began jumping up and down. "A meteor shower. By the Five, how amazing," she gasped and twirled in a circle, unable to tear her eyes away from the sky.

Jules stood and moved close to her, staring at the meteors with an expression of wonder on his face. Natalie couldn't help herself; she clasped his hand. "Isn't it stunning?"

"It is," Jules said, his voice catching.

His tone of voice made her turn from the miracle occurring in the heavens above. Mesmerized by his eyes, all at once the energy flowing between their clasped hands overwhelmed her senses. It swept up her arm and made her heart pound. Heat pooled in her middle, and she took a step back as the sensation nearly made her ill.

She lifted the hand not holding his and traced the side of his cheek with it. He pulled away; her lips curled into a small, unsurprised smile.

"What's wrong?" Natalie whispered.

"You ... you're my student. I can't. I shouldn't. And I'm—" He shifted his gaze over her shoulder.

Had this been the problem all along? Natalie wanted to laugh out loud. Smiling, she pulled him toward her with the hand that clasped his, and then she let go and cupped his face gently in her hands. "Juliers Rayvenwood. I am eighteen years old, Healer in my own right, and I haven't been your student in years. If you don't kiss me now, I swear by all we both hold holy, there will be consequences."

Jules's jaw fell open.

Natalie shook her head. "Insufferable man," she whispered and drew his face down to hers. She brushed his lips lightly with her own and nearly whimpered with pleasure when his lips responded. Jules ran his fingers through her hair and wrapped his other arm around her back, and Natalie moaned as he pulled her closer.

With his body pressed against hers, desire and energy bubbled to the surface of her skin, mixing to form a combustible, intoxicating blend of desire and lust. Natalie slid her hands through his silky dark hair and deepened their kiss and struggled not to wrap her legs around him and pull him to the ground.

Some conscious corner of her mind thought to pull away to be sure he was all right, but he growled and drew her back into an even deeper kiss. Her heart soared at the knowledge he wanted her just as much as she did him.

After several minutes, Jules trailed a series of kisses along her jaw and cheek and then rested his forehead against hers. "Natalie Desmond, if those are the consequences of not kissing you, please know I am absolutely never kissing you again."

Natalie's joyous laughter filled the star-filled night until Jules bent his head to capture her mouth again.

"What would happen if we didn't go back to the Abbey?" Natalie said against Jules's back. They rode double on Elric, leading Benji, who carried all the supplies and tack. It was a blissful way to spend a morning, bareback on a tall, sleek horse with her arms clasped around the man she'd spent the night kissing before falling asleep curled up tight in his arms. The tree-dappled sunlight shone on her back, the birds and insects sang in the trees, and aside from wanting to get Jake, it was hard to think of a reason to return to the Abbey and walk into Aldworth's web of lies and intrigue. Jules had already lost enough.

Jules sighed. "I know how you feel. However, Aldworth is after me with a powerful will. I don't think he's given up entirely on me helping him put a brand new megalith on the mainland."

"Is there anyone who can protect you from him?"

"So far, Anli, Onlo and the soldiers they command have been my greatest allies. I am not certain even Headmistress Gayla and Healer Hawkins know of the extent of his treachery."

Natalie made a rude noise. "We have to get him off the

Council."

Jules raised his eyebrows and glanced over his shoulder at her. "How?"

"I don't know. Can't we tell someone? The King and Queen? Or the Council of Isles?"

"Ah, that's where it gets interesting. Their Royal Majesties support the effort to put a megalith on the mainland."

Natalie almost fell of Elric. "What?"

"Yes. Think—if they had an army of Healers who could Heal on Lorelan, they could invade Lorelan by land and have much fewer casualties."

Several puzzle pieces clicked into place—Jules's lack of respect for the monarchy, Aldworth's betrayal, the timing, duration and nature of the war. Of course the King and Queen wouldn't negotiate for peace; why would they if Aldworth succeeded with this new megalith and they could invade and take Lorelan for their own? Natalie swore.

Jules nodded. "And the Council of Isles is intent on keeping the Isles to themselves. Which is not a bad idea; the Isles are self-sustaining, each Isle with its own unique magic and skills to offer. However, when we face threats from both within and without, being isolationist is not a wise viewpoint."

Natalie swore again.

"Which means it's down to us to save us all, and you know it," came a smoky voice from the woods. Natalie jumped and Jules drew his dagger.

Two dark-haired figures materialized from the underbrush on the right. Jules put his dagger away and grinned.

"Greetings, brother," Onlo grinned.

"Onlo." Jules threw a leg over Elric's withers, jumped down and strode over to clasp his friend's hand, and then turned and gave Anli a hug.

Anli poked Jules in the chest. "I wasn't kidding, Jules. We're here to save you. Again."

"We got your message," Onlo said.

"Message?" Natalie asked from Elric's back, baffled.

Jules turned to her. "I sent Anli and Onlo a message from Mistfell at the same time I sent a message to the Abbey. I suspected things weren't going to go well for us. I hate being right."

Natalie put her hands on her hips and glared at Jules. "I thought you weren't going to keep me in the dark anymore." She dismounted and stalked off into the nearby woods, viciously pulling her way through nearby vegetation to see if she could find something edible. She kept one ear toward the conversation nearby.

Jules proceeded to tell his friends what had occurred in Mistfell, their current disgraced status with the Abbey and the summons from Aldworth. Anli spat on the ground at the mention of the traitorous Healer's name.

"There is much more you need to know, brother," Onlo said, his voice grave. "But first and most important—the sweating fever has reached Roseharbor. The capital city is falling."

CHAPTER 19

Natalie tore raspberries from a raspberry patch she'd found, her fingers turning a macabre shade of red in the process. She did not turn around when she heard footsteps behind her.

"Natalie, please come listen to what they have to say. You need to hear this."

"No," she turned and pointed a red finger in Jules's face. "You three seem to have everything under control, good old buddies that you are. So figure out how to help Roseharbor, and I'll ride back to the Abbey and get out of your way."

"Nat, stop being childish."

"Childish? I wasn't the one who went behind my partner's back making plans. Childish." She huffed and turned back to her raspberry patch. The silence lengthened as berry after berry dropped into Nat's satchel.

"Nat, please? We—I need you at Roseharbor. I can't Heal without you."

Nat whirled back to him, nearly spilling the berries. "You can't Heal without me, but you can plot and plan our fate without me? Is that how you think this works, Juliers Rayvenwood? If so, then I'm out. I have had it up to the back teeth with people and diseases determining where I go and what I do."

"Nat, I'm sorry."

"Damn right you're sorry."

Jules took her free hand in his "Nat, please, I—we— need your help. I promise we won't leave you out of the loop again.

Natalie looked over his shoulder. She could just see Anli and Onlo in the distance. *The capital city was falling,* they said. Judging by their stances, they looked pretty agitated. She'd been left out—again—but maybe she needed to hear what they had to say. She rubbed her thumb along Jules's hand, warm inside hers. Images of a thousand shared kisses from the night before flitted across her mind.

She brought her gaze back to his face and made sure he saw the warning in her eyes. "All right."

The four companions ate lunch as Anli and Onlo told them all that had transpired since their last meeting.

"Whitestrand harbor is under Obfuselt's protection," Anli said, "and Lorelan tried to get past us. They know Whitestrand is weak and they want it."

Jules's mouth hardened into a thin line. "Which means there are spies telling Lorelan of the sweating fever and what it's done to our people."

Onlo nodded. "Soon after we heard reports of Lorelan's attempts to get past our coast guard, we got your message from Mistfell. We told our Council the fever had spread to another town. Even now, they mobilize more protection for Ismereld."

Natalie breathed a sigh of relief. Thankfully, some Isle folk still took care of their own, despite the treacherous machinations of a few.

"Right before we left, an Imperial messenger arrived

asking for aid defending Roseharbor," Anli said, her face sober. "She said a great illness had befallen the city. From her description, we knew it was the same illness you fight."

Natalie put her hand on her heart and shook her head. "All those people in Roseharbor. The Abbey will send many Healers since it's so close." She caught Jules's eye. She saw the same desperation in his countenance she felt in her own soul.

"Give us a moment, please," Jules asked his friends. He and Natalie walked some distance away so they wouldn't be overheard.

Jules turned his intense green eyes on her. "What do you want to do?"

"We have to get there. Fast." Natalie's tone brooked no argument.

Jules nodded. "I agree. It's down to us to stop this thing."

Natalie put a hand on his arm. "I worry for your safety. If you'd asked me this morning, I'd have said we should find a remote corner of the island, change our names and be ordinary town Healers to keep you hidden away. But …"

Jules shook his head and put his own hand on hers. "I am a Healer like you, Nat. I can't turn away from a city full of dying people. Particularly when that city is my home."

"But Aldworth …"

Jules grimaced. "I'm scared, too. But I've got you. And Onlo and Anli. We'll find a way, the four of us together."

Natalie swallowed the lump in her throat, reached for his face and kissed him as if he might disappear right in front of her. Jules kissed her back with a ferocity that made her knees weak. With a last determined look at one another, they took hands and walked back to his friends.

"We ride for Roseharbor," Jules declared.

Anli swore. "Jules, you can't go back. This is the perfect time for Aldworth to make another play for you. Besides, neither of you is allowed to Heal right now."

Jules crossed his arms. "What would you have me do, An? Let my home city die while I hide? Besides, I don't think the Abbey is going to turn away two experienced Healers while everyone in the capital dies."

Anli turned to Natalie with her hands on her hips. "And I suppose you're going to let him do this."

"I'm not his mother. This is his choice," Natalie retorted. "I am a Healer and so is he. We have to save those people."

"Let someone else save them," Anli shouted.

"No," Natalie yelled back. "This disease killed my father and I failed to save him. I'm going to go save those people if it's the last thing I do."

"And get Jules killed in the process?" Anli was in her face now.

"What Jules does is his own decision. I don't know how to keep him safe from Aldworth, but let's bloody well figure it out after we get there. Who knows what worse horrors await us if we return to the Abbey? You are wasting our time. We need to get on the road." Natalie pushed past Anli and stalked over to Benji.

Natalie fumed as she transferred Jules's supplies from Benji to Elric, making sure everything could sustain a fast pace. Taking Jules into Aldworth's domain and disobeying the Council of Healers to fight the sweating fever again was bad enough without having someone yell at her for doing it. There was no way to explain the passion driving her; despite the danger, she had to try and save Roseharbor. *For Da.*

With everything ready, she mounted her horse as Jules mounted Elric.

"Onlo and Anli are coming with us. They will be our eyes and ears while we're taking care of the city," Jules informed her.

"Wonderful," Natalie drawled. The thought of spending more time with Anli set her teeth on edge.

When everyone mounted, they set off at a canter on the

road toward Roseharbor.

Natalie sat on her bedroll that night, certain dust inhabited every bit of her body. It stung her eyes when she blinked and crunched in her mouth when she bit down, and her hair felt stiff and strange. Was it only this morning she rode Elric bareback, her hands clasped around Jules with the sun shining blissfully on her back?

Jules entered the tent and she smiled wearily at him. He took off his boots, sat next to her and bent his head to hers, his lips touching hers lightly. She returned the kiss with equal gentleness. When they broke apart several minutes later, Natalie rested her forehead against his.

"I'm sorry about Anli's behavior today," Jules began. "When I was on the mission …when I was kidnapped, she was on the same mission. She blames herself for my capture."

Natalie sighed. "I don't understand why she doesn't like me though."

Jules rubbed her back. "Anli can be a tough nut to crack. I don't always understand her myself, sometimes. But her loyalty, once given, is unswerving."

Natalie picked another glob of dirt out of her eye. "But I also see her point. I would give anything to keep you away from that spineless excuse for a human being."

Jules kissed her forehead. "First we have a city to save."

Natalie laughed and kissed him. "Oh, well then. Easy as pie."

Jules's deep laughter filled the tent. He put his arms around her waist and tugged her against him so they lay spooned with her back against his. Sleep claimed them both quickly.

The next morning's hard ride brought them in view of Roseharbor. Onlo scouted for and found a secluded campsite, while Anli hunted game they could eat. Jules and Natalie prepared to go into the city for the first time.

"What are the odds the other Healers have heard of our punishment and will tell us to get out when we arrive?" Jules mused.

Natalie considered this. "I suppose it depends on what Aldworth's true motives were when he told us we couldn't Heal."

"So. The Five only know."

"Pretty much."

Natalie checked her satchel for the umpteenth time. She had plenty of supplies, though she'd need to buy a pot of honey in the city. Finally, she mounted Benji.

"Five be with you," Onlo said. "We leave today to scout the Abbey and learn what we can of Aldworth's whereabouts and plans. We hope to return in four or five days."

"Oh," Natalie exclaimed, her face lit with excitement. "Can you do me the biggest favor? Can you find my friend, Emmeline Arnold? She's taking care of my dog, Jake. Can you please bring Jake back with you?"

Anli grunted in frustration and stalked away.

Onlo's forehead wrinkled in concern. "How will your friend know to trust us?"

Natalie thought for a second and then reached into her satchel and tossed Onlo a vial. "Tell her this is from Natalie Desmond, Jake's owner."

Onlo looked at the vial and back at her dubiously. "All right." He pocketed the vial and turned his horse to follow Anli.

"What did you give Onlo?" Jules asked.

Natalie glanced at him and grinned. "A bottle of moonbark extract."

Jules laughed so hard he choked, his face bright red. "Contraceptive herbs as a message to a midwife. Only you, Nat."

Unlike Whitestrand, Roseharbor's streets still had people going about their business. However, they looked over their shoulders as if something might grab them from behind at any moment. No one talked with anybody else, and everyone seemed in a hurry to get off the streets.

"Should we go find your family and check on them?" Natalie inquired.

"Maybe later. We don't get along well and I haven't been home since … well, let's just say they don't approve of me, and I doubt they'd approve of my new look."

He's joking, right? How could his family not welcome their son home after everything that had happened to him? Deciding to save the matter for another day, she changed the subject to their current mission. "I need to find a place where I can buy honey."

"This way."

As they navigated the streets, Natalie and Jules observed occasional broken doors, abandoned shops and signs of looting.

"The Queensguard should stop this. Are they ill with the fever?" Jules wondered.

Thankfully, an open-air market was still doing business, and Natalie bought her much-needed pot of honey.

"We're Healers newly arrived from the Abbey," she told the beekeeper innocently. "Where are the other Healers tending the sick?"

"Up at the palace," the beekeeper replied. "The King and Queen fled the city in fear of the illness." Natalie pinched the bridge of her nose. If they'd taken the disease with them, then their job had just gotten a whole lot harder.

"Is that why there's been so much looting? Did the Queensguard go with them?" Jules asked.

"No, most of the Queensguard took ill with the fever," the beekeeper replied.

"Thank you," Natalie said. She stored the honey safely

in her satchel and mounted Benji.

"With the Royal family gone, the Queensguard decimated, and the population dwindling, it's a good thing Obfuselt knows to protect the coast. Lorelan could attack at any time."

"If the Royal family took the fever with them, this Isle is in deep trouble," Natalie added.

Jules swore and they asked their horses to go faster. Once at the palace stables, Natalie handed both horses to Jules. "Just to be on the safe side, stay here with the horses while I go see who is Healing."

Jules nodded reluctantly and took both horses. Natalie pulled the hood of her cloak tightly over her head and strode toward the palace gate, stomach churning. A room full of the sick and dying she could handle; a threat to Jules's life made her quake in her boots. She wasn't about to lose another person, whether it be to illness or to threats by an old man. She took a deep breath and strode through the doors.

A portly, formally dressed, mustachioed man with red cheeks greeted her. "Ah, another Healer. Hello. Please follow me. Everyone is in the ballroom."

"Thank you," She followed him through a maze of ornate hallways. After the last turn, Natalie gasped and craned her neck at the largest room she'd ever beheld. Tiled in white, the floors stretched on forever. The ceiling stretched wide over her head like the sky above an open field painted with elaborate depictions of the Isles' history. Glittering on the floor-to-ceiling columns were five types of stone, each one representing one of the five megaliths of the Isles. The orange sunstones of Solerin, golden-yellow citrines representing Citherin and lustrous amethysts symbolizing Methyseld combined with Ismereld's emeralds and Obfuselt's obsidian to form intricate mosaic patterns that twisted and swirled in and out of one another. Large floor-to-ceiling windows let in plenty of light—quite practical for Healers treating a room full of people dying.

Scanning the room, she estimated about twelve Healers present. She thanked her escort and made her way through the room to put her supplies in an empty corner. She kept her eyes downcast and looked out under her eyelids at the Healers, trying to identify any who might be a threat to her or Jules. Her heart soared as she spotted Headmistress Gayla. Carefully, she made her way over to the elder woman.

Gayla's face lit up. "My dear girl," she said, giving Natalie a big, warm hug.

"It's so wonderful to see you. I missed you so much." Natalie returned the hug quickly and then grasped the Headmistress by the arms. "I am here to help. I've learned a great deal about how to treat this illness. But first, can we talk for a moment, please?"

Gayla wiped her hands on her apron. "Certainly. Where is Healer Juliers? He's not ... did he catch the illness?"

"No, but I must ask you," Natalie whispered, taking the Headmistress's elbow and walking with her away from the patients and other Healers. "Gayla, what do you know of the charges the Council brought against us? And what do you know about what Aldworth did to Jules?"

CHAPTER 20

The Headmistress's shoulders sagged. "I do know of the charges against you. For the record, I think they are flat-out rubbish."

Natalie breathed a sigh of relief. "Please believe us; we left Whitestrand for good reasons. The people who were going to contract the disease had already done so. Then, someone broke quarantine and went to Mistfell. We couldn't help Whitestrand, but we could try to help Mistfell."

Gayla nodded. "Logical. And were you able to help Mistfell? Can you help us here?"

"I believe so. The most important thing we learned was to begin treatment as early as possible, and in addition to tanyaroot and dullanbark tea, keep patients hydrated with a honey and salt mixture in the tea to help replace the fluids they lose. As of when we left, the mortality rate did seem better in Mistfell."

Gayla's eyes lit up. "I'll convey that to the others. Now, what about Jules. Is he here? What is this about him and Aldworth?"

At first it was hard to speak, with knowledge of Aldworth's betrayal so fresh a wound. Natalie summoned year after year of memories with the Headmistress—taking tea with the Headmistress, crying on her shoulder, cringing under her hawk-like stare after getting in trouble—and Natalie found the trust to tell her old friend the story of Jules's abduction and injury at Aldworth's hands.

Gayla sat in the nearest chair shaking with fury. "A short time ago, I had some of my own start watching him. I found out about his experiments. I had no idea he'd involved any of our own—" she clenched her fists. She stood and leaned close to Natalie. "You should know Aldworth believes an actual mage is alive right now. Finding that person is the sole focus of all his current efforts."

"A mage alive now?" Natalie said, stunned. "But he doesn't know who or where the mage is?"

"No," Gayla confirmed. "But all current leads point to the mage being here in Roseharbor."

"So if Aldworth gets his hands on an actual mage and some descendants of the Five Mages—which we know Jules is one …" Natalie mused.

"There will be no stopping him." Gayla finished.

"So we need to find the mage before he does. We'll just add 'find a mage' to our to-do list along with 'save capital city from certain death,' shall we?"

"I have trusted people looking for the mage. In the meantime, let us do what we do best."

"Jules is out in the stables. I will tell him to come in if he is welcome and safe to Heal here," Natalie said.

Gayla's eyes fixed her with a fierce stare. "As long as I'm here, he is. You tell that man to come in here and get to work."

Natalie grinned. "Yes, ma'am," and she ran off to the stables.

Late that night, Natalie and Jules stumbled into their tent and collapsed side by side.

"If I never move again, it will be too soon," Natalie said, her bedroll muffling her voice.

"I agree." Jules turned her toward him and kissed her gently. When she moaned, they both deepened the kiss. Natalie ran her fingers through Jules's hair, pulling him closer as his fingers traced her jawline to her chin and then down her neck to the dip in her shirt. She broke the kiss to stretch her chin up like a cat. Jules took advantage and planted sensuous kisses along her neck. She sighed as he tantalized her by lifting one side of her shirt and slowly undoing the buttons one by one. He growled as one stubborn button wouldn't come undone; she laughed throatily, undid the pesky thing herself and tossed her shirt off to the side.

His touch on her skin sent delicious shivers down her spine. In between kisses, she undid his shirt, and it soon joined hers on the tent floor. When they grasped each other again, the melding of their bodies lit a fire in Natalie's stomach. She fanned it by tracing random shapes on Jules's back with her energy all while teasing his lips with her own.

When Natalie thought she might go mad with desire, she pulled away from his sweet kisses to stare into his emerald gaze. "I want you."

He caressed her cheek. "Sweet Goddess, I want you too, woman. But not here."

Natalie touched her forehead to his. "Why? I have another bottle of moonbark extract."

Jules pulled back and ran his fingers through her hair, shaking his head. "It's not that. I … I want our first time to be when we're not on the run, covered with road dust and the stink of sick people. Maybe even where there's a bed."

Natalie swallowed her disappointment, blushing a bit. "But you … you do want to, right?"

"Sweet Five, yes," he growled and kissed her with renewed passion.

Later, their lips swollen with hundreds of kisses, Jules turned on his side and gathered Natalie against him. They pulled a light blanket over themselves, making a cocoon in which they could hide away from the world.

"When did you first know? About your ... feelings ... for me, I mean," Natalie whispered into the dark of the cocoon.

"Hmm." She felt her lover's voice vibrate against her back. "Besides the feeling I wanted to throttle you?" Natalie bit him. "Ow! All right, woman. I know you're hungry for me, but that's a little much." He sighed. "Maybe when you promised to make me mud pies."

Natalie fizzed with giggles.

"But if I'm being honest, when I returned to the Abbey and saw you standing in the greenhouse doorway, I thought you were the loveliest woman I'd ever beheld."

Tears filled Natalie's eyes and she stroked her fingers along one of the arms embracing her.

"How about you? When did you first take a liking to me?" Jules asked, planting a kiss behind her ear.

"My first Naming lesson," Natalie confessed.

"Natalie Desmond," Jules scolded. "You should not have crushes on your teachers. That's just wrong."

"Oh? Well, I'll just leave then, shall I?" Natalie moved to stand, and Jules snagged her around the waist, dragged her back and covered her with kisses while she giggled uncontrollably.

It was quite some time before they fell asleep.

Natalie's kerchief covered her mouth every time she yawned the next day. Still, the cause of her late night was worth it. Jules caught her eye just then, winked and continued treating his patient. Heart pounding and face blushing, she spilled a bit of tea on her own patient. She stumbled to clean it up as her cheeks grew even hotter.

A motion at the ballroom doorway closest to her caught her eye. It was one of the ubiquitous palace pages with a message for the Headmistress.

Headmistress Gayla materialized at her elbow, startling her. "Quickly, come with me," she murmured. "Aldworth is on his way. Get Juliers."

"Jules," she hissed. She beckoned him to follow as the Headmistress rushed her out of the room.

The Headmistress led them just outside the ballroom and into one of the many curtained-off alcoves that ran along the corridor there. "In here, now. I must return so he sees me."

They ducked in and Natalie pulled the velvet curtain closed behind them. They sat on a red velvet bench. She clutched his hand in both of hers. "Why would anyone have several curtained-off closets with benches next to ballroom?"

"They're for, uh, couples who want privacy from a ball," Jules explained.

Natalie slapped her hand over her mouth, trying not to giggle. It proved difficult with the hysteria pressing in her chest trying to get out.

"What's going on?" Jules hissed. "Why are we hiding?"

"Aldworth is here."

Jules swore under his breath. Natalie thought his grip on her hand might cut off the circulation. Natalie was certain Aldworth could find them by the sound of her heart pounding alone.

Sitting and waiting was excruciating. No sounds reached them from the ballroom-turned-healing ward. All they could do was wait for Gayla to fetch them when the coast was clear. Eventually, Jules leaned his head back against the wall, and Natalie put her head on his chest and listened to his heartbeat, holding his hand like a lifeline.

After what seemed like hours, footsteps sounded outside their alcove. "It's me, dears," called the

Headmistress. "He's gone."

They thanked the Headmistress, who waved them off. "It's lucky I have the pages on the lookout for him."

"Does he come often?" Jules asked.

"No, at this point, he doesn't like to get his hands dirty when there are others to do the work."

Jules snorted.

"But he does like to put on a show about being in charge, even though three of us are on the Council," Gayla added.

Jules muttered a string of insults under his breath regarding Aldworth, Aldworth's possible parentage and something anatomically impossible involving a donkey.

After returning to her patients, Natalie fought the urge to glance over her shoulder at every unfamiliar sound. Her paranoia grew as the day progressed. Whenever someone helped her change a patient's bed linens, she kept her eyes averted, hoping the person didn't know she was wanted by Aldworth. By late evening, she had a headache from the stress. She eagerly mounted Benji and led the way out of the city to their campsite, where they ate cold rabbit and fruit Natalie had gathered earlier.

"I have a headache," Jules complained as they finished the last of dinner.

"I do, too. I feel like I've been watching over my shoulder all day long. Plus we didn't sleep well last night. Do you want me to Name you? Just to be sure?"

"No, you're right; it's just stress. Come on," Jules offered Natalie his hand. "Let's try and get some good sleep."

Natalie took his hand, smiling at him. "Good idea."

They made a cocoon in the tent again, needing a safe space after the day's events.

Natalie started out of a sound sleep when Jules vomited up his dinner. Natalie tended to him before she even knew she was awake, checking his fever and pulse.

"I ... I've got ... the sweating fever," he rasped.

Natalie felt the blood drain from her face but kept her composure. "Well, let's do a Naming and find out."

She closed her eyes, her heart pounding, and connected with the ley lines deep in the Isle below her. She imagined the emerald megalith generating the ley lines, and she prayed as she never had to the Five Mages that created it. Shaking, she put her hands on Jules's body and directed her energy into his. A few minutes later, she yanked her hands off. "No! Let me do it again." She breathed and tried again when she felt a hand clasp hers.

"Nat, I can feel it … for myself. You have to … start treatment … now." Jules cracked his eyes opened, his emerald eyes glassy and bloodshot.

Natalie burst from the tent and stood indecisively between the horses and the dead campfire. It would take time to rebuild the campfire to make tea. Then, she'd need to douse it and take him to the palace. On the other hand, it would take about twenty minutes to get to the palace— twenty minutes before starting treatment. She'd seen firsthand the difference in patients who started treatment right away, versus those who waited. As she stood, paralyzed, a raindrop struck her head. She held out her hand. Two more drops fell. The pattering sound of drops on the forest leaves indicated more rain. Palace it was. She ran for the horses and tacked them.

She led Elric close to the tent. Natalie somehow got an arm under Jules—*Goddess, the man must weigh as much as the megalith itself*—and the two of them staggered over to Elric. Natalie made sure Jules had a hold of the saddle before giving him a leg up. She was only able to get him hanging sideways face down, which made him vomit again. Natalie helped right him and then mounted Benji. Blessedly, Elric followed Benji without question.

The rain came down in sheets, plastering Natalie's hair to her face. Rivulets of water became small streams across her path and she feared losing her way into the city. Five minutes into the journey, she stopped when Jules vomited and fell off Elric into the mud. Slipping, sliding and pushing with all her might, she got Jules back up onto Elric's back. *Get up. Get up, damn you, get up on this horse or I swear I'll kill you myself.* She managed to get him mounted again, only to have him slide off a minute or so later.

Tears added to the rain pouring down her face, and it took her three tries to get Jules into the saddle this time, as covered in mud and vomit as he was. Each time she failed, she knew it was lost time getting him the treatment he needed. When she finally succeeded, she removed Elric's reins from his bridle and tied Jules to the saddle. Arms limp and burning and fingers dripping blood, she surveyed her work. If he came off now, it would be because the Goddess really hated her.

She tied Benji's reins to Elric and led Elric down the road on foot. She stumbled and slipped down the dark road in the downpour. How long had it been since they'd left camp? And where was the city? Shouldn't they be there by now? She blinked and wiped water and mud from her eyes as best she could. In her stupor, she didn't notice a rock in the path; she stepped on it, twisted her ankle and fell in the road.

"Goddess damn it all to hell!" she shouted at the sky. Tears welled up as she pounded the ground next to her and succeeded only in splashing herself with more mud. Sobbing in earnest, she got to her feet and took stock of her injuries. Some superficial cuts and likely a sprained ankle.

Sniffing and hiccupping, she grasped Elric's bridle and limped forward. After an interminable time, she saw the city lights. *One foot in front of the other*, she recited to herself over and over until the palace door loomed before her. No one was outside the palace at this time of night, so she dragged Jules off Elric herself. Her back and legs strained with the effort to catch a man a full head taller than she, and her bad ankle threatened to give way entirely. He was only able to walk a bit as they stumbled together toward the ballroom. Thankfully, several Healers came to her aid.

"Please," she begged all of them. "Help me save him."
And she collapsed.

CHAPTER 21

Once the Healing staff situated Jules on a cot and began his regimen of teas and rehydration, Natalie allowed a Healer to treat her. With her ankle wrapped, scrapes cleaned and bandaged, and her own cup of tea, she retreated to a palace bathroom to clean up. One of the other Healers provided her with a change of clothes, and after taking a quick bath, she gingerly changed into them, her back and legs screaming in protest. Somehow, facing the possible death of her love felt more doable now that she was clean.

Her love. She froze. It was one thing to have a crush on someone for years; to daydream about them and pretend you were in love. Now by some twist of fate, she'd actually fallen in love with the man. And she'd never told him. She stared at her face in a mirror. Her wet hair hung in loose scraggles around her face. Her eyes had dark circles underneath them, and her face was drawn and pale with worry and lack of sleep.

Damn it, the insufferable man would have to live so she could tell him she loved him. How did he get this bloody disease anyway? They'd been together the whole time since arriving in Roseharbor. She needed to find out before he was too far gone to answer her questions.

After re-braiding her hair and covering her face with a kerchief, she hobbled out into the ballroom. She took the cup of tea from Jules's current Healer, thanked him, and knelt to caress Jules's face. "Jules. I need you to come back to me now. I know you're far away, but I need to know where you think you got the sweating fever." Jules moaned and turned his head. She helped him drink some more tea. "Jules," she hissed, not wanting to disturb the nearby patients. "It's Nat. Open your eyes and look at me. Tell me where you got this Five-forsaken disease." He opened his eyes, but they didn't focus on anything.

Natalie stood and bit her thumbnail through her kerchief. When had they been separated the past few days? Had he eaten or drunk something she had not? She paced next to his cot as she mulled over every detail of what had happened since they'd arrived in Roseharbor. They rode into the city, they bought honey, and then …

She stopped pacing, flew to his bedside and shook his shoulder. "Jules, look at me," Natalie demanded. Jules groaned. "Goddess dammit, Jules, I need to know how to fix this, you insufferable man. I need to talk to you. Now." She shook his shoulder again, cursing the disease and fever affecting his brain. Looking around to make sure no one was watching, she slapped his cheek. "Jules."

He opened his eyes and stared blearily at her. "Leave me be … you damned … pest of a woman," he rasped.

She laughed, eyes tearing up. "Jules, when I was in here making sure it was safe for us to Heal and you were in the stables, was there any place you could have gotten the sweating fever? A water or food source you used?"

Jules lapsed into silence; she thought she might have to slap him again. "The feed room … stables … fed … horses."

Natalie clasped her hands together. "Thank you, love.

That's all I needed. Now rest, get better and come back to me soon." She stroked his forehead. She'd have to wait until daylight to search the stables. For now, she'd stay by his side. She gratefully accepted cups of tea and cool cloths from passing Healers. Jules barely roused when she helped him swallow tea and Activated it. She took the cloths and wiped his skin tenderly, willing the fever to leave and his skin to cool. Unbidden, the sensation of running her fingers over his chest in the dark came to her. She sniffed and wiped tears from her eyes.

"I don't want to fail you," she whispered to Jules as she wiped his sweaty hair away from his face. "Don't you die like my Da. You say it wasn't my fault, but … if I'd just been faster or thought about dehydration sooner or been a better Healer …" she rested her forehead on his, her tears falling onto his face. "Please don't leave me."

Natalie's self-pity kept watch with her as she administered as much hydrating fluids and Activated as much tea as she dared. Time ceased to have all meaning and became an endless cycle of tending to Jules and staring at his face as if to memorize it.

Natalie jumped when she felt a hand on her shoulder; it was Headmistress Gayla. "We need to move him, sweeting. If Aldworth comes back and finds him here, there will be hell to pay. There's a small alcove near the main supply area; let's move him there." A cold lump of dread formed in Natalie's stomach. The time for their Council of Healers "review" was long past. Aldworth must be combing all of Ismereld for them now.

Together, Natalie and three other Healers moved Jules from the main ballroom to the alcove. Jules groaned as his cot moved; Natalie bit her lip and said several prayers as she carried her corner of the cot, hoping the move didn't make his health worse and that her ankle held out. With a lot of grunting and not a few muffled curses, Natalie and her three compatriots got Jules settled in one of the curtained-off alcoves near the Healer's main storage area;

hopefully a place Aldworth wouldn't check should he pay one of his surprise visits. Natalie set about making sure Jules was as comfortable as she could make him and then returned to the main ballroom to thank the Headmistress.

Natalie blinked at the sun's rays pouring in the ballroom windows; it was dawn.

"Headmistress, could someone keep watch over Healer Juliers? Before he became too ill, he told me how he might have contracted the disease. With your permission, I'd like to investigate," Close enough to the truth. Natalie bit her lip. She didn't want to get anyone's hopes up.

"Absolutely, dear." Gayla turned and issued orders, which Healers obeyed promptly. Natalie admired Gayla's ability to run an efficient operation. Every single patient in the room received organized and efficient care and the Healing staff listened without question. It was a skill she envied.

"Thank you. I am so grateful to you—for everything." Natalie put her hand on the Headmistress's shoulder before limping back to Jules's alcove. She kissed his forehead. "Wish me luck," she whispered to his still form. Then, much as it pained her, she stood, swirled her cloak around her and left the palace.

As she stepped into the shade of the palace stables, Natalie reflected that the smell of clean barn, horses, leather and hay might just be a close second to the smell of a library. A long row of stalls lined each side of the palace barn; some had inquiring heads poking out of them, ears pricked in her direction, curious about the newcomer. She walked down the aisle, patting the occasional soft nose and keeping her eyes peeled for anything that might transmit disease. She found Elric's stall, and after scratching him behind the ears in his favorite place as a greeting, she entered his stall. His water seemed clean. There were flies about. Could it have been flies? No, if flies transmitted this disease, she and Jules would've been infected long ago, having camped in outdoors for so many days. Besides, Jules said he fed the horses. She had to get to the feed room.

"Oi, can I help you miss?" demanded a voice from the stall door. "You're not supposed to be messing with the horses." A grizzled old man glared at her.

Natalie felt her face redden and a frisson of embarrassment shot through her chest. "Oh, uh, hi. I'm Healer Desmond and this is my partner's horse. My partner's name is Healer—I mean this horse is Elric. He belongs to my partner and I was visiting him to be sure he was all right. And you are?"

"I'm Gaffigan, the head groom," he replied in a gruff voice.

Natalie tried to make the best of it. "Is my own horse, Benji, here? He's a small chestnut."

"Yeah, he's here."

Not the most forthcoming man. Natalie sighed and did her best to smile charmingly. "I might need Benji's tack soon. Could you show me where the tack room is please?"

After a few seconds' silence during which Gaffigan seemed to be figuring out whether she was a horse thief or not, he said. "This way."

She let herself out of Elric's stall, closed the door behind her and followed him to the tack room. "Thank you very much. And if I wanted to give him some grain, where is the feed room?"

"The grooms do all the feeding," Gaffigan grunted.

Obviously, she'd do much better exploring the barn on her own. "Oh, of course. Thank you for showing me the tack room. I'll go visit Benji and go back to the palace."

Gaffigan showed her to Benji's stall. She let herself in and made a big to do, fussing over him and petting him such that Gaffigan rolled his eyes and left them alone. Once he left, she opened the stall door and closed it, hoping to give Gaffigan the idea she'd left, and then she squatted against the front of Benji's stall and hid. Benji nosed her and nibbled at her cloak, and she scratched his nose and ears.

Her legs had fallen asleep by the time she thought the coast was clear. She stood and peeked over the stall door. The barn aisle seemed empty, so she opened the door as quietly as she could, slipped out and closed it behind her. On the alert for other surly grooms, she headed back toward the tack room. She guessed the feed room was nearby. Sure enough, a large solid door stood across from the tack room. With one last furtive glance around, she unlatched the door and slid it open just enough for her to slide in and closed it right behind her.

If Jules was right, this was where he'd contracted the sweating fever. She searched frantically, fearing discovery at any moment. She checked in the feed bins, up at the ceilings and around the windows. Nothing seemed out of the ordinary. The feed room was as clean as the rest of the palace barn. She spun around slowly in the middle of the room with her hand on her forehead. She must be missing something. And dammit, she was out of time. The whole city was running out of time.

Something skittered behind her and she turned to the door, holding her breath, praying no one had discovered her. But the door stayed closed. Letting out her breath, she peered over her shoulder. It was almost like … she walked around to the side of one of the feed bins, squatted and grabbed it by the corner and tried to move it out from the wall as best she could, her sore body protesting.

Something banged against the feed bin, ran between her legs and across the room, making her jump. She put a hand on her pounding heart.

Rats in the barn.

She'd been in another barn this summer where she suspected rats made a home—Oswald's in Mistfell. Where her parents used to eat. And then they got sick. Rats liked feasting off human food supplies. Rats would love a brewer's grains, a brewer such as Morley. If diseases lived on rats or if diseases lived in their excrement and if Morley had accidentally transported rats in his cart from Whitestrand to Mistfell to Roseharbor …

Well, it was a theory, but dammit, it was the only one she had that made sense. And theories could be tested.

Natalie limped out of the feed room as fast as she could, closing the door hastily behind her. Gaffigan was on the other side, red-faced and ready to explode.

He did not expect Natalie to take him by the shoulders and give him orders. "You have rats in the feed room and possibly the whole barn. Kill them all and clean the feed room thoroughly. Kill all rats you see anywhere. All of Roseharbor depends upon you doing this, do you understand me?"

CHAPTER 22

Natalie limped as fast as she could back to the ballroom, cursing her sprained ankle. Spotting Gayla, she beckoned the Headmistress aside.

"It's rats," Natalie said, panting from her run. "The disease is transmitted by rats. Somehow, we have to kill all the rats in the city."

Gayla raised her eyebrows. "How do you propose to do that? Traps? Poison?"

"I don't know," Natalie admitted. "I need time to think. How is Jules?"

"He's started coughing."

Natalie gimped back to the alcove. A Healer tended to Jules as coughs racked his body. Natalie waited until she could take over his care.

"Jules," she whispered, "It's me. I've figured out what's been transmitting the disease. It's rats. Thanks for telling me to look in the feed room." She kissed his burning forehead. "Now, do you have any ideas about how to kill every rat in the city? Fast?"

She sat against the wall and adjusted Jules so he lay

propped up on her chest with her arms around him. All his teas were within easy reach, and she administered and Activated them when needed. A knot formed in her stomach when she felt how much lighter he was than when she'd hauled him here. "What we need," she whispered in his ear, "are a bunch of hungry cats. Or I need you to miraculously wake up and tell me how to find Anli and Onlo so they can teach me how to build rat traps."

She tried to recall when Onlo said they'd be back. Four or five days. How long ago did they leave? Everything was a blur.

"So, my love, how do you catch a city full of rats?" Natalie leaned her head wearily against the wall behind her. Over the next few hours, in between giving medicine to Jules, Natalie came up with ideas, each one sillier than the last. "We could build mechanical cats. We could put a wheel of cheese in City Square and hope they all come for a visit. We could put a thousand tiny huntsman on a thousand tiny horses and hunt the rats down. Maybe Gayla will find the mage who will then magically kill them all with lightning bolts." With each of her own suggestions, she giggled a bit more, but she had to stop when the giggling made Jules cough.

Dammit, there had to be a way. She grabbed her Healing diary and thumbed back and forth through it. Something caught her eye on a particular page and she flattened the book and ran a finger down the page. "Listen to this Jules, but three hundred years ago, there was an illness like this one, killed only adults in their prime. Children and the elderly were largely spared," she read her notes aloud to Jules. "Having a strong immune system seemed to work against the human body in this case. As if the immune response overwhelmed the body and it was too much. Children and the elderly, having weaker immune systems, didn't have this problem. Bloody hell, I didn't put it in with my notes on epidemics, I put it in with my notes about immune systems," She dog-eared the page to show Jules the entry when—if he woke up.

It seemed to be a day of discovery. Still, she had yet to figure out how to kill every rat in Roseharbor. Natalie only knew about the spring snare traps Jules had shown her how to make, and those depended on having a tree nearby. Perfect for the rats outside, but for the ones inside houses or barns, she needed another idea. Lack of sleep and the cumulative exhaustion of the past few weeks made thinking feel like wading through mud. Traps and poison, Gayla had said. Traps and poison ... Well, poison might be nice, but people would need to touch the dead rats to dispose of them, increasing their chance of contracting the sweating sickness. And poison might kill beneficial animals as well.

"Dammit, Jules, I'm a Healer, not some builder from Obfuselt. Why didn't you ever tell me how to contact your friends without the whole Isle finding out?" she grumbled. He didn't reply, so she stuck her tongue out at him and went back to brainstorming. Would there be anyone else from Obfuselt in the city? If so, how would she find them? Obfuseltans were notorious for being hard to find unless they wanted you to find them. But perhaps there was a builder, an architect, a wood carver—someone she could ask. Maybe she should've brought Aaron along after all. He'd know what to build.

But it meant leaving Jules's side again. Her heart squeezed painfully. She gently hugged him tighter and put her lips next to his ear. "I have to go," she said, choking on the words. She pressed a kiss to the side of his temple. "Don't you go anywhere while I'm gone. You fight, do you hear me?"

Slowly, she extricated herself from behind Jules and laid him carefully on his cot. With a final brush of her fingertips across his forehead, she turned and left before she lost her resolve.

She told Gayla where she was going, made sure good

Healers were tending to Jules, and left the palace once more.

Stepping into the bright sunlight, Natalie stopped short; she had no idea where to go. Roseharbor was a huge city, one with which she was utterly unfamiliar. Taking a breath, she began asking passersby where she might find a builder or architect. Some people ignored her and some people gave her terrible directions using landmarks in the city she had a wretched time finding. Eventually, with her ankle throbbing and her temper significantly worse for wear, she arrived at the door of one Siaraa Kamal, Builder. She knocked impatiently. After what seemed like an eternity, a tall woman with long dark hair, burnished tan-colored skin and striking topaz eyes answered the door.

"I don't remember calling for a Healer," the woman said.

"I'm looking for Siaraa Kamal, Builder. I'm Healer Natalie Desmond and I need to build rat traps. Rather a lot of them, I'm afraid."

The woman raised her dark eyebrows. "I am Siaraa Kamal, Builder. How does one Heal with rat traps?"

Natalie raised her own eyebrows. "One kills the rats who are killing everyone else."

Siaraa considered this, then gestured for Natalie to enter. "Please come in."

Natalie followed Siaraa into her workspace, a spacious, rectangular room with sunlight shining through large windows onto an enormous wooden worktable covered with paper and thin charcoal sticks. Several of Siaraa's sketches hung on the walls.

Siaraa gestured to a chair. "Please sit and tell me more."

Natalie sat, wishing desperately she could take off her boots.

"My partner and I followed this disease from Whitestrand to here. The only time we were separated was right before he fell ill. He was in the palace barn, the feed room to be exact. When I went to investigate, I found rats."

"How certain are you rats carry the illness?"

Natalie raised her hands and let them fall to her lap. "Nothing else fits. When the disease left Whitestrand, it left with a brewer carrying ale. And I am completely certain the disease is not passed from person to person. If I am wrong, then … I am wrong. But I really don't think I am, and this is the last chance we've got to stop it."

Siaraa steepled her fingers. "So. Rat traps. Even if we design a simple one, who is going to build them—you and me? We have a whole city to cover."

"Indeed," Natalie agreed. "I thought about that on my way here. As it turns out, this disease does not kill children. Children—at least children above a certain age—should be able to build a rat trap if it's simple enough. They have access to their own homes, whereas we do not. Plus, they can often sneak into places adults cannot."

Siaraa considered this, a dubious expression on her face. "An army of children building and deploying an army of rat traps in the capital city of the Isles."

"Yes."

"That sounds absolutely crazy."

Natalie's stomach fell.

"My kind of project," Siaraa grinned and began sketching like mad.

Siaraa's hand flew over the paper as she muttered to herself, occasionally balling up a drawing and throwing it away in frustration before beginning anew. Natalie paced Siaraa's workroom, unable to be of use. Perhaps this was how patients and their family members felt waiting while Healers worked—desperately hoping for a good outcome but unable to help in any way.

"Stop pacing; you'll drive me mad," Siaraa snapped, not

looking up from her work. Natalie slumped in a chair and brooded instead. How close was Aldworth to finding her and Jules? How close was he to building another megalith for Lorelan? What were Anli and Onlo up to? Were her mother and Aaron all right? Had anyone from Solerin responded to her mother? She tried not to think of Jules; any thought of him and she might leave the room and run back to the palace.

After an interminable amount of time, Siaraa sat back in her chair with a grin of satisfaction on her charcoal-dusted face. "There."

Natalie stood up, walked over, and peered at the drawing. "How does it work?"

Siaraa took a piece of charcoal and pointed to the relevant parts of the drawing as she discussed them. "So, it's basically a rectangular tunnel that's closed off at one end. Inside the tunnel is a ramp with a hole bisecting its midsection. A dowel will go through the hole and hold the ramp in the middle of the tunnel."

Understanding crossed Natalie's face. "So once the rat enters the tunnel and crosses from the lower end of the ramp to the upper, it weighs down the upper part of the ramp and the ramp drops."

"Exactly. If we build and bait the trap properly, once they cross from one side of the ramp to the other and fall off the ramp, they won't be able to cross back. They'll be stuck at the closed end of the tunnel."

"Fantastic."

"How many do we need?" Siaraa asked.

"As many as we can possibly make. Does Roseharbor have an orphanage? And a City Hall? We need to organize the children."

Siaraa nodded. "You get as many children as you can to be here tomorrow. Oh, and get City Hall to make signs and have the town criers announce it. People need to know. I'll get as many supplies as I can."

Natalie swirled her cloak around her. "I will. Thank

you. If the city lives, it will be because of you. I'll have the Abbey arrange payment for you."

Siaraa waved her hand. "No need. I'm a sucker for crazy ideas and impossible odds. Plus, I don't feel like dying just yet."

After breakfast the next morning, children from all over the city filled Siaraa's workroom. Natalie explained the need for killing the rats. A few children balked.

"Miss, must we kill them? They're innocent animals," a girl with brown pigtails called out.

Natalie smiled kindly at her, recalling her own first animal kill and Jules reminding her the animal must die so she could live. "It pains me, too, sweetheart. I love animals. Unfortunately, the rats carry the disease that's killing so many people in the city. Either we kill them or they kill us."

The girl with pigtails considered it for a moment. She still didn't seem pleased, but she didn't leave. Natalie could work with that.

Siaraa walked the children through building the traps, showing them a completed model first and then supervising them as they built their own. She inspected each one to be sure it worked properly. Soon, the children were working on their second and third traps.

Even Natalie learned how to build the traps and helped the children as well. She had to work to keep a silly smile off her face as she taught the children and watched them learn. *When this is all over, I'm going to speak with Gayla and ask to teach classes at the Abbey again.*

Natalie was helping a child with a trap when the workroom door opened and closed and a girl near the door said "Doggie!"

Natalie turned around in time to get a face full of fur. "Jake!" She fell to the floor, arms flying around him as he covered her with kisses, wiggling from nose to tail. "I missed you so much," she sobbed into his fur.

When her sobs quieted into hiccups, she wanted to bury her face in Jake's fur again. The whole room was staring at her, including Onlo, with a bemused expression on his face, and Anli, whose expression appeared both bored and disgusted.

"Sorry everyone," she said sniffing and dabbing her eyes. She turned to Anli and Onlo. "Thank you for bringing Jake back with you."

Onlo raised his eyebrows. "Our pleasure. He is a good dog. We come with news, but first I must ask—what project are you working on here?"

Natalie informed them of Jules falling ill, her theory that rats were the disease vector, and the idea to build and place as many traps as possible throughout the city.

Anli stomped over to her and stopped with her nose an inch from Natalie's "You let Jules get sick? Why aren't you Healing him now?"

"Oh, enough! I did not let Jules do anything." Natalie explained how it was Jules feeding the horses that had inadvertently led to the discovery of the most likely disease vector. "And I am not Healing him, because I am here, leading the effort to kill every rat in the city. We have to save the city, remember? Isn't that why you came to us in the first place?" Natalie turned and walked away from Anli to count the number of traps made so far that day.

"People should make sure to keep cats about," Onlo added, inspecting one of the traps.

"And snakes," Anli added, shocking Natalie.

Snakes. Oh, the parents of Roseharbor were going to love her.

At the end of the session, the children each received a collection of empty traps and instructions on how to bait them, where to place them and what to do once they caught a rat.

"Do not ever touch the rats or their droppings," Natalie said. Some of the children giggled and Natalie grinned. "Empty the rat out and burn it. If you can't get the rat out, burn the trap, rat and all. Make sure you have an adult help you. Other animals good at hunting rats are cats and snakes." Several children perked up at this. Natalie held up her hand. "Please, only collect non-venomous snakes like black rat snakes. Meet back here at the same time tomorrow and we'll make more. Tell your friends to come, too. Thank you all so very much, you did a great job."

One by one the children filed out. Natalie and Siaraa each slumped in a chair.

"My workroom is a disaster area," Siaraa said mournfully. "What am I going to do?"

"The only thing we can do," Natalie said, letting her head fall back and staring at the ceiling. "Wait to see if this stops the damn disease from spreading."

Onlo's bass voice brought Natalie back to the present. "Natalie. We must speak with you. Alone."

CHAPTER 23

Natalie nodded wearily. "All right. I'm going to help Siaraa clean up first. We need to organize for tomorrow's trap building. Do you mind pitching in? We can talk sooner that way."

Between the four of them, they cleaned the space, using lessons learned from the morning's efforts to organize the supplies in a more efficient manner.

She left with Anli and Onlo, and she'd never been happier to have Jake trotting at her side. Onlo helped her mount his horse behind him.

"Let's ride to the campsite," he said in a low voice. "I don't want to risk being overheard."

That sent a frisson of panic through Natalie's stomach.

They rode the city streets toward the road out of town. Natalie spotted several signs instructing citizens to kill all rats and advertising the daily trap building sessions for children. She drew comfort from the city's support for her efforts; perhaps there was a chance of saving Roseharbor after all.

Passing the palace on the way out, Natalie nearly

begged Onlo to stop, but she knew if he did, she wouldn't leave Jules's side. So she tightened her arms around Onlo and turned her face away from the palace and rested her cheek on his long, thick cords of hair.

Reaching the campsite, Natalie dismounted and sat near the dead campfire while Anli and Onlo tended to their horses. She helped herself to rations from her pack, sharing some with Jake, while she waited.

"Aldworth was not at the Abbey," Onlo began, sitting down next to her.

"I know; he's here," Natalie told them of Aldworth's near discovery of them in the palace.

Anli nodded. "We quickly figured out he'd left for Roseharbor. What we wanted to know was why. From all Jules told us, he doesn't seem to be the sort to get his hands dirty with actual work."

Natalie snorted in agreement. "No, his visit that day was more a show of power."

Onlo shrugged. "So, we made some discreet inquiries. About the Council and Aldworth. Headmistress Gayla and Healer Hawkins, according to our sources, are honest people we can trust."

Natalie nodded.

Anli continued for her friend. "Aldworth, of course, is not. Since we already know his plans in terms of building and Activating a megalith in Lorelan, we wanted to see if we could find anyone working for him." Anli grinned like a feral beast. "We succeeded."

"Well, partially," Onlo qualified.

"Have you ever heard of the New Mages' Guild?" Anli asked.

Natalie knitted her eyebrows in confusion. "New Mages' Guild? Mages died out soon after the Five Mages created the megaliths on each Isle. Mages haven't existed since. Only their magic is left behind."

"So we've all been told. Aldworth is the head of this guild and he—well, they—seem to think they can train to be mages." Onlo said.

Natalie let out a sharp bark of laughter. "Did he even read history? Mages were born, not made. You either had the power or you didn't. You couldn't just learn it from books in the library."

"Nonetheless, they are trying and experimenting," Onlo continued, a sober expression upon his face. "Some experiments don't go so well—look at what happened to Jules."

Natalie swore.

"Indeed," Anli agreed. "And here's where it gets interesting. The Guild, while aware they are not actual mages, believe an actual mage is alive right now. Finding that person is the sole focus of all their current efforts."

"I know. Gayla told me."

Anli and Onlo raised their eyebrows. "Did she tell you why?" Onlo asked.

Natalie shook her head. "She says she has people she trusts looking for the mage, but they haven't found anyone yet."

"If Aldworth finds the mage, he will be able to create his megalith for Lorelan with ease. It's likely the mage will die in the process. The Isles will then be able to invade Lorelan. And we will become a country of conquerors."

Bile rose in the back of Natalie's throat. She loved her island home; why had Aldworth and—didn't Jules say the King and Queen support him? —want to invade Lorelan? To change the nature of the Isles forever? These people did not stand for what she believed in. It was violent and horrible. "How do we stop them? How do I find the mage? I'm already trying to Heal at the palace and build the rat traps."

Onlo chuckled. "We'll search the city for the mage. You work on the disease. To communicate with each other, we'll place a rat trap just inside Siaraa's front door. We can put written updates in it for each other. It will be less conspicuous than meeting up."

Natalie nodded. "Sounds good. Would one of you mind giving me a ride back to the palace? I'd like to check on Jules and help them out until it's time to build more traps tomorrow."

To Natalie's relief, she found Jules still slept and coughed, but had not declined further. A small ember of hope glowed deep inside her, but she hardly dared acknowledge it. Throughout the rest of the day, she helped her fellow Healers tend to the patients in the ballroom. She also gave Gayla an update on the rat eradication plans for the city. She asked the Headmistress to start keeping track of the number of new patients each day. Tomorrow, she would tally how many rats the children caught. Surely— hopefully—as the number of dead rats increased, the number of new patients would decrease.

That evening, Natalie and Jake curled up next to Jules's side. Natalie gently kissed his brow and told him of her day—leaving out the bits the Obfuseltans discovered, since she didn't know who was listening. She was just drifting off to sleep when Jake growled. Natalie jumped awake, trying to find the source of his alarm.

She heard a soft, "Miss?"

Natalie placed a calming hand on Jake.

A teenage girl in a dark cloak was in the hall with her. A pale face with stunning silver eyes the likes of which Natalie had never seen stared out at her from under the hood. "Miss, I'm sorry to bother you. Are you a Healer?"

Natalie wished she knew where Jules's dagger was. "I am."

The girl removed her hood, revealing hair so blond it was silver-white. "Please, I need your help." Jake leaned forward to sniff the newcomer.

The girl smelled of woods and travel and her boots were caked with mud. Her eyes implored Natalie to trust her; Natalie could find no deceit there. "Are you sick?"

"No. I ... well, it might be best if I show you," the girl rubbed her palms on her cloak. "May I take your hand?"

Natalie hesitated, then placed her hand, palm up, between them. The girl clasped it and Natalie gasped as her own energy and the girl's merged as easily and powerfully as hers and Jules's did.

"You're a Healer?" Natalie hissed. "I don't remember seeing you at the Abbey." Natalie didn't know everyone at the Abbey, but she was certain she'd recall someone this powerful and striking.

"I am, but I could not go to the Abbey to study." The girl's face fell.

"Why?" Natalie said, dumbfounded.

"My name is Charlotte Fairisles, princess heir to the throne of the Isles. My parents, that is the King and Queen, do not know I'm a Healer."

Natalie's mouth gaped open like a landed fish. *Manners*, she reminded herself after several seconds of uncomfortable silence. "Pleased to meet you, Your Highness. How—why did you leave your parents? And did they take the fever with them when they left the city?"

"No, no one is ill at the other palace. And I left because I needed to find ... people like me. To help me learn about what's happening to me and how to control it. Things have been ... much harder since I had a mild bout with the sweating fever. There's more, you see," Charlotte continued, swallowing hard. Taking a deep breath, Princess Charlotte held her right hand in a tight fist, and quick as a flash, unfurled her fingers to reveal a small ball of white-blue light hovering above her palm.

"You're the mage," Natalie breathed.

Princess Charlotte nodded, silver eyes wide as saucers.

"Why did you seek me out?"

"Please help me. I am being hunted."

Natalie put the heels of her hands in her eyes. "I know, I know. But why come to me?"

"I returned to the palace two days ago. I've lived here

since I was born. I know almost all the secret passages. I've spent all my time watching and waiting to see who best to approach. None of the Healers are ever alone, except you. Every night, you are here by yourself, tending to this man. You are the only one I could approach without risking greater exposure."

Natalie closed her eyes for a moment. "I know people who can help you. They are people I trust and they are from Obfuselt. They can get you out of the city and hide you. I just need to find a way to get you to them in the morning. But I'll be honest with you—one of the men hunting you is also hunting me and my friend. And he's already been here once already. Plus, you'll need to start hiding your hair. The Five only know what we can do about your eyes."

The princess hung her head. "I don't even know a spell to hide their color."

"Hey," Natalie lifted her hand and put her hand on the girl's shoulder. "The only people who could have trained you died two thousand years ago. Go easy on yourself. For now, you can sleep in the alcove next to ours. I'll go find some blankets."

The princess heir tucked in for the night, Natalie lay next to Jules's side and stared at the wall for a long time before falling into an uneasy sleep.

Natalie kissed Jules goodbye in the morning, and then she, Jake and the Princess left the palace for Siaraa's. Natalie found a spare Healer's cloak for Princess Charlotte. Fortune favored them: it was drizzling, so no one looked twice at two women with hoods pulled over their heads. When they arrived at Siaraa's, Natalie dashed off a note to Onlo and Anli and left it in the rat trap inside the front door. Princess Charlotte sat at the worktable, unsure whether to trust Siaraa.

Siaraa, on the other hand, was not one to be put off.

"Who is this?" she demanded.

Natalie explained the basics of the situation, leaving out the bits about Charlotte being a Healer and mage.

Siaraa rolled her eyes. "Save the city, save the princess. I knew it, I'm stuck in some third-rate tavern bard's song." She stomped off to double-check the supplies for the day.

Natalie burst into a fit of giggles, earning her a strange look from the princess.

"Healer Desmond?"

Natalie waved at her weakly, tears streaming down her face. "It's Natalie, please. And it is rather like some awful made-up bard's song, isn't it? The city is dying while we try to kill rats to save it. Now we must rescue you, Princess. Knights with sh-sh-shining r-rat traps!" Natalie collapsed in a chair in a fit of mirth.

The humor lost on the princess, she selected one of the traps and examined it. "Why are you trapping rats?"

Natalie explained their theory that rats transmitted the sweating fever and how the children of the city assembled every day to help build and disperse the traps.

Alarm washed over the princess's face. "When will the children be here?"

"Any minute now, I expect. Are you all right?"

"I must hide." The princess's voice sounded tight and nervous. "The children will recognize me. I've tried to—well, it doesn't matter now, where can I hide?"

"Upstairs," Siaraa commanded as she returned to the room. "Follow me."

The princess's cloak disappeared up the stairwell as the first child entered the door. Natalie schooled her face so as not to show her relief. "Good morning," she addressed the little boy, who must have been around eight years old. "What's your name again?"

"Jenson," he announced proudly, with a slight lisp.

"Did you catch any rats, Jenson?"

"Oh, yes miss, I caughted two. And I burned them just like you said." His gap-toothed smile of pride was so precious.

"Wonderful. I'll mark in my log that you caught"—Natalie glanced at him making sure he caught her correction of his grammar—"two rats. Well done. Let me get you some more supplies, shall I?"

A large crowd of children entered Siaraa's workroom bragging about the number of rats they'd caught. Natalie carefully noted each child's name and the number caught in her log. The older children, who already knew how to build traps, taught other children the technique with minimal supervision from Siaraa and Natalie.

"We're going to need a bigger space," Natalie observed.

"Mmm," Siaraa agreed. "I'll see if I can think of someplace."

The cacophony of children's voices faded as they took their creations out into the city. Siaraa left to see about getting them more workspace while Natalie tidied the workroom, and Princess Charlotte descended the stairs to help.

"Well," Natalie began. "I need to get today's numbers to the palace. We need to compare it with—"

Natalie put her hand to her heart as a large, tall figure darkened the door.

CHAPTER 24

S he breathed a sigh of relief; it was just Onlo. He strode toward her, her note crumpled in his palm, and pulled her to the side.

"Natalie, is this true?" His deep voice was hoarse with disbelief. "You found the princess and the mage?"

"I didn't find her; she found me," Natalie turned to Princess Charlotte and nodded for her to join them. "I trust him. He saved the life of my friend countless times."

Princess Charlotte stepped forward and whispered. "Yes. I am Princess Charlotte. I am Attuned to this Isle and I am a mage."

Onlo regarded the princess with skepticism, then bowed at the waist. "An honor to meet you, Your Highness. I am Onlo, from the Isle of Obfuselt. If I may ask, how do you know you're a mage?"

Princess Charlotte gave Onlo a very small version of the same demonstration she'd given Natalie the day before. Natalie thought Onlo might have gone a bit pale underneath his dark skin.

"We must get you into hiding," he said. "My partner is

outside; we have a safe house we can take you to." Onlo offered her his elbow. "Do you trust me to keep you from harm?"

The princess nodded and accepted Onlo's arm.

"Onlo, where are you taking her? Where is your safe house?" Natalie demanded.

Onlo paused. "Natalie, it is best you do not know. If Aldworth finds you, you can honestly say you have no idea of the princess's whereabouts. Before we leave, I must warn you. During our search of the city, we did see agents of the New Mages' Guild present. Be careful, my friend."

"Then wouldn't it be best if we all stayed together? Strength in numbers? Besides, she needs training." Natalie hissed.

Onlo arched an eyebrow. "You can train a mage?"

"No, but I can train Healers. She needs to get at least some of her power under control. She needs me."

"So does Jules. So does this city. Will you abandon them for her?"

"I'm not abandoning anyone. She needs to stay here."

Onlo's fist clenched. "Natalie. The city is crawling with people hunting you, Jules and the princess. Let's not make it easy for them by keeping the three of you together. And you have a palace full of sick people and a massive project here that desperately needs your help. You can't be everywhere and do everything. Let us keep her safe until you can train her. Do you trust us to do that?"

Natalie swore and pinched the bridge of her nose. Finally, she nodded and swallowed past the lump in her throat. "Safe travels."

As she finished tidying Siaraa's workshop, a morose cloud descended upon her. Onlo was right—it was best she didn't know the princess's location. Plus, her priority lay here in the city. But she wanted to learn more about the princess, her abilities, and how she'd managed to escape her parents and the host of people who must have been guarding her. Oh, hell in a kettle, she'd forgotten to ask

Onlo how she'd be able to communicate with him. What if she needed him or Anli? Should she still use the rat trap in Siaraa's shop? Or was Siaraa's place being watched?

She sat wearily in a chair and leaned her head against her palm. A few minutes later, she felt a hand on her shoulder.

Siaraa sat next to her, her face filled with concern. "You have the weight of the world on your mind."

Natalie huffed softly in agreement. "Well, these past few weeks have been all about saving cities and towns—one of which I totally failed to save—"

"Excuse me, Miss Healer," Siaraa interrupted, "But from what I heard, Whitestrand was mostly dead by the time you got there. So unless your Abbey taught you the ability to raise the dead, then Whitestrand is not on you."

Natalie picked at her fingernails, trying not to conjure in her mind's eye visions of bodies burning and long spires of smoke rising toward the sky.

"Next was my hometown, Mistfell," she said in a flat voice. "My da was the first to die. I couldn't save him." Natalie clasped her arms over her chest as if to cover the hole in her heart where her da used to be. Tears spilled down her face and she was grateful Siaraa's hand stayed firmly on her shoulder. "And I don't even know how Mistfell is doing because the Abbey called us back; they—or most likely Healer Aldworth—blame us for leaving Whitestrand. He thinks we should have stayed. To make it worse, we ignored his summons and came here to help with the epidemic instead. And now ..." Natalie threw her hands up in the air, not wanting to reveal anything about the princess.

"If you had to do it all again, would you do anything differently?" Siaraa asked.

Natalie mulled over the events of the last few weeks for several minutes. If there were times when a different choice could have been made, it would only have been if she'd had the ability to predict the future with any sort of accuracy. She hung her head. "No."

Siaraa squeezed her shoulder. "So, these times when you think it's all your fault, just remember you are human. You make only the best choices you can at the time. All of this? This fever, the princess and this horse's ass Aldworth? It's not your fault."

Sobbing now, Natalie turned to hug Siaraa, who awkwardly patted her back. "Eh, you have a lot of snot coming out of your nose."

Natalie laughed and blew her nose on a handkerchief from her pocket.

"Listen. I've made arrangements with the milliner next door for us to use her space tomorrow as well. Let's get things ready, all right?"

Hiccupping, Natalie nodded and helped Siaraa prepare the trap-making materials for the next day. "Siaraa, why are you here instead of on Obfuselt? I've seen your drawings; they're amazing."

"Pfft. I am talented enough without a big rock helping me. Besides, I would rather take my own jobs when and how I choose without being governed by some council."

"You've never even been to the Isle just to see?"

"Never been. Do you think I could do this job for you for free if I were latched onto a rock on Obfuselt waiting for approval from a council to do it?"

Natalie wished she could explain it wasn't like that; that her connection to Ismereld's ley lines made her feel warm, welcome, and like she was a stronger person. But she'd had it up to the back teeth with councils herself, so she shook her head at Siaraa and finished tidying.

Natalie settled into a grueling routine the next few days. Mornings were spent with Siaraa building traps with the children of Roseharbor, whose number seemed to grow each day. Siaraa and Natalie spilt the children up; Siaraa in her own shop and Natalie in the milliner's. The milliner, a hawk-like, standoffish woman, made Natalie quite uncomfortable. The glares she often shot over her spectacles made it clear she resented the invasion of her space. She refused to help build traps and was soon making her own creations in a very small space indeed.

One memorable day, the mother of Jenson, the small boy who'd been the first to report to Natalie his success catching a rat, entered the milliner's shop with a red-faced Jenson in tow, screeching at Natalie. Apparently, Jenson had taken Anli's advice to heart, captured a snake and set it loose in his family's kitchen pantry to help catch rats. Natalie apologized profusely and made Jenson promise to keep the snakes outside.

Later, she whispered in Jenson's ear. "Great job. Just put the snakes in barns or grain warehouses next time, deal?"

He turned to her with his adorable gap-toothed smile. "Deal."

With trap building done for the day, Natalie took the day's rat total to the palace to enter into the log she and Gayla kept to compare the number of rats killed to the number of new patients. After three days of intense effort by the children, the number of new patients had stayed the same for two days in a row. Natalie held her breath. Was it too early to hope?

She threw herself into helping the patients in the palace sickroom, administering and Activating the teas, making sure the balance of salt and honey was just right and doing whatever she could to ensure as many people survived as possible. She was scared to confirm with Gayla, but it did seem like fewer people were dying than at Whitestrand.

Asleep on her feet by late evening, she collapsed next to Jules's side, propped up her aching ankle on Jake's back, and updated them both of the day's events. Jules was still unconscious, feverish, coughing and sweating, but he had not progressed beyond that. If he was going to die, he wasn't doing it as fast as her father had. On the other hand, if he was going to get well, he wasn't recovering as fast as her mother.

She longed to talk to him again, hear his voice, the deep timbre of his laugh. She longed to caress him lovingly again instead of treating him so clinically. She yearned to kiss him and taste all the promises yet unfulfilled between them.

Lying next to him, she stroked his brow with cool cloths and made sure he drank his teas. After she told him the day's stories, she talked about anything that came to mind. She told him once Roseharbor was safe, they'd escape late one night and head for a remote village on the coast of Ismereld. She'd dye her hair black and he could dye his hair red. They'd change their names, learn to fish and be small-town Healers. No one would ever bother them again. She whispered to him until she fell asleep, snuggled against his side, grateful for the Healers who tended him overnight in her stead.

A week after the children of Roseharbor deployed the first rat traps throughout the city, Natalie took her midday dead rat total to Headmistress Gayla, who reported they had five fewer new patients than the day before. Natalie spun around and covered her mouth to stop the whoop of joy that nearly escaped her lips.

She grabbed Gayla's hand. "Do you think it's working?"

Gayla put her hand on the small of her back and sighed, but Natalie swore one side of her mouth curled up. "It's possible."

Natalie twirled in a circle again and began treating the day's patients with renewed vigor. For the first time, she allowed herself to hope she'd found the answer. Maybe this once, she had not failed.

"But, we definitely need to wait," she whispered to Jules later that night, her head resting on his chest. His fever was down and his cough had let up a bit; she enjoyed listening to his easier breathing under her ear. "We have to be absolutely certain before we send this big a message to the whole Isle." She stroked her fingers along his collarbone, which stuck out prominently after a week of no solid food. She wished she could use her Healing abilities to put flesh back on his bones.

"When you get better, I'm going to take you to my mother's and make you the biggest meal of your life," she promised. "Roast goose, mashed potatoes, and whatever vegetables are in our vegetable garden. And my mother is going to bake you the biggest, best apple pie you've ever eaten."

"You ... promised ... me ... mud ... pie."

Natalie jumped up on all fours. Hands shaking, she reached out with her fingers and smoothed Jules's hair across his brow. His eyes were open and they drank her in greedily. While her eyes fell into in his endless green gaze, her hand on his forehead slid over and cupped the side of his face. "Am I dreaming? Did you just say something?"

Trembling, his hand drifted up to stroke the side of her cheek. "So it seems. You saved me. And the city."

Tears overflowed Natalie's eyes and she shook her head. "No. No, I had help. You told me to go the barn feed room and I found the rat, then Siaraa, the children and I built the traps and the children put all the traps out—cats and snakes, too—and all the other Healers have been Healing you, too, and—"

"Shh." Jules took two fingers and hooked her chin and pulled her face toward his.

Once her lips touched his, Natalie felt their energies connect and swirl around one another, and she felt how alive he truly was. She whimpered with drunken euphoria, cupping his precious face as if it might disappear if she let go. He wrapped his arms around her and pulled her close so she was laying on top of him, the full lengths of their bodies pressed against one another.

"By the Five ... woman ..." he said, his voice hoarse from disuse. "If I wasn't ... recovering from near death ..."

A heady thrum jolted from Natalie's head through her heart. The desire to grasp him by the neck, kiss him passionately and touch him in ways that alleviated all the delicious aches in her body nearly overwhelmed her. But she refrained. She couldn't risk him overexerting himself. She ran her thumb across his cheek and placed a kiss on his forehead. "It would be cruel of me to take advantage of a man in such a weakened state." He rewarded her with a faint snort. She curled up next to his side and pulled a cozy blanket over the both of them. "Let's get some sleep. It's best for both of us."

Jules let out a frustrated sigh. "I've been sleeping for ... a long time. I want to start ... living now."

"Don't worry," she whispered, closing her eyes. "We have time."

CHAPTER 25

Ordinarily, feeding broth to a patient would be a mundane task, but helping Jules eat breakfast felt akin to working in a garden on a perfect spring day. In between taking bites of rations from her own pack, she told him all that had happened while he'd been unconscious. She especially loved telling him about the children in Siaraa's workshop, how Siaraa had developed the design for the traps, and how she and Siaraa had helped the children build them.

She paused for breath describing the tenaciousness of one girl who could build almost ten traps in a morning when Jules asked: "Why am I not with the other patients? Why am I back here?"

"Aldworth was here the day before you fell ill, remember? The Headmistress suggested we move you back here in case he returned."

"Has he?"

"No," Natalie replied, hesitating to tell Jules more during the early stages of his recovery.

"I sense a 'but' in there. Come on, Nat, out with it," he

smirked at her. Goddess, even recovering from near death the man could be insufferable.

In a quiet voice, Natalie told him about the New Mages' Guild, Aldworth's possible role in it and the arrival of the princess right here next to his bed.

Jules's eyes widened. "I remember Princess Charlotte. She's a Healer and the first mage the Isles have seen in two thousand years? Bloody hell. Where is she now?"

Just in case, Natalie leaned close to his ear and whispered. "Onlo and Anli have taken her to a safe house. For my own protection, they didn't tell me where."

Jules nodded. "Wise."

Natalie put her rations back in her pack, hiding her grimace. It still irritated her that the princess couldn't stay at the palace to begin her Healer training. To cheer herself up, she dug out her diary and showed Jules the dog-eared page where she'd found evidence of a historical epidemic that had had a similar demographic impact as their own.

Jules smiled reading her entry. "This sounds strange, but I don't feel so crazy now. I was pretty sure no one would believe us when we got back to the Abbey and told them that the epidemic only rarely killed the young and the old."

Natalie nodded vigorously. "Same. Okay, I have to get going to Siaraa's. The numbers are finally starting to look good. Every day, the dead rat tally grows, and yesterday, for the first time, the number of new patients went down."

Jules smiled. "I'm so proud of you."

Natalie ducked her head and hid her embarrassment by kissing him. "Keep getting better. Take care of yourself."

She donned her green cloak, called Jake, and left before she spent the day with Jules and ignored the whole city entirely.

Natalie returned to the palace later that afternoon, Jake trotting behind her, with the day's dead rat count. She thought of the colorful stories the children had told her of snakes with bulges in the middle sunning themselves in inconvenient places and the city's burgeoning cat population. Headmistress Gayla, in return, reported they had fifteen fewer new patients that day. Natalie finally had the courage to ask the Headmistress about how many patients had died every day.

Gayla sighed. "It was a lot in the beginning. It makes me ill to even venture a count. Since you and Juliers arrived with your knowledge, it's been much less. I'd say now we only lose a maximum of five patients a day. Most people, if they were healthy to begin with, recover with the blend of teas, honey and salt you developed."

Natalie put a hand to her forehead and released a big breath of air. Gayla pulled her in for a hug; Natalie's eyes opened wide with shock at the rare display of affection from her Headmistress. After a moment, Gayla released her, grasped her by the shoulders and said, "You've done an amazing job."

"No, I —"

"Oh, be quiet, Healer, and get to work," Gayla said with mock sternness.

Natalie giggled. "Yes, ma'am. Oh, and we need to spread word to the other cities and Isles about the sanitation measures required to prevent this disease."

Gayla nodded. "I'll take care of it."

Natalie did some quick rounds on the patients in the ballroom. She knelt next to one patient who looked remarkably like Aaron, or what Aaron would look like in ten years or so. She blinked to hide her shock at his appearance as she offered him tea. He smiled and accepted it. Her hands shook as she placed them on his shoulders to Activate the Herbs. Gayla and Jules's pride in her was not unwelcome, but this was why she did not want to fail. Saving another life, another family, another city— somehow, she'd always believed it must be possible. And it'd been hell getting there, but she'd figured it out. During the Activation, a sense of freedom washed over her, as if someone had cut the strings that had always tied her to Gayla and Aldworth's approval. Her shoulders relaxed as if a great weight had been removed. As the magic of Ismereld flowed through her, her lips curved into a beatific smile.

After Natalie finished tending to her patients, she sneaked back to visit Jules, something she'd previously never permitted herself to do during the day. She found his cot empty.

A jolt of panic shot through her stomach. She spun around and spotted him at the other end of the hallway, holding on to the wall and trying to walk.

"What are you doing?" she hissed, ran to him and put his arm over her shoulder.

"What does it look like I'm doing? I'm walking," he said irritably.

"You're lucky you haven't fallen flat on the ground," she retorted, observing the sweat dripping profusely down his face and soaking through his shirt.

"I'm tired of lying down," Jules grumbled.

Natalie rolled her eyes. "Thank Goddess you're a great Healer because you're a terrible patient. Come on, let's walk back."

Carefully, they turned around. Natalie assisted him back to his cot and helped him lie down. Once he was settled, Natalie hovered over Jules with one hand on either side of his head and fixed him with a gimlet eye. "Now, you stay here until your Healer tells you it's okay to try walking."

"You're a mean Healer," he whined.

She grinned. "I am. I don't want my half handsome patient falling and breaking his arrogant face."

"What if I try again anyway?"

"Oh, you won't," Natalie said smugly.

"Why is that?"

"I think you like your face the way it is." She giggled. Goddess, she had missed him so.

"I won't fall," Jules protested.

"Well, just keep in mind if you do fall and break your face, you'll be missing out," Natalie whispered.

"On what?"

Without a word, she bent and kissed him thoroughly, her mouth slanting over his, one hand spreading through his hair and pulling him to her. His Healing energy surged through her, mixed with her own, fueling her passion. They both sighed as her tongue flicked along his lower lip. When he opened to her, they lustily explored each other's mouths, drunk on the ardor and energy swirling between them.

Pulling back with a tiny nip on his lip, she grinned. "That's what."

Smirking, she stood. "I have to get back to the ballroom. I'll send someone with something more substantial for you to eat than broth."

Jules growled loudly and Natalie laughed all the way to the ballroom.

Two days later, Jules could walk steadily and pestered all the Healers treating him to let him out of the palace. At last, Natalie relented and agreed to let him come to the morning rat trap building session.

"But you have to cover yourself with your cloak and you have to take it easy. I don't want you being discovered by the New Mages' Guild or getting worse," Natalie commanded.

Jules rolled his eyes. "Yes, Mother."

Natalie made a face at him, double-checked both their cloaks, and took his arm, and they wended through the cobblestone streets to Siaraa's, Jake padding behind them.

They no longer needed the milliner's shop for building space. Jules helped Natalie move the supplies from the milliner's back to Siaraa's. The milliner wore an expression of glee as they cleared out.

Only a few children came to Siaraa's, and Natalie found she missed the crowds of enthusiastic children wanting to learn and help. But, she sighed to herself, if it meant the city wasn't dying anymore, she could handle it. Working with Roseharbor's children made her miss her Naming students at the Abbey keenly. That was the problem with her daydreams of running away to a remote part of the Isle—she really wanted to teach again. But Aldworth had decreed she couldn't Heal until after the farce of a review he'd called, and Goddess only knew what else he had planned for her, let alone Jules. Thanks to Aldworth, the Abbey, her home for the last five years and the center for Healing education, was off-limits. Anger and betrayal burned in her chest.

Natalie shook her head and returned to the present. Jenson sat next to Jules, teaching him how to build a rat trap and regaling him with stories of all the rats he'd caught and burned, and the time he'd gotten in trouble with his mother about the snake. Natalie smiled affectionately at Jules's dark head bent next to Jenson's light one as they worked.

Natalie and Siaraa thanked each child by name as they left.

Natalie plopped her logbook on the table, startling Jake from his nap underneath. "Only sixteen dead rats reported today. Siaraa, together with a raggle-taggle band of children, we've nearly eliminated an entire species from the city."

Jules raised an eyebrow at her. "This orchestrated by the woman who once hesitated to kill a rabbit so she could eat."

Natalie stuck her tongue out at him. "The irony is, the number of years of study and practice we have using magic to Heal, and how do we stop the epidemic? Some wood, cats and snakes. Bridhe herself would laugh."

"You see? I told you I will never attach myself to one of those big, stupid rocks," Siaraa said. "Didn't help you here, did it?"

Unable to contain her joy, Natalie kissed Siaraa on the cheek before the other woman could pull away and dashed out the door.

Arm in arm, she and Jules made their way back toward the palace. Soon after they left Siaraa's, she noticed Jules staring at her.

Natalie stared at her toes and fussed with her cloak. "What?"

"It really is amazing what you organized here." His emerald eyes glowed with pride as they walked. "This disease stumped us at Whitestrand and again at Mistfell, and then you—"

Jules fell silent.

Natalie gazed at the ground with embarrassment. "Please. Any one of us would have—"

Jules squeezed her arm tightly. Before she could protest, he muttered, "We're being followed."

Natalie's eyes widened and her heart leaped into her throat.

"Keep walking normally, don't speed up. Bloody hell, I didn't bring my dagger," Jules swore.

Natalie clung tight to Jules's side. She could tell by his face he was trying to figure out a plan as fast as possible.

"I don't think we can make it to the palace," Natalie said between clenched teeth.

"Not the normal way," Jules said grimly. "Pretend we're going to the bakery over there." He smiled and pointed as if they were two ordinary lovers finding a place to get something to eat. They strolled toward the bakery, making every effort to appear as casual as possible.

"Do you see the alleyway to the left of the bakery?" Jules still smiled in an effort to maintain their relaxed demeanor. "What we'll do is look in the window of the bakery, pretend we don't find anything, continue walking up the street, then turn fast as we can and run down the alley. I know a way to get from that alley to the palace."

Natalie glanced at him, a dubious expression on her face. Would he make it? "Are you up for running?"

Jules stared straight ahead. "Do I have a choice?"

They traipsed to the bakery window and peered inside. Natalie attempted several times to swallow her pounding heart back down into her chest.

"I don't see anything I like," Jules said in a loud, snobby tone. Had Natalie not been shaking in her boots, she would've been impressed with his highborn affectation. He took her arm and they proceeded along the street. As soon as they were both even with the alley, they dropped hands and ran.

Natalie's fingers grabbed her bag and flung it to the ground so she could move faster. Trying to stay even with Jules, their pounding feet echoing in the alley and the sound of her ragged breathing rasping in her ears. Jake ran with them, his tail tucked low. That scared Natalie even more; Jake sensing danger made the threat too real. Turn after turn through the back alleys of Roseharbor had Natalie quite lost, but Jules seemed to know exactly where he was going.

"Does your family live nearby?" Natalie gasped. "I know you don't get along, but— "

Jules shook his head. "Outskirts of the city."

Please let the palace be close by. Jules, so soon out of his sick bed, faltered quickly. He had not recovered enough to be running for his life. Her own ankle throbbed painfully, reminding her that she couldn't continue much further either.

The dark, wooden sides of the alley loomed on either side of them, and their boots were wet from splashing through puddles full of liquid best left unidentified.

Natalie risked a glance over her shoulder; a figure clad in dark leather wielding a gleaming sword followed close behind them. The sight gave her flagging energy a burst of speed. "Are we … almost … there?"

"Yeah," Jules gasped. "Five more turns … if I remember correctly."

Natalie glanced behind them again. The dark figure still followed but had not gained on them. She had just enough time to be puzzled by this when they rounded the next turn and something hit her head with a thud. The world went dark.

CHAPTER 26

For Goddess's sake, what was the blasted bumping that wouldn't stop jostling her body about? And dammit, she couldn't see or hear very well. She took a deep breath and wished she hadn't; apparently, she lay on a floor covered in fetid ... something, maybe straw. Her hearing slowly returned with creaking and muffled clip-clop of hooves on a dirt road.

Grit coated her eyes when she opened them. It was dark and the fetid straw floor moved. She must be inside a cart. A tiny amount of light flickered across a small row of wire-covered windows above her. It was night, but some sort of firelight was outside. She squinted; sometimes there seemed to be two rows of windows. Double vision. She'd been hit on the head in Roseharbor. Right.

Gingerly, she tried levering herself into a sitting position. This proved difficult, as her hands were tied behind her back. They must've been tied for some time, as she'd lost all feeling in her hands. Wiggling back and forth, she was able to get mostly upright, though her stomach rebelled at all the motion combined with her pounding head. She leaned to the side and retched, but nothing came up.

Jules was next to her, still unconscious. His arms were tied to his sides and his ankles were tied as well.

Natalie's head fell forward and she swore silently until she'd said every foul word she knew. Aldworth must've found them. She scooted as close as she could to Jules.

"Jules," she hissed. She poked him with her knee. "Wake up. We've got to get out of here." After several minutes of trying—and failing—to rouse him, she scooted to the back of the cart and attempted to open the door, fingers fumbling behind her back. There seemed to be no part of the door mechanism accessible from the inside.

She swore again, this time more loudly. This woke Jules, and his eyes blinked in confusion. She made her way on her knees over to him.

"Shh, it's me. We're locked in a cart. I can't find a way out of it. I think Aldworth's got us."

She expected Jules to swear but he didn't. He closed his eyes and took a deep breath. "Are you able to untie my ankles?"

Natalie ignored the slight shake in his voice. "Possibly." She shifted around uncomfortably and began working away at the thick cords binding his ankles. No matter what angle Natalie tried, she couldn't loosen the knot. Jules tried to guide her, but the end result was an argument between the two of them and a knot no less tight than it was before.

Sweat poured down Natalie's back and she was pretty sure her fingers were bleeding when the cart came to an abrupt halt. Shouts sounded outside and the horses whinnied. Natalie and Jules glanced at each other in hope when one of their captors screamed in pain nearby.

The window next to Natalie darkened and they both heard a sharp thunk. A few more moments of scuffling went on outside. They heard someone shout, "Search the forests, find them and kill them."

After a few minutes, the cart continued its journey.

Natalie's shoulders slumped. "Well, whoever tried to rescue us just failed."

Silence met her pronouncement.

"Jules?"

"I … I think they weren't trying to rescue us. At one point, someone got close to the window right? And we both heard a noise." Excitement and hope bubbled up in his voice as spoke.

"Yes," Natalie said, still not understanding.

"Search the floor," Jules commanded.

"For what?"

"Something. Anything that doesn't belong."

Natalie took her bound hands and searched through the rotted straw behind her. Her back and knees ached from bending at an awkward angle, but she kept going. Her fingers hit something hard and it slid away from her. Heart pounding, she groped blindly in the straw, cursing the darkness. Finally, she was able to grab the object in question. She ran her thumb over it. Jagged in places but smooth in others, the item felt cool her palm. Possibly a stone?

She relayed this information to Jules.

"How smooth would you say the stone is?" Jules said eagerly.

"Smooth as glass."

"Obsidian," Jules craned his neck to see the rock she held behind her back. He sighed and laid his head against the cart wall. "Not a rescue attempt; a message. It's a good bet Onlo and Anli are following us."

A spark of hope came to life in Natalie's heart. "How would they even know we—"

"We need to hide that stone," Jules said. "If our captors see it, they may recognize it as a message from an Obfuseltan."

Natalie thought for a moment. "Your arms are tied to your sides, right? Can you still bend your elbows?

225

"Yes, but not enough to get out."

"Getting loose isn't necessary for my plan. If I put the stone in your hand, do you think you could put it down the front of my shirt?"

"What?" Jules choked.

She cocked an eyebrow at him. "Well, if the guards look there, we've got bigger problems, don't we?"

Jules sighed. "All right. Give it to me."

Natalie awkwardly scooted on her backside over to Jules, who held his hand out behind him. After a few missed tries, she got her hand in his and carefully turned her hand over so the obsidian fell into Jules's hand.

"Got it," he said. "Uh, I think this will be easiest if you lay down."

Wincing at the pain in her bound hands and wrists, Natalie lay next to Jules, trying to line her body up with his hand. She giggled uncontrollably as he felt around for the top of her shirt.

"A bit further left," she guided. "That's it. Now j-j-ust p-p-ush it st-straight d-d-down." Natalie lost it entirely and laughed until tears ran down her face.

Jules swore and retreated to the other side of the cart.

The cart stopped along a dark stretch of road, and the guards allowed Natalie and Jules to relieve themselves. Natalie did her best to act naturally, hoping Anli and Onlo would burst from the brush and save them. But nothing happened. The small ember of hope in Natalie's heart faded. Why go to the trouble of giving her and Jules a rock if they weren't going to be rescued at the first opportunity? Perhaps Aldworth's henchmen had killed them after all.

The guards outnumbered Natalie and Jules five to one. Aldworth obviously wasn't taking any chances. Strange he would send so many guards to escort a one-hand man and a woman who knew nothing of the fighting arts.

Disheartened, she got back into the cart herself;

anything to keep the rough hands of the guards off her. Their captors gave nothing away. Clad in black with faces covered, the guards didn't talk, so she and Jules did not learn anything about their destination. Jules tried to demand of one guard where they were going and got a fist to the stomach for his trouble. Natalie found him curled up in a ball in the cart. She lay on her side, tucked her body behind his as best she could, wishing she could lay hands on him and Heal him.

"Are you all right?" she whispered.

"I've had worse," he grunted.

She kissed his back, rested her forehead against him, and closed her eyes. A tendril of thought took root in her brain and swirled until it became a raging storm. How dare Aldworth decide to seize power that did not belong to him and use it to hurt others—people she loved—in the process? He and the people he'd gathered to his side threatened the very fabric of life on the Isles. Though she was glad Onlo and Anli had tracked her and Jules through the night, she hoped they didn't catch her until she'd had a chance to speak to that spineless traitor. She wanted that farce of a review to which he'd summoned them. She was going to storm up to the Council table and let him have it. All of it. So long she'd been afraid of losing his good opinion. Not anymore. She'd make sure he bloody well knew she could care less he'd lost his regard for her. Not only that, she'd lost all respect for him; and that meant something in this world.

She wanted to hit or throw something, but since her hands were tied, she lay there, angry tears pricking her eyes and fists clenched.

Natalie started when the cart lurched to a halt and the door opened. The guards dragged Jules and Natalie out. She blinked in the torchlight as the outline of a familiar stately stone building took shape before her; they were at the Abbey.

"Ah. I see it's time for our official Council of Healers

227

review," Jules remarked, raising an eyebrow.

The guards seized them by the arms and escorted them to the front entrance. The door did not open as it customarily did, and no staff came out to meet them. The Headmistress's office was dark; Gayla could not possibly be here for their review. Not only was this review a farce, it was a trap.

Natalie stumbled and suddenly found it very hard to breathe. Her earlier bravado and ideas of giving Aldworth a piece of her mind dissolved into panic. Before she could stop herself, she yanked her arms away from her guards, twisting and trying to run away. The guards wrestled her to the ground. One guard sat on her back with his elbow jammed against her jaw, mashing her face into the road. With her mouth full of dirt, she clenched her teeth, swearing to herself she would not scream. *No. It's not possible. Aldworth won? Gayla's not here. Onlo and Anli are dead or Goddess knows where. After all we did, how has it come to this? If we go to that review, Aldworth will take Jules again. All we've done will have been for nothing.*

Bile rose in her throat, and she realized she must calm down so she didn't vomit and then choke. She struggled to breathe as the guard sat on top of her, yelling in her ear. She could hear Jules, too. He shouted something at her, but it was cut off quickly, likely by one of their escorts. She relaxed, giving up her fight. What was the point, anyway?

The guard hauled Natalie to her feet; she stood with her hair in a tangled mess around her face. She spat out a glob of dirt as the men in black dragged them toward the entryway. She gazed dully at the ground, stumbling behind her guard as they went around the cloister that contained her greenhouse, and into the antechamber just outside the Council of Healers chamber. The guards untied Jules's arms and her wrists and sealed them in the room without a word.

Natalie jumped when Jules grabbed her elbow and put his mouth next to her ear. "The Inn of the Three Pearls in

Saltwick, do you know where it is?"

"Jules, I—what?"

"The Inn of the Three Pearls, do you know it?" he hissed.

"Yes, I've been several—"

"Good," Jules cut her off and cupped her face with his hand and gazed at her intently with his emerald eyes. "No matter what happens to me in there, if they let you go, you go to that inn with the obsidian. Onlo and Anli are at the inn; they will see you safe. Promise me, please, Nat."

Natalie shook her head. "How do you know? And what about you? Jules …"

"Nat, please," Jules begged, running the pad of his thumb along her chin. "I must know you are safe."

"And I must know you are safe," she cupped the side of his face.

Jules shook his head and lowered his forehead to hers. "Aldworth is in those chambers. And he's more likely to let you go than me. Since that's the most logical outcome, we must plan for you to get away. Come find me if you can. But whatever he has planned for me, I can only bear it if I know you are alive and well in this world." He kissed her deeply and then let her go, taking a full step back. "One more thing. Don't—"

Natalie stood helpless as the Council Chamber doors opened and a guard escorted Jules inside first. *Don't what?*

Aldworth sat by himself at the center of the long table at the back of the room, his fingers steepled on the table in front of him, the candlelight in the room causing his frog-like face to seem quite grotesque.

Natalie stared at him for a moment and then shuffled to her seat.

Aldworth put his palms flat on the table. "This review is now called to order."

Natalie couldn't help herself. "Excuse me, Healer. Where are Headmistress Gayla and Healer Hawkins?"

Aldworth considered her calmly. "My esteemed

colleagues, unfortunately, passed away from the sweating fever in Roseharbor."

Natalie's jaw fell open. "But the fever doesn't kill people their age. And Healer Hawkins wasn't even in Roseharbor."

Aldworth's gaze narrowed at her. "That is what happened."

Horseshit. Her heart threatened to beat out of her chest. Tears pooled in her eyes, but she refused to let them fall. No, she would not give this man the satisfaction of seeing her tears. She would not cry in front Gayla's murderer. Gayla … how could he? She crossed her arms over her stomach as if to stem the damage of her soul shattering into a million pieces. How would she live without Gayla? Had Aldworth already decided upon a death sentence for her and Jules?

Before she knew it, she stood in front of Healer Aldworth, slapped her hands palms down on the Council table and leaned across.

"How dare you? I trusted you. You were my mentor during my apprenticeship and you betray the Abbey like this?"

"Order. Please have a seat, Ms. Desmond."

"No! You sent us to a city we had no hope of saving. And now you want to punish us for the town and a city we *did* save. We did our jobs as Healers and just because you have—"

"Ms. Desmond, if you will not come to order, I will have you summarily declared guilty, stripped of your Healer status permanently and exiled off this Island."

Natalie glowered at him and sat down.

Aldworth continued, unfazed. "Until such time as Healer Hawkins and Headmistress Gayla are replaced, I will conduct your review. The charges against you are: abandoning your assigned post and neglecting your duties, contributing to significant loss of life in Whitestrand. How do you plead?"

CHAPTER 27

"Not guilty," Jules drawled. "By the time you sent us to Whitestrand, it was beyond saving. We arrived to empty streets and pyres of bodies on the beach. But you knew that would happen, did you not?"

Uncertain of how Jules wanted to play his game with Aldworth, Natalie crossed her arms, slouched in her chair and glowered at her former mentor.

Aldworth turned to her. "Is that accurate, Healer Desmond? Was Whitestrand beyond saving when you both arrived?"

"Yes," she said through clenched teeth.

"And why did you leave Whitestrand?"

Natalie explained the story of Morley, his recovery from the disease and his escape past the quarantine guards to Mistfell. She didn't know why she bothered though. This man would never treat her or Jules justly.

"There was no one left in Whitestrand to save," she concluded. "But we could save Mistfell if we were fast enough. And we did. Through what we learned at

Whitestrand and our early treatments at Mistfell, mortality rates from the disease fell."

"You still left your post without permission," Aldworth snapped.

Natalie gripped the arms of her chair and dug her fingernails into the antique wood. "There was no time for permission. This disease kills too fast."

"And was disobeying a direct order worth it for you, Healer Desmond? Your own father was the first to die in Mistfell," Aldworth's eyes narrowed.

Natalie stood, fists clenched. "And my mother was the first to survive. Because of us."

"Sit, Healer Desmond. I will not warn you again."

Natalie sat and crossed her arms over her chest.

"Her father's death was coincidence, Aldworth," Jules cut in. "Besides, at Mistfell, I learned more about the disease, so like she said, mortality rates fell. Then I took that knowledge to Roseharbor."

"Ignoring my summons for this review in the process," Aldworth put in.

Jules waved his hand. "Yes, well, I thought Their Majesties might want fewer of their subjects dying. You could wait. Besides, in Roseharbor, I figured out how the disease is spread."

Natalie gave in and glared at Jules. *He* figured it out? He was behaving like a complete ass to both of them. Did he want Aldworth to kill him right there? Because if Aldworth didn't, she might.

"And how is that exactly?" Aldworth asked.

"Rats near the food supply," Jules replied.

"I did not see you during my inspections of the palace infirmary," Aldworth stated.

"Yes, well, someone had to coordinate the elimination of the city's rat population," Jules said, spreading his hands. "I deeply regret missing your visits."

"And what of Healer Desmond in all this? What did she contribute?"

Jules eyed her with a bit of distaste. She shot him a glare that promised death at his earliest convenience. "She's a tolerable Healer, I suppose. All right at Naming, administering and Activating herbs and so on. She tended to the patients well. All in all, a good assistant."

"You were working on Naming patients together before you left. And may I remind you that it was only the crisis in Whitestrand that got you out of a review for killing a patient," Aldworth reminded Jules. "Did Naming patients together help fight this epidemic in any way? Are you stronger for it, Healer Rayvenwood?"

Jules shrugged. An ominous silence descended upon the room.

Natalie clenched her teeth. Who was this version of Jules before her? Belittling her, after all they'd gone through together. After the nights and kisses they shared. The man had made her swear to keep herself safe after the trial. After he'd told her in Mistfell that he'd stopped withholding secrets from her, had he been keeping some great unknown secret all along?

"Very well. Healer Natalie Desmond: For the charges of abandoning your assigned post and neglecting your duties as Healer, you are stripped of your Healer status and are hereby exiled from Ismereld at once. You have one day to leave. You are dismissed."

Natalie blinked at Aldworth. Holy Goddess, he planned to exile her no matter what was said here. She sized him up, the elderly frog-faced man with elegant silk robes and well-groomed hair. He'd taken everything—her trust, her home, her calling, her greenhouse, her budding teaching career, her beloved Headmistress. And what would he take of the man next to her? Despite everything, she still felt protective of him.

"What about Healer Rayvenwood?" she demanded.

"I will sentence him once you leave."

There is more truth sitting in the bottom of Benji's stall than coming out of this man's mouth. She shuddered to think of what Jules's sentence might entail. "We committed the same crimes. Surely we deserve the same punishment?"

Healer Aldworth leaned forward. "You are not on the Council, *Miss* Desmond, and I strongly suggest you leave before I make your punishment worse."

Sighing, she turned to Jules, who gazed back at her. He lowered his gaze to her chest then back to her eyes. She blinked and almost cocked her head, confused.

But then the solid, stone weight between her breasts reminded her: the obsidian and her promise to find Onlo and Anli. Her promise to be safe. She schooled her face to betray no emotion, but inside, what was left of her heart shattered completely. She gazed fiercely into his eyes and blinked once. *I swear by all I hold holy, we will come for you. Stay alive, Juliers Rayvenwood.*

She made her expression neutral and turned to Aldworth. "Yes, Healer," she whispered and exited the room. The chamber doors slammed behind her, the sound reverberating through her tattered soul like a death knell.

Natalie stood in her room, a paralyzing numbness filling her heart. Her arms and legs felt wooden, and dizziness overtook her. The Healer part of her brain kicked in and recognized the early stages of shock. When was the last time she'd eaten something? Between her capture and everything that had followed, it was all a blur. Where was Jake? Oh no, Aldworth's men must've killed him when they captured her and Jules. She put a hand over her heart and fell to the side.

A knock on the door startled her out of her dull haze.

"Nat?" Em's concerned face appeared in the doorframe. "I heard you were— By the Five, are you all right?" Em enfolded her in a hug. "Ugh, you smell awful."

Natalie took a deep, shaking breath that was half laugh and half sob. "I do. I mean, no, I'm not okay. I'm so glad to see you. You're the first friendly face I've seen in ages.

But I have no time to talk, unfortunately. I need to leave here, fast." Em sat on the bed and Natalie told her as much as she could.

Em pounded her fist on the bed when Natalie said Aldworth had taken away her Healer status. "He can't do that."

"Shh," Natalie hissed. "He's a dangerous man, Em. He's killed the Headmistress, Healer Hawkins and Goddess only knows what he's going to do to Jules. I have to get away and get to his friends. They can rescue him."

"I'm coming with you," Em declared.

"What? No. Em, people need you here—"

"Oh, hush. You are *not* doing this all by yourself." Em stood and strode toward the door. "Give me twenty minutes. I'll meet you in the stables," she said over her shoulder.

Natalie sat on the bed blinking at the doorway. In their years together as students, she and Em had often snuck into each other's rooms after lights-out to talk and giggle. Later, as their classes got harder, they'd studied late into the night by the light of carefully guarded candles, sustained by food they'd stolen from the Abbey kitchens.

Natalie lay down and hugged her quilt. Despair crept up and threatened to suffocate her with its cold, dull fingers. She should just stay in bed.

But she'd promised Jules she'd be safe. Knuckling away a tear, she wondered why she should do anything Jules said anyway. Taking credit for her work and demeaning her stung. But he'd seemed so sincere just before they'd entered the Council chamber and he'd made her promise to find Anli and Onlo. And what had he been about to say when the doors opened? Which Jules did she believe: the one before the review or the one in it?

Probably the one before, she thought, flopping onto her back. Anytime Jules is near Aldworth, he's going to act strangely. I would if I were him. Plus, I wouldn't trust a pig I liked with Aldworth.

Sighing, she ordered her body to stand. Stumbling as she went about her room, she changed into a clean pair of clothes, grabbed a spare knapsack and packed what few possessions she had left; most of her belongings were still with the tent near Roseharbor. And her Healing diary was lost in some back alley in the city proper. Natalie swore. She'd put so much work into making her Healing diary, and its knowledge had saved her hide so many times. Five damn it all, as if it wasn't enough to be stripped of her Healer status. Now her diary would be lost to the elements, or worse, used by some drunken vagrant to wipe his bum. She kicked her clothes dresser, seething and barely registering the pain in her foot. She put her hands on the wall and breathed deeply until she calmed down at least a bit.

Natalie took one last turn around the room that had been hers for the past five years. She carefully made the bed where she'd slept countless nights curled next to Jake. She ran her hand along the desk where she'd stored all her herbs and studied for exams with Em. She couldn't see a thing, but she took one last look out the window where she'd spent countless hours reading. It wasn't much, but it had been home.

With her bag slung over one shoulder and her other arm clutched over her chest covering the void left where her heart had been, Natalie closed the door and left her room for the last time.

Sticking to the shadows, she snuck down to the greenhouse and filled her bag with useful herbs for her journey—wherever it was she might be going. Her bag full, she traced her fingers along the worktable and smelled the delicious scent wafting from its surface, the combined scents of years of herbs being mashed into its surface. When memories of Jules sitting in the moonlight sprang unbidden into her head, she pushed them away and leaned on the table, praying it would give her strength. Taking a deep breath, she whispered "Goodbye," and shuffled toward the front door of the Abbey and out to the stables. She had refused to look at either the corner where Jake used to sleep or the Headmistress's old office. Every Healer knew some wounds needed time to Heal before being poked and prodded.

Em peered at the buildings lining the streets of Saltwick. "What tavern are we looking for again?"

"The Inn of the Three Pearls," Natalie mumbled, not lifting her gaze from the cobblestones. The town of Saltwick was ten minutes from the Abbey by horse. They had walked straight past the stables and traveled on foot, not wanting to add theft to Natalie's troubles. Natalie's mood on the walk shifted from despair to another beast entirely. Her stomach growled loudly, her head spun, and she still couldn't remember the last time she'd eaten. If one more thing went wrong today, Healing oath be damned, she'd probably kill someone on sight.

"Oh, that's just ahead," Em said.

Natalie staggered along behind Em. "Mmm."

They entered the Inn's taproom, squinting against the light. Natalie hoped Onlo and Anli would be easy to find. She bloody well wasn't in the mood for some lengthy adventure hunting two hard-to-find people. Thankfully, she spotted two familiar black cloaks at a table near the back of the bar.

She walked over, pulled a chair across the floor and sat next to them, causing both Obfuseltans to reach for their weapons. "Good, you're not dead."

Onlo observed her for a moment. "Things did not go well."

Natalie arched an eyebrow. "You don't say?" She reached into her shirt and placed the obsidian on the table. "Our mutual friend said I should come to you for protection. By the way, this is my friend Em. And frankly, before I explain anything else, I'm going to need food or I will pass out." She swayed then, causing all three people at the table to reach for her.

A few minutes later, plied with a chunk of hearty bread and a glass of ale, Natalie told her friends what had transpired at the Abbey.

Anli was the first to speak. "We need to leave Ismereld."

Onlo nodded. "Let us go to Obfuselt for a bit. We need our intelligence network. And," he said, nodding at Natalie, "we need to keep you as far from Aldworth as possible."

She pounded her fist on the table. "We need to get Jules away from him now."

"Shh," everyone chided her.

"You would have the two of us ride in with no knowledge and try to get him?" Anli hissed. "That would be suicide. Think, woman. We need intelligence, numbers and time to plan."

"I would go with you," Natalie protested.

Anli scoffed and Onlo put a hand on his partner's arm. "Admirable as your sentiments are, you know nothing of defending yourself or others in a fight. And we will need to fight to get Jules back."

"So I have to stay behind while you all go find him?"

"Yes."

Natalie glared at a droplet of ale on the scarred, wooden table.

"But first we must plan and strike out from a place of strength. We leave for Obfuselt in the morning," Onlo said. "Come, let's get some sleep. You should know that a mutual female friend is with us."

The princess.

"And your stinking dog," Anli added.

Natalie stood so fast she spilled her ale. "Jake?"

"Hey," Anli grouched, grabbing a napkin to clean up what ale had landed on her.

"I thought he was dead." She hugged the prickly

Obfuseltan woman, who protested and pushed Natalie away. "Where is he?"

Onlo chuckled. "Follow me."

Natalie nearly tripped Onlo five times following him up the taproom stairs. She rocked from foot to foot while he unlocked the door. When it swung open, she was greeted by a flying ball of fur to the face, and she fell to the ground laughing and crying all at once as Jake covered her with kisses.

"Aw, Jake buddy, are you all right? Are you hurt?" She did a quick Naming on him, and other than his normal arthritis and a few scratches, he was fine.

"That is a good dog," Onlo observed in his warm, dark voice. "He tracked us to the safe house and we knew something must have happened. Then he helped us find you along the road to the Abbey."

Natalie scratched behind his ears. "What a good boy," Jake's tail thumped on the inn floor until he flopped over on his belly so Natalie could scratch it.

"Hello again." A young woman with silver-white hair and striking silver eyes stood and approached Natalie.

"Hello, Princess."

The Princess smiled. "It is good to see you again. I am glad you are well."

Em and Anli entered the room. Onlo said, "Let us get what sleep we can. We make for the coast in the morning."

Two days later, Natalie heaved the contents of her stomach over the side of the boat. Again. She collapsed on the deck and tried to take a sip of water. Jake pressed his nose against her and she patted him weakly. Her herb satchel lost and Em's stocked with herbs to help women's maladies, Natalie was left to wait the sickness out. Why was she the only one bothered by the motion of the sea?

The boat crew moved around her, hard at work. Onlo worried over her in between his duties helping the boat crew, which made her feel a tad guilty.

Em and Anli stood at the deck rail, heads together, chatting animatedly. Natalie could hardly believe it when she saw Anli smiling and laughing at something Em said. *Wonders never cease.*

Princess Charlotte stood tall near the bow of the ship, the sun reflecting off her billowing silver hair such that it made Natalie's eyes water. She envied the equanimity emanating from the princess.

Natalie rested her head on a small coil of rope and watched as the shoreline of Ismereld—her home— retreated in the distance. The ache of all her losses seemed to grow deeper as the shoreline faded.

She felt a warm, strong hand on her shoulder. She turned her head, squinting in the sunlight.

"We will make things all right, Healer," Onlo said. His deep voice sounded so confident she nearly believed him.

"I'm not a Healer anymore, remember?" Bitterness crept into her voice.

"You would let Aldworth define who you are?"

"I can't Heal on any other Isle."

"On Obfuselt, people get hurt and sick all the time. Although we are not Ismereld, we have people who tend the sick and injured. Are they Healers any less than you?"

Natalie didn't have an answer, so she returned her gaze out to sea. She felt Onlo's hand squeeze her shoulder, and then he left her to her thoughts. Jake curled into a ball against her back and sighed. She sighed, too, her thoughts swirling along with the winds carrying her away from the Isle of her birth. Her stomach settled for the moment and her eyes drifted closed.

A memory bubbled to the surface of her mind of a patient she'd treated in the ballroom in Roseharbor. It had been the moment she'd first realized that, ultimately, she'd fought to stop the spread of the sweating fever because, deep down, she'd believed she could. The desperate desire to please Gayla, Aldworth or Jules, people whose admiration she so desperately used to crave, had fallen by the wayside somewhere on the road between Whitestrand and Mistfell.

Natalie's eyes snapped open. Onlo was right; she would not let Aldworth—or anyone—determine her future. She would come for Jules with every bit of skill and knowledge she had.

She levered herself slowly to a sitting position. *I believe I can Heal people no matter where I am.* She took a sip of water and grabbed ahold of the deck railing. *I believe I can find a way to help get Jules back.* She pulled herself to a standing position, wobbling slightly, hair whipping about her face in the sea winds. *I don't know what I will need to do or what I will need to learn, but I* will *do it.* She swallowed twice, ordering her rebellious stomach to settle.

Digging her nails into the deck rail, she mulled over the one thing that still bothered her. In the review with Aldworth, Jules had done everything he could to make it appear as if he were the brains behind all their decisions and actions. Why would he do that unless ... unless he'd wanted to downplay her intelligence in front of Aldworth on purpose so she would receive a lighter sentence; to focus even more of Aldworth's wrath upon himself. The side benefit of this subterfuge was that Aldworth now also underestimated her.

"Oh, Jules, you idiot," a small grin tugged at her mouth. "I won't waste the freedom you gave me. I will Heal, I will fight, and I will come for you, my love," she swore.

Gripping the rail with both hands, with Jake leaning against her leg, Natalie looked at the horizon. The slate blue ocean stretched out to meet a cerulean sky, whitecaps dancing in the distance. She had no idea what lay over the horizon, but for now, there were clear skies and following winds. Natalie tilted her face toward the sun and let the salt-sea air cleanse her face and begin mending the pieces of her tattered soul.

Keep reading for a preview of

the extraordinary sequel:

SUNSTONE'S SECRET

Book Two of the "Isles of Stone" Trilogy

CHAPTER 1

Natalie Desmond stared at the boat—now a small dot on the horizon—sailing on the glittering sea until her eyes watered. Traveling away from Obfuselt, northbound to save the man she loved, all her hopes and her heart traveled with the tiny speck that disappeared into the bright morning sunlight.

"Will you leave me in peace now?"

She glared at the dark eyes regarding her. "Onlo, you know bloody well I think they've left three days later than they should have." Natalie whirled, wishing she still had her emerald green Healer's cloak so she could be more dramatic, and strode along the Ebenos Point docks, almost stepping on her dog Jake as she brushed past her friend. She struck out for Ebenos Point Keep, fists clenched and chin high—and said a silent prayer she would find her way to the keep without Onlo's help. *I just want to be alone in my room; Five willing, I'll get there before my temper explodes.*

"Natalie, it took the Special Operations Guild three days to—"

"Oh yes, the Special Operations Guild. Please don't start. People whispering behind closed doors who didn't even want my knowledge of Aldworth or Ismereld and didn't even want me in the room when they were planning

Jules's rescue."

When they first landed in Ebenos Point, a small spark of optimism took root in Natalie's heart. If there was ever an Isle equipped to find a missing person, it was this one. Obfuselt, like each of the Five Isles, had a megalith in the center, imbued with magic by one of the five mages that had founded the Isles two thousand years ago. Those people Attuned to Obfuselt's obsidian megalith were skilled in building and crafting. Because this ability extended not only to structures and ships, but to weapons, many Obfuselt Attuned were also spies, hunters, and trackers; people perfect for mounting a rescue mission. It must've been fate, then, that her friends brought her to Ebenos Point Keep—the headquarters of the highest-trained spies and trackers who formed the Special Operations Guild.

It was to their meeting chamber Natalie dragged herself, two days after arriving, disheveled and dehydrated, intent on bringing them her knowledge of Aldworth. Once he'd been one of the best Healers, and her mentor for a year, and now, their ultimate enemy. Certainly, they must need her knowledge of Aldworth in order to find him, right? Did they know he'd kidnapped and killed people in pursuit of his goals? Did they know what she knew about his plans to build his own megalith and imbue the country invading them, Lorelan, with Healing magic?

When mustering her courage to face the guild, she thought her only worry would be dropping to her knees in tears, begging them to leave right away to find Jules. Instead, the *boom* of the guild chamber door slamming a hairsbreadth from her nose, leaving her alone in the deserted hallway, was the final nail in the coffin of her ability to help the man she loved.

Natalie shook her head. "I sure hope they know what they're up against. Fools."

Natalie's voice rose half out of anger and half out of necessity; she and Onlo now strode along a busy section of the dock markets. Well, she walked as furiously as the crowd would allow and Onlo followed behind like a guard dog. *An unneeded, unwanted guard dog. Leave. Me. Alone.*

Hawkers cried out from under colorful awnings covering displays of a myriad of wares. Scrumptious smells wafted this way and that prompting Natalie's stomach to remind her she hadn't eaten much more than broth these past few days. People from all five Isles and the continent to the northeast shopped and wandered the streets. If she wasn't so determined to stay ahead of Onlo, Natalie might have stopped to wander amongst the shops, running her fingers along the soft textiles, sampling the foods and admiring the way the trinkets sparkled in the sun. The markets in Saltwick were never this colorful or bustling with such a variety of people.

"Natalie, that's my guild you're speaking of."

Biting the inside of her cheek, Natalie tried to recall if she'd ever heard Onlo use that tone of voice with anyone. She swallowed, stepping around someone going the other way be sure she didn't let her anger show on her face. "Yes, well, I don't appreciate being told to stay in bed and mind my own business. Especially for something as important as this."

"When we arrived, you were so dehydrated—you were delirious."

Even the thought of the unrelenting sea sickness she'd suffered during the voyage from Ismereld to Obfuselt made Natalie's stomach curdle.

"Besides, the Guild has a right to keep its own counsel."

"I've had enough of councils, thanks." Healer Aldworth, the last remaining member of the Council of Healers, exiled her and kidnapped Jules. The Special Operations Guild shutting her out of the rescue mission pushed her patience with governing bodies over the edge.

Warm fingers seized her elbow, spun her around and Onlo's deep, brown eyes bored into hers. "What happened to you and Jules was a terrible thing, it's true. All I am asking is for you to trust my Isle. Just as I would trust you if I—" Onlo's eyes shifted over her shoulder. Panic unfurled in her stomach as a bright, orange light flashed against the whites of his eyes.

A deafening roar made Natalie turn in his arms. A wave of heat rolled over her body and she lifted her hand to protect her eyes. Flames engulfed one of the marketplace stalls; Jake spooked and ran the opposite way, disappearing behind a shop. *Good boy, Jake, stay there until it's safe to come out.* Natalie shoved out of Onlo's embrace and ran toward people in front of the inferno, screaming as their clothes caught fire. Heart pounding in her throat, Natalie darted into a nearby weaver's shop and grabbed several blankets. Ignoring the shopkeeper's protests, she raced back outside. Dropping all the blankets but one, she used the thick blanket to tackle the person nearest her to the ground.

"Roll," she shouted giving the person a hearty shove. "Roll and put the flames out."

Grabbing the next blanket, she repeated the process with another person, and then another. She grabbed the last blanket and noted with relief that many people were following the example of the victims on the ground and rolling to smother the fire on their clothes.

"We need to move these patients away from the fire to make room for the fire wagon."

Natalie raised her eyes from the person she was helping. Five people carrying leather cases, black cloaks billowing behind them, listened to orders from a tall, dark-skinned woman with long, spiral hair secured at the nape of her neck with an intricate silver clip. They dispersed and carried people away from the conflagration, evaluating injuries as they went; Natalie couldn't help but admire their efficiency. A painful thread of longing tore through her heart. *I used to be part of a team like that. But I can still help these patients. Solenloe leaf works on burns even if you're not on Ismereld to Activate it. And I can bandage with the best of them.*

Natalie stood, looped her arms under her patient's shoulders and heaved. "I need help here," she called to the nearest medic.

"It's all right miss, we'll get him. Are you injured?"

"No. I'm a Healer, I can help," Natalie stated, but her words fell on deaf ears. "I can help," she yelled at another medic, but they all proceeded about their business, treating patients.

Rolling her eyes skyward, she dragged the patient inch by inch toward the triage area. "Hell … in … a … kettle …" *I couldn't have picked a petite woman, no, I picked a tall man with all the muscles on the planet.*

She'd nearly made it when the woman in charge of the medics grabbed the man's ankles. "What are you doing? Leave this to my team."

Glaring across the man suspended between them, Natalie squatted and set him next to the neat row of patients. "I am a Healer," she said through clenched teeth.

"Why should I believe you?"

Spotting an open leather case nearby, Natalie spied some mashed solenloe leaves in a labeled jar next to a row of carefully rolled bandages. Before the other woman could protest, Natalie snatched the glass jar and expertly applied the leaf poultice to the burns marring the skin of the man she'd carried, starting with the worst. This finished, she wrapped her work with the bandages, all the while conscious of the other woman's scrutiny tingling over her skin like lightning during a storm. Humph. An eighteen-year-old Healer could Heal a burn victim in their sleep. *Or am I nineteen now? The weather's just turned wretchedly hot so I'm likely nineteen.*

She put her hands on the man and reached into the island with her mind and found nothing but silence. Ismereld was the only Isle on which she possessed the ability to access the magic buried deep in the island.

Right. I'm not on Ismereld. I'm in Ebenos Point, Obfuselt and his body and the leaves will have to do their best.

"Who are you?" the head medic demanded.

Natalie shook her hair out of her face. "My name is Natalie. Like I said I'm a Healer. From Ismereld. I cannot Activate these poultices as I normally would. But if someone changes them every other day for two weeks, his burns should be fine by then."

The head medic considered her for a moment, and then her expression relaxed. "Take the woman with the red hair and the child in the dress. Help yourself to our supplies." Turning on her heel, the woman directed her own medics while treating her fair share of the patients.

Natalie grabbed as many items as she could carry from a nearby bag and knelt next to her assigned patients. Her hands danced over their skin and she hummed comforting words to them. The loss of Ismereld's magic felt like a ragged hole torn in her chest but she shoved her own aches aside. The wounded people on the ground needed her skills, and she had more to offer than the gifts her home Isle gave her.

Her last bandage wrapped, Natalie sat on the ground and dragged her forearm across her forehead. Her shirt had soot all over it; no doubt her face did, now, too. She pressed a hand to her lower back and bent backward trying to ease the nasty ache lodged there. Thirst burned her mouth and throat. *Not good. I just spent four days recovering from dehydration.* She spotted canteens of water amongst the medic's supplies and helped herself. The cool liquid soothed her parched throat a pleasant coolness filled her stomach; shivering, she gulped so much she had to make herself stop.

Drawing a soot-stained sleeve across her mouth, Natalie surveyed the burning building for the first time since she'd treated her first victim. A large wagon drawn by several horses had arrived carrying six large vats. Onlo and several others operated a pump on top of the truck that fed water to a hose which several other people held to douse the flames. The fire was much lower than when

Natalie literally tackled her first patient. Thankfully, it had only spread to the two shops on either side of the original building. Natalie breathed a sigh of relief, coughing as she did so. She and the medics didn't lose a patient and the Ebenos Point market didn't burn to the ground.

The head medic appeared next to her and squatted, taking a pull from her own canteen. Natalie stared at the fire as if it were the most fascinating thing she'd ever seen.

"Thank you," the medic said.

Natalie blinked in surprise. "You're welcome."

"Having competent help is always welcome around here. I didn't recognize you as a Healer. Where's your green cloak?"

Natalie picked up a piece of wood on the market walkway and tore it to shreds. "It's a long story."

"Must be. Well," the other woman put her hands on her knees and levered herself to a standing position. "I'm Asha. If you're staying here for a spell, we welcome your help anytime."

Natalie pressed her lips together in what she hoped was a smile. "Thanks."

Most patients walked home, under strict instructions to visit the medics to have their bandages changed. Only a few patients left the scene on stretchers carried by Asha and her team.

Natalie watched them leave. Coming in the other direction was Jake, trotting with his tail between his legs. Natalie held a hand out to him. "Hey, old buddy, the fire's all gone. It's okay," She kissed his head and returned her gaze to the retreating medics. The patients who still needed medical attention nagged at her conscious and her soul ached to help them. And Asha said she'd be welcome. Why didn't she follow them? She had nothing else to do until word came about Jules. She pushed to her feet, knees creaking after treating burns for so long.

"Natalie, are you all right?"

Turning, she found Onlo standing behind her, water

dripping from the thick cords of his dark brown hair and soot covering him from head to toe. The flames extinguished, the horses now pulled the cart with vats of water down the street.

"I'm fine. No burns. You?"

"Why did you run toward the fire?"

"People were *on* fire. I had to help them. What started it?"

"Come, let's walk back to the Keep."

With one last wistful glance at the retreating medics, Natalie crossed her arms and walked with Onlo up the hill to Ebenos Point Keep. Maybe she'd seek them out later.

"It was a luthier's shop that caught fire; his storage area in the back to be more specific. Someone was careless with a candle and, with so much dry wood, the whole shop went up in seconds. It's too bad, he's a good luthier and often sells violins and guitars to the finest musicians on Methyseld. I hope he can recover his business soon."

"Mm."

"Still, next time, let the fire crew and the medics help. I promised Jules I would keep you safe. I can't do that if you are running toward flaming buildings."

Natalie stopped and put her hands on her hips. "Excuse me? About a week ago, you told me I could be a Healer no matter where I was. That I shouldn't let Aldworth's sentence define me. Do you take it back?"

Onlo shook his head. "Natalie, by all means, be a Healer wherever you'd like, just don't run toward burning buildings."

"Healers *do* run towards burning buildings. And cart crashes and rooms full of sick people. Healing in hazardous situations is part of the job."

Onlo pointed a finger at her. "Stay out of danger while you are under my protection."

"So I shouldn't let Aldworth define me as a Healer, but I should let you? Hypocrite."

Natalie stalked ahead of Onlo to the Keep. If the world

was so intent on telling her where and how she could Heal, what was the point of being a Healer at all?

ACKNOWLEDGEMENTS

To Tammy who asked me when don't I hurt. I don't hurt when I write.

To the artists who've inspired me throughout my life, especially Lin-Manuel Miranda who taught me to write my way out. To Felicia Day who not only stepped outside the system and created loads of amazing TV and media content, but also created the Vaginal Fantasy Book Club, through which I met my best friends.

To my beta readers Sami, Erin, Melissa, Sue, and Billie: thank you for being the second pair of eyes I so desperately needed.

To my street team for believing in me and my dream and spreading the word about this book. Y'all are amazing.

To my editors, Katie McCoach and Stephanie Riva who taught more about writing and story craft than any book, website, or YouTube video ever could. I'm so grateful and I can't wait to work on book two with you.

To my book club for being the best friends a nerdy, Broadway-loving, MST3K-obsessed, movie-quoting mom could ever ask for.

To my husband, daughters, mother, sister, and the rest of my family who've picked me up off the floor and set me to rights more times than I can count. You've been there for me when I've been bedridden and you've ridden the roller coaster of chronic illness with me. You've gone beyond the call of duty so many times. I am eternally grateful; I have been and always shall be yours.

ABOUT THE AUTHOR

KATE KENNELLY started writing creatively when she was ten years old. She let a bad grade on a creative writing project in seventh grade get her down and stopped writing altogether. Many years later, now suffering from chronic pain, someone asked her "When are you not in pain?" The answer was "When I do creative things." Kate challenged herself to sit down and write something – anything – for the therapeutic value. Thirteen chapters later, not only was she writing, but she was reading books on writing, watching YouTube videos, learning all she could to try and craft a good story.

In her free time, Kate loves to Irish dance, play fiddle, do yoga, meditate and play World of Warcraft with her book club friends. She lives in Maryland with her husband, two daughters and two rescue dogs.

Made in the USA
Middletown, DE
21 March 2019